WRITING A WRONG

WRITING A WRONG

Betty Hechtman

**SEVERN
HOUSE**

First world edition published in Great Britain and the USA in 2021
by Severn House, an imprint of Canongate Books Ltd,
14 High Street, Edinburgh EH1 1TE.

Trade paperback edition first published in Great Britain and the USA in 2022
by Severn House, an imprint of Canongate Books Ltd.

severnhouse.com

British Library Cataloguing-in-Publication Data
A CIP catalogue record for this title is available from the British Library.

ISBN-13: 978-0-7278-9019-1 (cased)
ISBN-13: 978-1-78029-810-8 (trade paper)
ISBN-13: 978-1-4483-0548-3 (e-book)

This is a work of fiction. Names, characters, places and incidents
are either the product of the author's imagination or are used fictitiously.
Except where actual historical events and characters are being described
for the storyline of this novel, all situations in this publication are
fictitious and any resemblance to actual persons, living or dead,
business establishments, events or locales is purely coincidental.

All Severn House titles are printed on acid-free paper.

Typeset by Palimpsest Book Production Ltd.,
Falkirk, Stirlingshire, Scotland.
Printed and bound in Great Britain by
TJ Books, Padstow, Cornwall.

ACKNOWLEDGMENTS

It was such fun working with my editor Carl Smith. I loved all his comments while I went through the edits. Once again his suggestions were all right on. Thank you to my agent Jessica Faust as there wouldn't have been this series without her guidance.

I enjoyed writing about Chicago and my Hyde Park neighborhood. It gave me a chance to look at it with a fresh eye. Though thanks to the pandemic, only at a distance. It helped to have the amazing shots that David and Leslie Travis posted on Facebook to remind me just how beautiful the Point and Lake Michigan are at sunrise. William Vandervoort posted wonderful pictures of the area right around where Veronica lives. I am grateful to the whole Hyde Park Classic Facebook group for all the photos of the past and present, along with lots of background stories on my neighborhood.

Writing about Veronica's buildings stirred up a lot of emotions. I know her condo only too well and it's filled with memories of my family. I met Penny Fisher Sanborn and Pam Fisher Armanino when I was two and they lived on the first floor. It's nice to say that we're still friends and they're my backup memory.

Thanks to Burl and Max for sharing your Chicago experiences.

ONE

The doorbell rang, startling me even though I was expecting it. Bell was a misnomer. It sounded more like a buzzer or someone gargling under water. But it got the job done and I knew someone had arrived. I pressed the button that unlocked the downstairs door without using the intercom to check who it was. It was Tuesday, a little before seven, and I assumed it was someone from the writers' group a little early.

I opened my front door. 'Oh it's you,' I said, surprised by who stepped on to the third-floor landing. Not only was Tony Richards not part of the writers' group, but well, he stuck out like a . . . Before I could finish the thought I stopped, castigating myself for the cliché even if only thinking it. As the leader of the writers' group, I was supposed to be better than that. The problem with clichés was they got the job done, as in Tony's case.

Maybe in the Lincoln Park or River North neighborhoods, Tony would have blended in. But here in Hyde Park, with the casual vibe of the University of Chicago, the black cashmere overcoat, gray slacks and black shoes without the hint of a scuff stood out. He had an overall polished look, expensively styled dark hair and skin with a hint of tan despite the fact it was the end of March.

'I'm sorry for not texting you. I remembered you said your writers' group met Tuesday evening,' he said, giving me a friendly smile. It was the kind of smile that could melt an iceberg and of course, I said it was fine and invited him in. Before I could shut the door, Ed Grimaldi came up the stairs and crossed the landing. He gave Tony a dismissive look as he walked into my entrance hall. He was part of the writers' group and in stark contrast to Tony was dressed in track pants and an unzipped down jacket. No tan, no stylish haircut for his salt-and-pepper hair. He worked in maintenance at the university.

'New member?' he asked, turning to me. When I answered with a simple no, Ed shrugged and headed down the hall to the dining room where the group met.

A moment later, Tizzy Baxter came in as I was about to shut the door. She gave off such enthusiasm, it gave me more of a boost than a cup of coffee. She lived down the street and was fascinated by everything.

Daryl Sullivan pushed open the door and joined us in the entrance hall. She had a totally different vibe. As always she was dressed in a trendy outfit. The styles of clothes had gotten so crazy now it was hard to tell if she was wearing an eclectic mix of pieces or she'd run out of clean laundry. Her face was locked in a tense expression. That is until she noticed Tony. Both she and Tizzy did a double take when they saw him. It was an awkward moment and I wondered about introducing them, but decided not to.

'You can go on into my office,' I said to Tony. 'I'll be with you in a moment.'

He smiled at them and tipped his head, and they both melted. 'I'm sorry for interrupting,' he said. 'I don't want to keep you from your workshop.' Neither woman made a move to leave. He seemed completely at ease and kept smiling at them.

'So, are you a friend of Veronica's?' Tizzy asked.

'I like to think so,' he said, before introducing himself and letting them introduce themselves. 'Veronica is a wonderful help.' He glanced toward the frosted French door that led to my office. 'I really should go in there and take care of things.'

Before anyone made a move, there was a sharp knock at the door, and I let Ben Monroe in. He and Tony locked eyes for a moment. Though Ben was dressed in jeans and a long sleeve burnt orange T-shirt, his manner was all cop. Tony smiled and held out his hand as he introduced himself. Ben gave me a quizzical look, which I answered with an uncomfortable smile before he reluctantly accepted the handshake and offered his name. Tizzy and Daryl seemed a little disappointed when Tony finally went through the frosted doors into the next room. 'You can go join Ed,' I said to the three, pointing down the long hall. I waited until they started to walk before going into my office. It was always nice to see Tony and I wanted to make sure he had what he needed. He might have implied that he was a friend, but he was actually a client.

Besides running the writers' group, I was a writer for hire. I'd write whatever someone needed. In the past I'd polished wedding vows and composed love letters, written promotional material for a dance gym along with descriptions of all the classes. On a sadder note I'd written material for funerals or, as I preferred to call them, celebrations of life. I could write just about anything for anybody except, it seemed, for myself. I'd written a successful mystery called *The Girl with the Golden Throat* and was struggling with the sequel.

I'd had a flutter of notoriety after I actually solved a crime. But by now it had settled down, though it had gotten me a lot of local publicity for the kind of writing I did, which is how Tony had found me. He'd seen me interviewed on a PBS show devoted to unusual professions. The program had focused on the love letters I'd written.

Tony had hired me to write love letters and now love notes for him. Well, more correctly, as him. I chuckled inwardly at how Tizzy and Daryl had reacted to him. I couldn't blame them because I'd done the same. There was something about him. It was more than good looks. I'd tried to put my finger on it; the best I could come up with was that he had a magnetic smile and there was something about how he treated me that made me feel noticed and valued.

I was upset with myself for reacting to his charm. There wasn't an ethics organization for writers of love letters, but if there had been I was sure part of their rules would be that it was bad form to feel attracted to the clients. I was sure I wasn't his type anyway, though I knew almost nothing about his lady love, not even her name. He had me use terms of endearment like Dearest or My Love.

Though I'd been writing the letters for him for a couple of months, I still didn't know much about him other than that he traveled a lot. After meeting him, it was hard to believe he needed any help in the romance department, but he'd explained that it had to do with all the time he spent away and he wanted his lady love to know he was thinking of her while he was gone. He said he wasn't much of a words man. That was the reason he needed the letters and notes. When I asked about the person the letters were going to, he'd been all charming and mysterious and given no details. At least I wanted an idea of what sort of tone he had in mind, but when I asked if he wanted it to be serious or cute, he just said to write something that I would like to hear.

I went into my office and opened a file on my computer. 'Here's what I've got,' I said, offering him the chair in front of the desk. He was reading over what was on the screen as he slid into the seat. 'I don't know what I'd do without you,' he said, turning to face me. 'This is great stuff. You have absolutely saved my life with her. It's made it so she doesn't make a fuss when I have to leave.'

'Glad it's helping,' I said with a smile. 'If you have what you need, I'll leave you to it.'

My arrangement was different than it had been with my other clients. Since he was on the move a lot, he always came to my place. I had what I'd written for him set up on my computer. I left him alone to make any changes he wanted and he printed up the final version on some stationery he kept there. He gave me a nod and I walked out into the entrance area near the front door.

Thanks to the design of the apartment, I could just hear the hum of the group's conversation. I'd heard the style described as either shotgun or train-car design. Personally, I thought train-car sounded more appealing. The living room went across the whole width of the place, with windows looking out on the tree-lined street. There was also a door to a balcony. My office had another set of French doors that opened into the living room. I often wondered what that room had been intended for when the building was built over one hundred years ago.

I started down the long hall to join the group, thinking that the hallway was the only part that seemed to resemble a train-car. There were doorways to two bedrooms, several closets and a bathroom before the hall ended at the dining room. Beyond it there was a butler's pantry, the kitchen and a small bedroom and tiny bathroom. It was a lot of space for one person. But it hadn't always been that way. There had been three of us for years when my parents were both alive. When my mother died, it had been my father and me. And when he died I became the sole inhabitant. Despite the age of the place, it was now a condominium, with a paid-off mortgage meaning I could get by on my writing jobs. Many of the other tenants in the building had turned their dining rooms into dens, but I'd kept mine for its original purpose, along with being a place to host the writers' group. The rectangular wood table sat in the middle of the room. A buffet filled with drawers that held things I didn't use like tablecloths and candles was against the wall. On the other side of the room was a bookcase with some books and a lot of pretty things I liked to look at. The couch seemed a little out of place, but it had been there forever.

'Who's the guy?' Ed said, dropping his voice slightly and gesturing toward the front of the apartment. The four of them were gathered around the cleared-off dining-room table which was already covered with their pages.

While I was thinking of how to answer, I heard footsteps coming down the hall. A moment later Tony stuck his head in the room. 'I have everything I need.' He held up a manila envelope. 'Everything looks great as always. You're a wonder at what you do.' I felt myself blushing. It wasn't just the compliment, it was the way Tony said it in full-on flirt mode.

'You're lucky to have her,' he said to the group. 'Sorry to interrupt; you can get on with what you're doing.' I went to get up to walk him to the door, but he assured me that he could let himself out.

'Wow, what a dreamboat,' Tizzy said. 'Sorry for the cliché, and a dated one at that.' She rocked her head in regret. They all knew I had an aversion to clichés in writing and even in my own thoughts. I didn't have to say anything, and Tizzy went into substitute ways of describing Tony's attributes. 'He seems like the whole package: classy Cary Grant sort of demeanor but with some Brad Pitt thrown in. So what's he to you?'

'No fair,' Ed said. 'It's cheating to describe him in terms of other people.'

'That's only in writing,' Daryl said. 'I think Tizzy hit it on the head.'

'Thank you,' Tizzy said, smiling at Daryl and giving Ed a pointed nod. She'd taken off her outer jacket revealing a kimono-style covering made out of patches of different materials. She tended to gesture when she spoke and the sleeves fluttered with the movement. She turned back to me. 'Are you going to tell us who he is and what was he doing going in your office?'

'Whatever,' Ed said with an eye roll. 'Let's get down to why we're here. What Veronica does in her spare time is none of our business.'

'He's a client,' I said, hoping it would settle things. 'He's on the road a lot, so I let him use my computer and leave some stuff in my office.'

'I get it, you don't want to talk about him,' Tizzy said. She turned to the others. 'But she has another client I'm sure she'd be glad to talk about. As soon as I heard that Rex LaPorte was looking for someone to write descriptions for the menu and copy for their website, I told him Veronica was perfect. And he hired her.' Tizzy took a breath. 'I just love to help people.'

'I appreciate it,' I said. 'I'm looking forward to getting started.' LaPorte's Bakery and Café was a neighborhood fixture.

'Their chocolate mint cake has been my kids' favorite since they were little. It's always my go-to for their birthdays. Any chance you can snag the recipe?' Tizzy asked.

'Do you really think they'd give me the recipe for their signature cake?' I said with a chuckle. 'It's about as likely as Colonel Sanders giving me his fried chicken spice list.'

'You're right. I wouldn't mind a piece of that cake right now with the buttercream icing,' Tizzy said.

'Enough about your cake fantasies,' Ed said. 'Can we just get to it? Some of us are anxious to get down to business because they actually have someone waiting to put their pages on their website.' Ed wrote stories about contestants on a fictitious dating show for a website. The kind of show where one guy had a choice of women. Ed liked to imagine them to be famous women. There was a lot of time spent in the Getting to Know You Suite. I was pretty sure that Ed modeled the guy on himself. His work had been pretty graphic and only recently had he started to make the characters a little more multidimensional. So, now there were fuller fleshed-out characters, still with a lot of flesh. Ed's head had gotten a little swollen from actually being published somewhere and I'd thought he was going to stop coming, thinking that he didn't need the feedback anymore, but we had gotten to be a tight-knit group and I think he felt adrift without coming to our weekly gatherings.

The writer was never allowed to read their own pages because it was more effective to hear somebody else reading their work. In Ed's case, it was always Ben who read his work. Ben was a cop and he was able to read the detailed descriptions of the meet-ups in the private suite in a flat voice as if he was reading a police report. When the rest of us had tried to read Ed's work, we'd been reduced to embarrassed laughter.

Ben and I had a friendship outside of the group, too. His sister was my downstairs neighbor and she'd initially gifted three months of workshops to Ben hoping it would give him an outlet from the pressure of being a cop. He worked in one of the suburbs – maybe not quite the mean streets of the city, but there were problems everywhere. Sara was hoping there'd be more to it than helping with his writing. She was doing her best to push us together. So far unsuccessfully. He was going through a very slow recovery from a divorce and wasn't ready for any new entanglements. I on the other hand might have been interested, but since he clearly wasn't, neither was I. I was not one of those people who seemed to only want someone who didn't want them. I was less complicated. I only wanted someone who wanted me.

Tizzy was practically a neighbor and I knew her outside the group. She was married with grown children and worked at the university in the business school. She was writing a time-travel romance that was heavy on history with just sweet G-rated romance thrown in. She'd gotten the opposite advice of Ed's. The group thought she needed to spice things up a bit between Campbell Jones, the guest at the Chicago World's Fair, and the very contemporary Lilith.

Tizzy had been close to being finished with her book and

then had decided she wanted to revamp it. Ed read her pages. It was hard to focus on the words because he kept rolling his eyes at the hand-holding and kiss on the cheek that had gone on between Campbell and Lilith. 'Can't you put some tongue in it,' he said finally in exasperation.

'Not if he's going to kiss her on the cheek,' Ben said, and we all laughed at the image of Campbell licking Lilith's cheek.

'You know what I mean,' Ed said.

Daryl read Ben's work. He was working on a crime story with a cop as the main character. It was full of short sentences and terse dialogue. The group had prevailed on him to give the main character more emotion. He was making headway, but still had a long way to go.

'OK, I get it,' Ben said. 'You're not going to be happy until my character is crying about something.'

It was Tizzy's job to read Daryl's pages. She was the most difficult person in the group. She managed a trendy clothing store downtown, which was probably why she always had on an eye-catching mixture of clothes. She was too tense to say much when we made small talk and when it came time to read her work, she sucked in a breath loudly and I was always afraid she was going to forget to breathe out.

Tizzy presented Daryl's work. It all went fine until Daryl burst into tears.

'We didn't even say anything,' Ed said, putting his hands up in a hopeless gesture. Daryl was ultra-sensitive about any criticism. She got defensive if someone even brought up a misplaced comma. But if everyone gave her bland approval, she reacted too, saying that it wasn't helpful. As a result, they left it all up to me to give her comments.

This time it wasn't just worry about what anyone was going to say. It turned out she'd had a bad day at work, somehow getting in the middle of an argument between a mother and daughter who were customers in the store. We all tried to make her feel better.

I walked them all to the front when the time was up and saw them out the door. I knew it was done, but not over.

TWO

The knock at the door startled me even though it was expected. There was something about the wood door that made any knock come out as loud and commanding. It was an automatic reaction to open the door quickly even though the door was on the latch. Ben was standing in the hallway holding an aluminum-foil-covered plate in his hand, waiter style. 'Dinner has arrived,' he said with a smile.

Part of his sister Sara's plan to push us together was to send him up with a plate of supposed leftovers from their dinner. They were meat-eaters and I was a vegetarian and it seemed a little suspicious how there was always something meatless left over. I wasn't about to complain, though, since it meant I didn't have to cook and it was always delicious.

Ben always had dinner at his sister's before coming up to the writers' group and at first he'd brought the plate of food then. But the group had given him a hard time about it, saying it was like he was giving an apple to the teacher to get special consideration. So we'd changed things up and he left with the others, picked up the food and returned. I'm not sure we were fooling them, but at least they didn't make a fuss.

The deal was that he would stay while I ate because his sister wanted her plate back and a review of the food.

This time there was something more. I had to ask him for a favor. It was awkward and embarrassing, but I couldn't think of anyone else to ask.

'Sara said to be sure and tell you to take off the aluminum foil before you put it in the microwave,' he said with a smile, since she basically said it every week as if I didn't know.

I didn't bother objecting and told him to make himself comfortable in the living room while I went back to the kitchen. Instead he followed me down the hall.

'It's just us now,' Ben said. 'So who's the guy?'

'Just a client,' I said, hoping he'd drop it. Once we were

in the kitchen, I made a point of removing the foil and popped the plate in the microwave. 'Would you like something to drink?'

'I came prepared,' he said, pulling a bottle of beer out of his pocket. I thought he'd dropped asking about Tony, but then he said, 'That guy doesn't pass the smell test. Cop instinct tells me there's something too slick about him. I would lose him as a client.'

'Thank you for your opinion,' I said, not being clear if I was going to take his advice. I got a glass of sparkling water for myself and when the microwave dinged, put the plate on a tray and we went back to the front room.

The living room was filled with color from artwork, pretty things my parents had collected and the crocheted piece I had hung on the wall over the black leather couch. I glanced out the window and got a view of the third-floor window in an apartment building similar to mine on the other side of the street. The lights were on and I could just make out a guy hovering over his computer. We sat in the alcove at one end of the room, taking what had become our regular spots. He sat on the couch and I took the wing chair.

I was glad that he didn't bring up Tony again. I wasn't so sure it was cop instinct that made him dislike Tony as much as he felt threatened by Tony's effect on all the women. I balanced the tray on my lap and looked down at the plate.

'It's mushroom stroganoff over egg noodles,' he said. 'My sister outdid herself. Of course, ours had meat.' He noticed me looking at the plate closely. 'Don't worry, there was never any meat in yours. She'd kill me if I told you, but she always makes your plate up first and then adds the meat or chicken for the rest of us.'

'I kind of figured that,' I said, scooping some on a fork. 'There's something I need to talk to you about.' I was actually dreading it and it must have shown in my expression, because he instantly tensed.

'It's my pages, isn't it?' he said. Before he could go any further, I assured him that it wasn't.

'No, no, you're really doing great,' I said, giving some specific details. I absolutely meant it. When the gifted sessions from his sister had run out, he'd decided to continue on his own. It seemed to be helping him on all accounts. He'd been so stiff when he first joined the group. It was like he had a crust around him, keeping his emotions and personality hidden. He'd barely even smiled. 'Actually, I need to ask you a favor,' I began. Now came the hard part. I was worried he'd say no and think the less of me for having to ask him. I'd been invited to the engagement party of a former client I'd written love letters for. Usually, the people I wrote love letters for didn't want their intended to know that I existed, but this case was different. Not only did she know all about what I'd done, but they were treating me like a guest of honor, crediting my work for bringing them together. They were even going to offer a toast to me. All that attention was likely to get me some business – either for romantic letters or for the other kinds of pieces I wrote. In other words, I needed to make a good impression. Simply put, it wouldn't look good for someone who wrote love letters to come alone.

Rocky made an appearance just then. He was a large black-and-white cat commonly referred to as a tuxedo cat because his markings made it look as if he was wearing one. He also had asymmetrical marking on his face which gave the impression he had a crooked mustache. The cat paused briefly in the entrance to the living room and then walked over to the couch and jumped up next to Ben. Rocky immediately started rubbing against Ben's side and knocking into his hand. 'You know who your best bud is,' Ben said, beginning to give Rocky long strokes on his back. The cat responded with a loud purr as he leaned into the petting.

Ben had legitimately earned the cat's affection. He'd helped me when I brought Rocky home and was a little unclear about the cat's immediate needs.

In addition to the paid writing gigs, I also did some pro bono work for a downtown pet store that offered pets from assorted shelters for adoption. I wrote what I called personality pieces from the animal's point of view, which were supposed to help them find forever homes. Usually the pets at the shop were extra cute and the kind of breeds that were most desirable. Rocky had been brought there because he was desperate.

He was seven, which was a strike against him, and he was on his last few days at the shelter. So, if he didn't find a home, well . . . I couldn't bear to think about it. I'd done such a good job on the piece for Rocky that I'd been the one to give him a home. The way he'd looked at me and reached out with his paw as if to say 'take me with you' had helped, too.

He was my first-ever pet and I was glad that Ben had helped me. I'm sure Rocky was, too, since it involved getting him a cat box.

'I'm waiting,' Ben said looking at me, and I realized I'd been using the cat's entrance as a stall. 'And using my cop observation skills, I'd say whatever it is makes you uncomfortable.'

I smiled weakly. 'You hit it exactly.'

'There's no reason to feel uncomfortable. We're friends, remember, friends with no benefits and no need to keep up an image or try to impress as you would if we were, say, dating.'

I put down the fork. 'Maybe you'd like a drink.'

He held up his hand with the bottle of beer in it and smiled. 'Whatever it is, just say it and get it over with. It's like we say to suspects. You'll feel so much better when you get it off your chest.' He stopped. 'Yes, the last part was a cliché, but when you're dealing with suspects, it's better to cut to the chase than worry about being original.'

I knew he was right about just throwing it out there. 'It's like this,' I began, taking a breath. I explained the invite to the engagement party and the fact that I needed to project an image of being in a relationship and I gave him the date. I'd made a point to give him the exact date so it would give him an easy out. All he had to say was that he was busy.

He thought it over a moment and shrugged. 'I could do that. In fact, you could return the favor. You could be my plus one the next time I get invited to a birthday party or event with someone I work with. I'm tired of getting seated with some-body's cousin or everyone making an issue that I'm alone.' He looked at me directly. 'How about it? Will you be *my* plus one?'

'Sure,' I said. It made it better that he wanted something in return. It made me seem less needy. 'There's something we need to consider, though. For this to work, we have to look like we actually are in a relationship.'

He laughed. 'How about I hang all over you?'

'It can't be that obvious or it will appear false. I was thinking more on the subtle side. Like you know how I take my coffee and I know you like beer.' It still amazed me to see how different he looked now that he was letting his personality show. When he'd first joined the group, his expression had always been blank, which had made him seem as if he had no personality and, worse, was cold. But now there was some light in his eyes and he didn't seem chiseled from stone anymore.

'As a cop you probably know about body language,' I said.

He laughed again and I noticed that it made crinkles around his eyes that made him seem so much more approachable. 'The body language I'm looking for has more to do with whether I think someone is going to pull a gun on me or make a run for it. Not that I haven't had women try to flirt with me to get off from a ticket, but I don't think it's what you have in mind.'

'Right. It would be way too obvious.' I thought about it for a minute. 'How about this. We go to some place like the Mezze,' I said, referring to a neighborhood restaurant. 'We can observe how couples react to each other.' He recognized it as similar to the kind of outings I had the writing group do and saw the point.

'Sure, that sounds like a good idea,' he said.

Now that it was settled, I relaxed and ate my food.

'You can tell Sara it was another winner,' I said when I'd practically scraped the plate clean. I got up to take it back to the kitchen to wash it before I gave it back to him. He grabbed my empty glass and followed me down the hall.

'Back to that guy,' he said. 'Do you really think it's wise giving him access to your office? You didn't give him a key, did you? How long has this been going on? You never said anything before.'

Men, I thought with an inward laugh. Ben sounded almost territorial, which was ridiculous under the circumstances. He was the one who'd told me it was nothing personal, but he couldn't deal with a relationship right now. I understood that he'd been blindsided by his divorce, but how long was it going to take him to move on?

I was also divorced. Mine had been a brief marriage in my early twenties to someone who'd felt trapped practically from the 'I do.' He'd dealt with it by never being home. I admit that it left me not so sure about marriage, but I was certainly up for a relationship with the right person. Rule number one was that the guy had to be in the same place. In other words, I wasn't interested in anyone who wasn't interested in having a relationship with me.

'He doesn't have a key to my place. I've been working with him for a couple of months. And I don't want to talk about what I'm doing for him,' I said, handing him his sister's dinner plate. 'It's confidential.'

'Well, then at least be careful,' he said. I walked him to the door. 'I better get this back to her or I'll never hear the end of it.' He put up his hands in a hopeless gesture. 'I'll never hear the end of it from her anyway.'

'By the way, you really don't have to knock. The door's on the latch, so you can just come in.' There was a brief pause and we awkwardly touched each other's arms. Just saying good night had seemed too cold and anything like a hug, too much. The arm touching was something in between.

I felt keyed up when Ben left and went through my ritual of putting everything back in its proper order hoping it would help. First, I straightened up the dining room. The table was clear except for a couple of paper clips and the stack of pages they'd left for me to read over. I moved the stack to the sideboard and set up the table for its regular purpose as a place to eat. I arranged my placemat in its usual spot, set a ceramic square decorated with sunflower nearby for anything hot I put on the table, and finally dropped off a small tray of condiments. I looked back at everything I'd set up in its precise place and shook my head. Had I really become so finicky that everything had to be in its correct spot?

If anything I felt tenser after realizing that unfortunate truth. I put the water on the stove hoping that some chamomile tea and crochet would help. While I waited for it to boil, I took the stack of papers to my office. I brushed the keyboard of my computer as I set down the papers and the screen came on. Tony's file was still open, but the screen was blank. As usual, once he printed it up, he'd deleted what I'd written for him.

The whistling of the kettle called me back to the kitchen. The water sputtered as I poured it over the tea bag into the mug. As the tea steeped, it filled the air with flowery scent that was almost too strong to be pleasing.

My thoughts went back to the evening and I wished that Tony and the group had never intersected. Talking to the group about doing some writing for a neighborhood place was not the same as them seeing an actual client and asking a lot of questions, particularly since I was writing such personal stuff for him. Ben's comments bothered me the most, maybe because they struck a nerve. The whole thing with Tony seemed a little odd. When he'd explained why he needed the letters it had seemed plausible. He traveled a lot and wanted to let his lady friend know he was thinking about her. He'd said he was good in person, but not so much with the written word. I knew almost nothing about him other than the obvious. And even less about the person to whom the letters were going. In the past I'd made a point to get at an idea who the recipient was, often meeting them, incognito of course. I thought back to what he'd said when I asked what her interests were, what he loved about her, even what she looked like. He'd been charmingly self-deprecating when he said he was hopeless when it came to describing her and his reason for not having me meet her was a little foggy now. It seemed as if he'd loaded me up with compliments about using my fabulous imagination. Somehow when he'd said that, I'd bought it without a second thought, but now it seemed a little shaky.

I took the mug into the living room and found a comfortable spot on the couch. Along with the tea, crocheting seemed to help smooth out the edges of the day. The bag with one of my projects was tucked behind the throw pillow with the purple iris pattern. I had been crocheting since I was a kid and had always worked on small squares of all kinds. Some had motifs like granny squares and others had different stitch patterns and were done in a variety of yarns. When I accumulated enough of them, I sewed them together into an afghan. I glanced up at the wall above the couch. A sample of one of my earliest finished projects was hanging there.

It brought on a flood of memories. It had just been my father and me then. We were inching our way back to normal after my mother's death a few years prior. I'd gifted the blanket to him and he'd kept it in his office at the university. He always bragged to his colleagues and students that his daughter had made it.

I glanced around the living room. It seemed bright and inviting with all the colors and personal touches. It was also so full of memories from the years when there had been more than just me living there.

Sometimes I just sat there staring at the room and thinking of all the moments that had happened in that space and I'd see a montage in my mind. A fall day with leaves fluttering by the windows. Then I'd almost feel the warm breeze coming through the open door to the balcony on a languid morning as my father sat in the wing chair reading the Sunday newspaper. The image of a darkened room, then the lights coming on as my mother came in the front door and everyone called out surprise. She had seemed so happy with all the people and presents. None of us could have guessed that it would be the last one we'd celebrate.

I saw a swirl of holidays. Christmas parties with the living room full of guests and the wonderful scent of pine from the decorated tree with its colorful lights. Then it was Halloween when I was dressed as a fairy ready to go out trick or treating as the leaves littered the sidewalk. I saw myself on my eighth birthday, dressed in pink, waiting for my party guests to arrive. Then there was me ready for my wedding, totally clueless about what I was about to get into. I stopped the mental pictures there before I could berate my former self for her mistake.

After that my mind still went back to Tony, and Ben's suggestion to let him go as a client. There was one thing I hadn't dealt with or told anyone. Tony was behind on paying me. It was confusing because he'd started off paying more than I'd asked. But the last few times, he'd said he'd catch up the next time or, like tonight, said nothing. He'd intimated that things were coming together in the relationship and they were on the verge of making a commitment. I told myself that he probably just wanted to pay me all at once.

THREE

The love-letter gigs like Tony's tended to last for a while, but most of my jobs were short-lived which meant that I was always looking for more work. I had two appointments about potential jobs and one about a job I was already working on. The nice part was they were all local, actually walking distance from my place.

It was a walking neighborhood and there were always people on the street. There were lots of tall trees and the apartment buildings were mostly vintage, brick, three-story buildings like mine. Most of them had been turned into condominiums. There were plenty of houses in assorted styles from Victorian to the boxy town houses that were relatively new in comparison.

I brought my coffee into the living room to check out the day before I decided how to dress. The TV weather report had been right for a change. It was the end of March and people were thinking about spring, but it was snowing so hard I could barely see across the street. The sidewalks and cars parked on the street were all covered in white. When I checked my balcony, the black wrought-iron railing of the fencing had a thick puff of white on top. The wind sent the big snowflakes into a swirl. All that white reflected light back into the living room making it seem very bright. Rocky joined me as I stood looking outside, drinking my coffee. He swirled around my ankles then jumped into the chair to get a view.

'Be glad you're an indoor cat,' I said, giving his head a stroke. He meowed which I took as agreement. Maybe it was wishful thinking. Melissa at the pet store had said it was safest to keep him as an indoor cat and, looking down at a truck rumbling along the street below, I had to agree with her. But it still seemed sad to keep him cut off from the outdoors. There was my balcony, but I worried that he'd see the sparrows that hung out in the tree out front and try to jump at them. I shuddered to think of the consequences. 'When the weather warms up, I'll figure something out,' I said to him. I'd heard that cats could walk on leashes and there were pet strollers that were enclosed. But for now, I was afraid he'd have to be content looking out the window.

There was something hypnotic about watching the snow fall, but I pulled myself away, having decided on wearing my meeting-a-potential-client outfit of black slacks and a black bulky turtleneck with a silk scarf thrown on for color.

It was an odd day to be dealing with ice cream. But I was meeting with the proprietor of a new place going into the small storefront tucked under the Metra train tracks.

The weather called for the full winter treatment and I put on a black wool jacket and a rose-colored beanie that I'd crocheted. I made sure there were gloves stuffed in the pocket and pulled on the boots that sat in the hall outside my door. The final professional touch was my peacock blue messenger bag.

I half expected Sara to open her door when I crossed the second-floor landing, but she must have been otherwise occupied. She always seemed to want to hear both Ben's and my take on our encounters. I know she kept hoping for something exciting like the fact that we'd kissed each other, but that wasn't going to happen. The only body contact we had was something akin to a pat on the arm as he left.

Outside it was like a winter wonderland. There was something so magic about fresh snow, even if I was longing to see violets and budding bushes.

As soon as I turned the corner on to 57th the scene changed. There were students with backpacks on their way to class. The coffee shop on the corner was busy. Someone was bringing a pack of laundry into the dry cleaner's and I had to dodge a man with a dolly filled with boxes as he rolled it across the sidewalk to the small market on the ground floor of an apartment building.

A sign that read *Coming Soon: The Ice-Cream Experience* hung over the small shop tucked under the viaduct. The windows were covered with white paper, making it impossible to see inside. A Metra train was just pulling in to the platform overhead and the train's bell clanged as I opened the shop's door. I expected it to be dim inside, but while the white paper made the windows opaque, it reflected back the light from the recessed fixtures in the ceiling. I gave the interior a quick survey. It didn't have the vibe of a usual ice-cream shop. The walls were painted a bluish gray and the whole place had an industrial feel instead of the usual pastels that went with the frozen treat. The counter was stainless steel and sat between two freezers with angled windows. Instead of bistro tables, a long common table ran along the covered window, with a few metal stools pushed under it. Natural wood shelves were built into a back wall and a doorway led into what I imagined was a kitchen area.

I'd just finished my appraisal when a woman came in from the back. She was younger than I'd expected and I guessed in her early twenties. Her dark hair was pulled into a ponytail and black-rimmed glasses dominated her face. There was something a little brittle about her that didn't seem to go with being a purveyor of ice cream. She seemed deep in thought and startled when she realized I was there.

'Sorry for surprising you. Maybe you should put a bell over the door,' I said in a friendly voice. 'I'm Veronica Blackstone. You wanted to talk to me about helping you with some copy.'

'Right,' she said, sounding none too happy. 'I'm Haley Hess.' She reached out her hand to shake mine.

'I'm just curious, how did you find out about me?' I asked.

She seemed distressed. 'They said I needed a professional and gave me your name. Just because they put up the money doesn't mean they can tell me what to do,' she said in a strident tone. 'They are not going to run this place from behind the scenes.'

'OK,' I said calmly. 'Maybe you should tell me what you're interested in having done.'

'Just so you understand. I could do it all myself, but they insisted it was a deal breaker if I didn't have some outside help.'

'So, I'm guessing you want something for your website. Sometimes it's better when the person writing it has a little distance. I'm sure that's what your backer meant. I'm sure you know that everything is about the story now. A business has to have a personality. Who's the owner and how did the place come about.'

She nodded. 'I need that and descriptions of my products. Apparently, you can't just list the ingredients anymore.' She let out a frustrated sigh. 'I don't really have a choice about hiring you, so we might as well get to it.' She came out from behind the counter and pulled out two stools inviting me to sit. 'The point of this place is that the flavors are going to be different and unusual.'

I was curious who had recommended me and considered asking her for a name, but on second thought I was sure it would set her off. What was the difference anyway? I took out my notebook and pen. She seemed surprised. I suppose she expected me to pull out a computer or at the very least a tablet. But I was old-fashioned that way; besides, a notebook and pen didn't require a battery.

'Just to reassure you, you would have the final say on anything I wrote for you. My aim is for you to be satisfied. Why don't you tell me a little about yourself and how this place came to be?'

She immediately brightened. 'I look at ice cream as a vehicle for mixing interesting flavors and textures. It is imperative that they are described in an interesting, complex way. This is not going to be the spot you go for a hot fudge sundae. If we have sundaes at all they will be original, like maybe a sauce made of smashed strawberries bathed in balsamic vinegar.' She went on for a few minutes about wanting her place to be unique and memorable.

I was beginning to get a picture here. This was not going to be a place hosting kids' birthday parties. I wondered if she'd even allow kids in, thinking they didn't have a sophisticated enough palate.

'I just graduated from the UChicago,' she said. 'I thought the money was a graduation present. You know, came with no strings. Ha! I can't wait until I'm paying my own way, then let them try to interfere.' It was like she was talking to herself and then she turned back to me and abruptly pulled herself together. I could have guessed the part about graduating from the university, probably with a degree in some area of science that taught her about the molecular makeup of ice cream. Her jaw looked so tense that I was sure she had to sleep with a night guard in her mouth.

'I've been fascinated with interesting mixtures since I was a child. And the history of ice cream,' she said abruptly. 'You have to put in something about that. It's been around for centuries, well, not exactly in the form we think of, but I think there is something in people that makes them crave frozen concoctions.' As she talked, I was beginning to understand why someone told her to hire me. She was a little all over the place. From talking about the world history of ice cream, she suddenly started talking about her own. 'When I was a child I'd take vanilla ice cream and mix in all kind of things – like fruits, vegetable and spices. I thought they were wonderful, but not everyone agreed.' She looked over at me scribbling some notes. 'I want the flavors described as different and innovative.'

'You mean something that would entice them to want to have a taste experience,' I said, and she nodded. It seemed like something I could easily do. It was all about making it seem like a taste adventure. Maybe I'd put in something about where the ingredients were sourced. I always thought it was fascinating that vanilla came from an orchid.

'I'll get something I'm working on for you to taste.' She went in the back and returned with a dish of it with a spoon stuck in. She'd brought some water to clear my palate between tastes. 'I'm not going to tell you what I call the flavor. Let me see if you can dissect the complexity and detect all the different layers.'

I got worried when I saw some pinkish flecks on top and noted a smoky fragrance. 'Is that bacon?' I asked and she nodded. I hesitated over what to say. I wanted the gig, but I also couldn't stomach trying something with meat in it. I finally decided to be honest and told her I was a vegetarian, though I'd eaten bacon before becoming one and remembered the flavor. She pursed her lips and, though her glasses made it hard to tell, I think she furrowed her brow. I started to push back on the stool, figuring we were done.

'I wouldn't want anyone to say I discriminated. Let me get you some without the bacon. It's actually an add-in,' she said. She went into the back and came back with another dish of ice cream that looked about the same without the pinkish flecks. 'Just be sure that you make the description of the bacon specific,' and I nodded in agreement.

'It's not enough to just say bacon anymore. The one I use is pasture-raised and smoked over maple wood.'

I took a taste of the ice cream and let it roll around in my mouth, taking in the flavor. It took a moment for it to register what I was tasting. 'It's breakfast ice cream,' I said. 'Mixed in with the creaminess, there are bits of buttermilk pancakes laced with the sweetness of real maple syrup that remind me of a Sunday breakfast.' I looked for her reaction and she nodded. 'Crowned with smokey sweet sprinkles of . . . pasture-raised, maple-wood-smoked bacon.' I put the spoon down and wrote down a shorthand version of what I'd just said.

'That's it, exactly,' she said sounding pleased. 'I think we can work around any ice creams with meat. Do you eat fish? I was thinking that smoked whitefish might make an interesting flavor,' she said. I kept my smile and forced my eyes not to roll. Vegetarian meant you didn't eat meat, fowl or fish. But people who weren't vegetarians often seemed to think fish didn't count. Besides, smoked whitefish ice cream? Just imagining the smell made me gag. I had to ask her what else she had in mind anyway.

'I'm working on a Caesar salad ice cream,' she said. 'Maybe I'll just leave the anchovies out of it. It was just a hint of their flavor anyway. Though you've given me an idea. I can make a vegetarian version of the breakfast ice cream and use coconut bacon instead.'

I kept what I thought of the flavors of ice cream to myself. It was my place to write the descriptions, not judge. Even though I wondered if I was doing her a favor by not telling her what I thought. For now I just wanted to get it straight if she was indeed hiring me. She had started muttering something about vegan ice cream and started to scribble down some notes. She seemed to have drifted off into space and I understood that I was going to have to pull her back to earth to talk business.

'I think I understand what you need,' I said. 'And you're OK with hiring me?'

She shrugged. 'Sure, I guess. So, yeah, go ahead and do your thing.' I could understand why her backer thought she needed help. I was casual with my business, but I needed more than that to start working.

'How about I write up a proposal – what I'll do and how much.' I looked at her to see if it was registering. She seemed to be half listening. 'If you like it, you can sign it and there's a matter of a deposit. Then I can start.'

'OK,' she said nodding. 'But what about the ice cream I had you taste?' She looked at my notebook as I shut it and dropped it in the messenger bag.

'Fine. I'll write up that description and it's yours no matter what.'

This was going to be an interesting gig.

FOUR

C aesar salad ice cream? I know I said it wasn't my job to judge, but still if she gave me an awful flavor to taste, I was going to say something. I couldn't help getting too involved when I worked for somebody.

Though I had managed to keep a distance with Tony, and had stuck to doing just what he asked for instead of telling him I thought the letters would be better if they were more personal, starting with using her name instead of the endearing terms he'd had me use. But what did I know? He'd said they were close to making a commitment, whatever that was supposed to mean.

I'd been so involved with Haley and her ice-cream flavors, I'd forgotten all about the snow until I walked outside and saw that not only had the big flakes stopped falling, but the sky had cleared and the sun was out, melting all the white away.

The sidewalk glistened, the water reflecting the sunlight, as I headed to my next appointment. I had to dodge a group of four students jogging toward the lakefront. There were others on the sidewalk going toward the campus. Student housing was spread around the whole neighborhood which meant there were always students going somewhere. There was plenty of other foot traffic as well since people in the neighborhood walked as a means to get somewhere, not just as a form of exercise.

There was a sprinkling of businesses on 57th Street, but 53rd was the main commercial street in the neighborhood and where my next stop was located. I was pretty sure I'd get the gig with Haley even if it seemed under protest, but I wasn't sure how the next one was going to turn out. Haley's ice-cream concept was almost too trendy while this next place was just the opposite. It was an old-fashioned kids' shoe store. It was where I'd gotten my Mary Janes when I was little, along with countless other neighborhood kids. But the world had changed a lot since then. It was a family-owned business and some of the younger members were interested in keeping the store going. I was there to pitch them on how I could help.

The front window featured a train set circling a display of little shoes. Walking inside the storefront brought back instant memories of coming in there holding my mother's hand. The interior looked exactly the same all these years later – good for nostalgia, but would it be good for business?

The store had been in the neighborhood for over sixty years, long before there was a need for personality pieces. It was enough to be local, with an occasional advertisement in the neighborhood newspaper to get more than enough customers.

It was also before the need for clever names for shops and it was simply called Handelman's Children's Shoe Store. Rows of chairs with red leatherette seats flanked the side walls. Stools shaped like elephants sat ready for a salesperson to sit on while they fit shoes on a pair of little feet. In the center at the back was a cow jumping over the moon. The cow was on a track and made a trip over the moon and then returned to its starting position. A far cry from all the digital stuff that decorated shops now.

The current Handelmans running the place were the grand-children of the original owners. I assumed the athletic-looking, dark-haired man about my age dealing with a customer was one of them. He was sitting on one of the elephant-shaped stools helping a kid about four dressed in a Spider-Man costume try on a pair of Spider-Man boots while the little boy's mother stared at her phone. I watched as the man had the little boy stand up and walk around. Then he did a lot of touching around the toe area. He was actually making sure the boots fit right.

A woman of similar age with a clear family resemblance was at the front counter. I walked up to her and put on a friendly smile. 'You must be Emily Handelman,' I said, taking out a business card. 'I'm Veronica Blackstone.' I glanced toward the man. 'I spoke to your brother on the phone about some copy you needed.'

Her wavy dark hair was cut short and her silver dangle

earrings jangled as she leaned toward me and kept her voice low. 'It was my idea to contact you.' She drew me over to the side. 'Our grandparents were running the place until they moved to Florida. Business had been going down and they wanted to close up the shoe store, but Lewis convinced them to give us a shot at running it. Well, and he convinced me to go in on the plan. It was always just a store for locals, but Lewis thinks we can make it into an iconic place through a website and some PR. That we can somehow convince people to come here where an experienced staff can properly fit their children's shoes instead of buying them online or picking them up at a store with shopping carts where you are on your own.' She let out her breath and I smiled at her, thinking that was sure a mouthful. She looked at her brother. 'Lewis thought he could create all the copy for the website – don't tell him I said it, but he's not a writer. Actually, he's a substitute gym teacher. We're sharing the duties of running the place while we both have other jobs until . . .' She rolled her eyes and I got the message until the place was profitable.

'I love this place. I know the décor is dated, but I think it's adorable.' She looked at me. 'I heard good things about what you do. You wrote a mystery and write all kinds of copy. I heard you even solved a murder.'

I bowed my head and blushed. 'I did write a mystery, and I do write all kinds of copy. The murder solving is more or less true,' I said. It was funny how I liked hearing good things about my accomplishments, but I was uncomfortable at the same time. I was anxious to change the subject and I looked around at the place. 'I think I understand what you're after. You need to give the store a personality, make it a star. Of course, I'd need background information to create a story.'

She stopped to think for a moment. 'Lewis and I know some stuff, but you'd really need to talk to our aunt. She worked here when she was in high school and college, but then she became a jewelry designer. She knows all about everything.' She glanced toward her brother who'd brought out several boxes of Incredible Hulk sneakers and was showing them to the boy's mother. 'I'm sure she'd talk to you. She's kind of bummed out over a bust-up with her boyfriend. She's in her fifties and I thought you took things better by the time you got older.' She stopped herself. 'Sorry, I shouldn't be telling you her personal business. Please don't say anything about it to her. I'm not even supposed to know.' She glanced in the direction of her brother as he held up a bright green shoe.

I was only half listening and nodded in agreement just as my smart watch binged, announcing my next appointment. 'I'm going to see another client after this. LaPorte's,' I said, pointing in the general direction of the bakery and café.

'They're your clients?' she said, sounding impressed. She was curious what I was doing for them. There was nothing secretive about the sort of copy I was providing for them, so there was no reason not to tell her.

'It's a family business like yours,' I began. 'And they've decided to open up branches in other neighborhoods. I'm going to be writing some publicity material for them with the history of their business. It's about the personality of a place, but then I think you know that.' She nodded with a smile.

'The original owners are neighborhood people like my grandparents. I heard they were expanding. I love their chocolate mint cake. It's been a birthday tradition for us.' She laughed. 'I'm making myself hungry. I think I'll grab lunch there today.'

She had a sudden thought. 'I didn't tell you, but we're bringing back the prize jar.' She left and came back with a huge barrel-shaped jar filled with clear cellophane bags. Each contained a toy or game.

'I remember the prize jar,' I said. 'I got my shoes here when I was little.'

Emily smiled. 'I got mine here, too, but then I guess that's obvious. We love this place, that's why we're doing whatever we can to keep it going. We need to change it from being a neighborhood place where people bring their kids to get shoes, to being a destination where people come from all over.' She smiled sheepishly. 'I know I'm repeating myself, but I'm afraid all I think about is how to make this store more successful. We want to sell the experience and the quality we offer. We don't just bring out shoes for kids to try on. We fit them. You can't get that online.' She sighed. 'Here I go again. I can't seem to turn off. Sorry.'

'It looks like your brother is going to be awhile,' I said. 'I think I understand what you want. How about I write up a proposal and come back tomorrow when we can all talk?'

'That sounds perfect,' she said.

She'd gotten me excited about the place and I was already rooting for them to succeed. I knew I'd get the gig, but I also knew that – with what they had on the line and the fact both of them were working at other jobs – there was no way I would charge them anything close to what I usually got paid.

Just then the cow started making its trip over the moon while below it a dish and spoon were holding hands and their feet moved. The movement of the cow was hardly smooth, but it was fun to watch anyway. I looked at the junior Spider-Man checking it out. To my surprise he clapped his hands with excitement. Good to know that they could still delight.

LaPorte's Bakery and Café was barely a block away. I jumped at the chance to do some work for them when I was contacted by Rex LaPorte. It was local and a place I liked. All the backstory I really knew about the bakery and café was that it had started with a cake and had recently relocated from a storefront on the ground floor of an apartment building to a newish structure that had housed a bookstore from a now defunct chain.

From what I gathered, everyone in Hyde Park knew about the place and probably had had one of the chocolate mint cakes as a birthday cake, but they were only known marginally outside the neighborhood.

It had been fine to have the menu of the café offerings on a dry erase board, but now that they were expanding they wanted to have something printed that had more detail. Rex had said they were looking for a way to play up the family angle for the new locations as well. They needed website copy, menu descriptions and promotional material – it was a big job for me and paid accordingly.

I walked into the ground-floor area of the two-story building.

Big windows looked out on the street and let in copious amounts of sunshine. The floor was a pale wood, as were the tables, all of which added to the brightness of the interior. In addition to the smaller tables, there was a long community table which had become the norm. A buttery smell of sweetness permeated the air as I looked around the interior. Several people were in line to order food at the counter. A dry erase board stood on a chair with their offering. I smiled at the soup offering listed simply as *vegetable* and thought of what I could do with it. Something like *a hearty broth with chunks of garden vegetables*. Maybe I'd be more specific and say *sweet kernels of corn, vine-ripened tomato quarters and corkscrew pasta*. I passed by another counter with a line waiting to buy baked goods and found the elevator hidden on the side, taking it up to the second floor.

The baking smells wafted up there, but it looked totally different. The space had been divided into offices with a communal area in the front with some tables and chairs. As I approached the door leading to the offices, I heard conversation coming from inside. Conversation was a nice way to put it, but it sounded more like a disagreement. Interrupting an argument didn't seem like a good way to start with a new client. No one was watching me, so I decided to give it a few minutes and see if the dispute was settled and then I'd knock at the door. I told myself I was only eavesdropping so I could tell when the argument was over.

'This is so last minute. I don't understand why you agreed to it,' a man's voice said.

'It will be fine. When people want to get married and want to keep it simple, there's no reason it can't be done,' the woman said.

'Don't you at least think you should consult with the family for their input?'

'No,' the woman said, sounding exasperated. 'They'll only make a fuss. It's best to leave it as is.' I could only hear part of what the man said, but it was something about all the information.

That seemed to be the end of their discussion. I waited for a breath and then knocked on the door.

Instead of inviting me in, they came out, both giving me a blank stare. I recognized Rex LaPorte as he was a familiar figure around the neighborhood and the person I'd been in contact with.

'Veronica Blackstone,' I said, reminding him who I was and that we'd spoken on the phone and emailed back and forth. His face lit with recognition and he shook my hand. The casual dress of jeans and a polo shirt made him look more like a worker than the boss. He seemed somewhere in his fifties and had the shape of someone who enjoyed a good meal.

He glanced at his watch and his face clouded over. 'I'm so sorry. I forgot you were coming. There's so much going on with the expansion and trying to keep this place humming. I'm actually on my way out. You can talk to my sister,' he said, indicating the woman.

She was wearing a white chef's coat over a pair of jeans. Her brown hair was tied back, a few tendrils falling free. I'd noticed that many people had one feature that seemed to define them. With her, it was her smile. It was big and a little goofy and hers turned her eyes into slits that carried the merry look.

He turned to her. 'Be sure and tell how we started.' The woman made a face.

'I know what to tell her,' she said. Then she looked at me. 'He's used to being the one in charge.' She shook her head in an exasperated manner. 'He forgets that I'm a grown woman who knows what she's doing.'

'I'm sure you like to think so,' he said. 'All I'm saying is not to rush into anything.'

I felt like I was in the middle of something between them, probably connected to whatever they were *discussing* before. It was as if she realized how they sounded and tried to smooth it over.

'Don't mind us. We had a disagreement about a wedding cake order. That's what happens when you have a family business,' she said with a shrug.

'Right,' he said in a flat tone. 'Now I really have to go.' He went to the counter and picked up one of their trademark sunny yellow boxes with LaPorte's Bakery written in a dark gold and hesitated.

'Go, already,' she said, waving him off with her hands before turning back to me. 'Excuse my brother's manners. I'm Cocoa LaPorte. My real name is Jennifer, but everybody calls me Cocoa.'

'Is that like Coco Chanel?' I asked. The mood had changed with the departure of her brother and she seemed ultra-friendly.

'No, C-o-c-o-a as in the chocolate powder. It's because of our signature cake. My mother thought Cocoa sounded better than Choco.' She looked at me to see if I understood. 'It's short for Chocolate.' She glanced toward the seating area. 'We can sit over there. After we get you something to eat. We never do anything here without food.'

She walked me over to the kitchen area. There was a plate of mini cinnamon croissants and two vacuum pots with coffee. One was labeled decaf and the other dark roast. I grabbed a paper cup and gave the top of the pot a push; a tiny stream of dark liquid came out, followed by some bubbles and a whoosh to indicate it was empty.

Cocoa looked displeased as she pulled out her cell phone and tapped something in it. She stepped away, but I still heard her chew somebody out for the empty coffee pot. A moment later, she was all smiles when she pointed me to one of the tables. 'Someone will bring you a fresh cup in a minute.'

I thanked her and pulled out my notebook and pen. I decided to start with a little small talk. 'Do you have children working in the business?'

'Twins, and not only do they want to be different from each other, but separate from me.' She added a sigh and it seemed as if she accepted their decision, but didn't like it. 'My brother thinks you are just what our business needs, now that we're expanding out of the neighborhood. We need to have something to make us stand out. To make us legendary.' She punctuated it with a big smile.

'I've heard good things about you,' she continued. 'I understand you write mysteries and anything that has words in it.'

'It's mystery,' I said. 'I like the way you described what I do. I may just use that and say I'll write anything that has words in it.' I looked down at the notebook. 'We probably should get started.' Just then my coffee arrived and I took a grateful sip. I set it down and took a dainty bite of the cinnamon croissant. It tasted so good it was hard not to swoon.

'Of course,' she said. 'I'll give you the deluxe version. The best place is to start at the beginning. Our whole soon-to-be empire began in my mother's kitchen. She was a fantastic baker and her signature cake was the chocolate mint cake with buttercream icing. Everybody who tasted it, loved it. She began to get orders for the cakes. It came at a good time because she'd been laid off her teaching job and we needed the money. The orders kept coming. I helped her with the baking and Rex was the delivery guy. The orders were from neighborhood people and he used our red wagon to carry the white cake boxes. Everyone was happy to see him because it meant there was a cake on the way. It's the same now. He does a lot of deliveries himself. And everybody is still happy to see him. Of course, now there's more than just our signature cake and the boxes are yellow.'

She stopped for a moment and took a piece of a cinnamon croissant. 'You'd think I'd be immune to all this by now. But I have to say our baked goods are fantastic. We use the best of ingredients, just like my mother did.' She shook her head and smiled. 'Sorry for getting off track. I was telling you how we got started. The chocolate mint cake was super popular, but I guess she got bored just making one kind of cake and she added a pound cake and carrot cake. Then she started adding some other items. These cinnamon croissants were next. And our kitchen became too small, so she rented a commercial kitchen. It got to the point where she was selling the baked goods through several stores in the neighborhood. That's when she and my father decided to take the leap and open our own place. There was some extra room, so they added a few tables. She started making bread which led to us offering sandwiches. Salads came next. The menu was small but we kept the prices low. Through it all my mother and I did most of the baking and my father handled the business.' Her shoulders dropped. 'But it all changed when he died. Now it's just Rex and me running things, though the expansion idea was mostly his. Soon the whole city will love the chocolate mint cake,' she said with a smile, then dropped her voice. 'We're the only ones who know the recipe.' She leaned closer. 'Top secret. If I tell you what's in it, I'd have to kill you.' Though it seemed like she was teasing, something in her expression made me wonder if she meant it. Before I could think much about it, she had sat up and moved on.

'One of the things we're going to want you to do is write up new descriptions of the menu items. We keep expanding our food offerings and changing them. We're trying more ethnic dishes. Up until now, the descriptions were really just a laundry list of what was in something. Like one of our sandwiches is listed as *ham and cheese on your choice of bread.*' She looked at me. 'That doesn't really work anymore. We need to say something more exciting. You know, something more descriptive.'

While she was talking my cup of coffee arrived and I took another bite of the croissant and was instantly lost in the deliciousness of the pastry. She gave me a knowing smile and continued talking, letting me savor every delicious bite. When I'd eaten the last crumb, I offered my suggestion for the ham and cheese sandwich. I had the gig and didn't have to audition anymore, but I couldn't help myself. 'I'd probably suggest something like savory slices of oven-roasted ham paired with flavorful English cheddar cheese on freshly baked bread or a flaky croissant.'

'That's excellent,' she said, giving me a tiny round of applause, 'but we're all about being authentic so we'd like you to sample everything and write your descriptions from your experience.'

My smile at the praise faded and I realized there was a problem.

'About that ham sandwich,' I said, feeling uncomfortable before explaining my dietary situation. I could see the job ending before it began.

'So you're a vegetarian,' she said, looking over my face as if there'd be some kind of telltale sign. 'I guess we can work around it. We like the idea of working with someone local. You can use your fiction skills on anything with meat. All you have to do is throw in some interesting adjectives,' she said with a friendly smile before looking down at my notebook. I had put down the pen when I'd gotten so immersed in eating and went to grab it back. 'To continue with the story, we're a family business and we've always kept things small. It took forever for us to move here. We're expanding because we have enough adult family members to run new locations. That should give you some background,' she said, standing. 'You can do it in a series of tastings. It's too much for one sitting. And there will be chances for you to get more information. This is all new to us. Thank heavens we have some help. Now, if you'll excuse me, there are some cakes waiting for me to bake.'

I walked home with an upbeat feeling, being pretty sure that I had three gigs. Next time I heard from Tony, I was going to tell him we were done.

FIVE

'I found the perfect place to check out romantic behavior. It's not in your neighborhood, but if you're free, we could go there tonight,' Ben said. I'd barely gotten in the house when he called. He'd just gotten off his shift and suggested driving into the city.

I thought about it for a moment. It was tempting. I was without a car and I used Uber and Lyft sparingly, depending mostly on the Metra train. The idea of being whisked away someplace interesting sounded great. I could start work on my three gigs in the morning, writing up the notes from all of them and preparing the proposals for Haley and the Handelmans.

'Yes,' I said. 'That sounds great.'

'I'd like to keep my sister out of it.'

'I agree.' I laughed, imagining if she saw us leaving together. 'She'd read way too much in it.'

'I could just stop out front,' he said, sounding a little uncertain.

'And you'll honk?' I was joking but he took it seriously.

'Honk the horn? Who does that?' he said, confused.

My usual behavior would have been to keep my thought process to myself, but I decided it was better to explain. 'I was joking. It's something out of the ancient past, if movies are true, where the nice girl in town gets picked up by her bad-boy boyfriend so her parents don't know.'

'Oh,' he said with a little laugh. 'I guess the modern version of that is a text, though it seems too bland for a bad boy to use. But exactly what I was going to suggest.' There was the hint of a smile in his tone.

I told him I'd be awaiting his message and we signed off. He hadn't mentioned the destination, so I dressed in my all-purpose outfit of black jeans and a black turtleneck sweater finished off with a scarf for color. I stuck to leather ankle boots as footwear. After a few runs with a hairbrush, I redid my makeup with a little more care than usual. The last touch was a spritz of rose-scented cologne.

When Ben texted me, I grabbed my jacket and purse and went downstairs. I tiptoed past Sara's, afraid she'd open the door. She'd smell the perfume and figure something was up.

I was pretty sure the black Wrangler double parked in front of the building belonged to Ben, but just to be sure I peered in the window as I crossed the sidewalk. Ben lowered the passenger window and gave me a wave. It was higher off the ground than the typical SUV and I was really glad this wasn't a date because I was hardly graceful as I launched myself into the passenger seat.

The first thing I did was check out what he was wearing. He'd stepped things up a notch and had on slacks and a sweater. I caught a whiff of cologne and he caught me sniffing.

'I hope you approve. I'm practicing for our fake dates,' he said.

'It looks good to me,' I said. 'So, where are we going?'

'I did a little research and found a fondue restaurant known to be a romantic spot. It seemed like a good place for us to study how people act so we can emulate.' He explained it was in Old Town which was located just north of Downtown and was filled with cafés, trendy shops and hip entertainment venues.

'This feels a little naughty,' I said as he headed toward the outer drive. 'I really should be home doing some work for my new clients.'

'New clients?' he said. 'More love letters?' There was a touch of disapproval in his voice.

'No, this time it's ice cream, food and kids' shoes.' We had started to drive north and I glanced toward the lake which was lost in the darkness. As we passed downtown, I watched a plane fly out over the water and then hook around to fly over the city, lowering to land at O'Hare. He chuckled when I told him about Haley's weird ice-cream flavors. He'd already heard about the chocolate mint cake. When I mentioned the décor at the kids' shoe store, he suggested I tell Sara to take Mikey there.

It was a challenge to find a parking spot, which turned out to be several blocks from the restaurant, but while it was cold there was no wind and there were lots of interesting shop windows to take in.

The restaurant was located in a storefront at the base of an apartment building. The lights were low enough to make everyone look their best, but bright enough to see the other patrons in the restaurant. It appeared Ben's research was right. All the people in the place seemed like they were on a date. They had their heads together as they dabbled long forks in the pots in the middle of the tables. I saw a man lift a fork with a cube of bread oozing warm cheese and feed it to his companion. Ben saw it too.

'I bet this is the kind of place your lover-boy client takes his lady friend,' he said as we sat down at a table in the middle of the restaurant. 'Too bad he isn't here. He'd probably have all the moves down and would be a good one for us to study.' Ben had reverted to his flat cop tone of voice, but his distaste for Tony was obvious.

It was ridiculous, but I felt as though I had to defend Tony. 'You don't know him,' I said. 'He's not the oily operator you seem to think he is. He's just like the rest of us, trying to get together with someone.'

'Is that what he told you?' Ben said, staring at me directly.

'Well, yeah, more or less. He said something about wanting someone who looked beyond his good looks and nice wardrobe. And I guess he found her, but he needed help in sealing the deal, which is where I came in.'

Ben rolled his eyes. 'He sounds like a con man who knows just the right thing to say to whoever he's speaking to. He pegged you as someone who wasn't sold by good looks and a cashmere overcoat.'

'I don't think so,' I said. I'd tried to keep my tone even, but I was sure it came out defensive. Ben had to be wrong. I was about to say that he hadn't conned me out of anything, but then I stopped myself. He had charmed me into working in a way I didn't like and now he owed me money. 'Maybe we should order,' I said, hoping to change the subject.

I was relieved when Ben picked up the menu and we began

to discuss what we would order. Since everything was meant to be shared, we decided on the cheese fondue. I got an ice tea and Ben ordered a beer.

We spent the time waiting for the food checking out the crowd. I watched as a woman's coat slipped off the back of her chair. I nudged Ben as her companion picked it up, replacing it and putting his arm around her for just a moment as he did. 'That's good, a subtle but affectionate touch.'

'You want to practice?' he said, eying my jacket. There was a twinkle in his eye and I knew he was joking.

'We're just here to observe,' I said, smiling as I held on to my jacket.

It took two servers to bring the fondue pot and the tray of dipping items. Then came a lot of instructions and warnings about hot liquids and the flame underneath the pot.

'Whew, that was a lot,' I said when they finally left. We both looked over the set-up.

'We're not going to feed each other, right?' Ben said. I thought he was being serious again, but then he cocked a smile.

We put our 'romantic body language' study on hold while we dealt with the food. It was definitely not for the famished. It was a slow process of loading a piece of bread on the fork, dipping it in the liquid cheese, letting the excess drip off before finally delivering it to your mouth. But it was sensual and I got why the place was a lovers' hangout.

'You were right about this place,' I said. 'Next date I go on, I'm coming here.'

'What happened? Did you meet somebody yesterday?' he said. 'I thought we were in the same place about that. You're still too bummed over your divorce.' There was no even cop tone now.

'No, I didn't meet somebody yesterday,' I said, rolling my eyes at the thought. Remembering that I'd made it seem like I was as standoffish as he was about getting involved with anyone, I was careful about what I said. 'I meant that when I'm ready for a relationship and I find that person, I'd suggest this place.'

He seemed disconcerted. 'So nothing has changed for us

and this project? You're not going to suddenly say you don't need me anymore.'

'Nothing's changed. I still need a stand-in, as you do. And we still need to figure out how to act so we seem authentic.'

'OK, then,' he said and he let out his breath. 'Should we get dessert? There's one called lovers' chocolate,' he said, reading it over. 'A pot of warm chocolate with ripe whole strawberries for dipping.'

We were interrupted by a noise coming from the next table. I couldn't describe what it was, other than maybe a grunt or someone gagging. We both turned to look. The man was staring at his companion as cheese dripped off the cube of bread at the end of his fork. Her eyes were bugged out as she flailed around.

'Hey, man, she's choking,' Ben said, already getting out of his chair. The man seemed frozen as Ben passed by him and rushed behind the woman. He hit her on the back a number of times and nothing happened. He bent her forward and grabbed her around the middle. After one strong thrust something flew out of her mouth. She started to fall forward, but Ben caught her and hung on until she collected herself. By now the whole restaurant was staring at him and broke out in applause. Ben took a bow and held up his badge as he said, 'All in a day's work.'

'Impressive,' I said when he came back to our table. 'You're a regular hero.'

'Hardly. It really is all in a day's work, and that's nothing. I had to put a tourniquet on a chef about to bleed out after he . . .' He stopped himself. 'There's no reason to give the gory details.'

We ended up not getting dessert, though the management encouraged us to have it and insisted on picking up the check. 'Sorry we didn't get much chance to observe couples,' he said on our walk back to the Wrangler.

'I'm sure that woman would think what you did was far more important.' I was still processing the whole evening and how effortlessly he'd stepped in and basically saved the woman's life.

When we finally got to my street, Ben pulled into a parking

spot right in front of my building. 'You're welcome to come up,' I said. 'I can offer you a glass of my cooking wine.' Since even a sip of wine went right to my head, I didn't drink, but I did use wine in cooking.

He glanced up toward the third floor. 'I'd like to, but my sister has a sixth sense and I know she'd manage to open the door as we were going by. One look at us in our dress-up duds and she'd be having Mikey fitted for a tuxedo so he could be a ring bearer.'

We both laughed at the idea and I opened the door to get out of the car. There was an awkward moment when I wondered how we should mark the end of our evening. It was like he read my thoughts. 'Do you think a hug would be appropriate?' he said. I nodded, reaching across the console and we embraced quickly before I made my exit.

It had been quite a night.

SIX

I was still processing the previous evening when I got up on Thursday morning. Rocky followed me back to the kitchen and as usual ate some of his dry food, while I made coffee and what had become my regular breakfast of an orange along with toast and a hard-boiled egg. I brought everything into the dining room and put it on the placemat on the dining-room table. I glanced up at the bookcase, filled with things I'd collected and others left from my parents. The only thing that seemed to change from day to day was the angle of the sun. Rocky had finished with his breakfast and had come into the dining room and as usual jumped on to an adjacent chair, waiting until he could move over into my lap.

As I sliced the egg and buttered the toast, I suddenly saw myself in a new light, and not a very happy one. I'd become a spinster lady, living surrounded by memories, whose only companion was a cat. Though since I had been married once, was I really a spinster or a divorcée? The term didn't really matter. I was stuck in a rut, either working or repeating the same routines. Even my crocheting of squares reeked of dullness. I was no fun. The outing the night before had made me realize how far I'd fallen, so that even a fake date was a big event.

It was natural for my thoughts to go to Ben. I thought back to when he'd first started with the group and seemed so one-dimensional. Even his writing was so bare bones with no emotion. As I'd gotten to know him outside the group, I'd glimpsed more of his personality. But last night had been different. The way he'd stepped in and saved that woman's life, as if it was nothing special, had wowed me. I only stayed on that thought for a moment before it morphed into me thinking of how he could incorporate that into his story. I couldn't help it, I was always thinking about writing. And then it morphed into thinking about my own work.

All my notes from the day before were waiting for me. I hoped I wouldn't freeze up. I hated it when I stared at the screen and nothing would come. It didn't happen that often with the writing I did for other people, but remembering how I was still struggling with the second mystery made me wary.

I made an effort to alter my routine, and didn't refill my coffee cup when I'd drunk half of it. My big stab at getting out of the rut was waiting until the whole cup was gone. And then instead of staying in the dining room, I took it into my office. I had to talk myself out of fretting that I was going to spill it over the keyboard.

Making an effort to do something different, I threw open the frosted French doors that led to the living room. I usually kept them shut so as to keep my office space separate. Sunlight streamed in, taking away the usual semi gloom due to there being only one window, which looked out on the narrow space between my building and the next.

I still had to turn on the student lamp with the yellow glass shades, but everything was brighter. Rocky came in and looked around. Instead of his usual spot in the burgundy wing chair, he settled in a sunny spot on the floor. Maybe we both needed to get out of our usual habits.

I thumbed through my notebook, reading over the notes I'd taken the day before. I typed them into the computer, fleshing them out as I did and adding questions that I had. I got lost in my work of writing the proposals. When it came to price, I went bargain-basement cheapest for the Handelmans and a fair amount for Haley Hess and her ice-cream business, since I sensed dealing with her was going to be a challenge.

When I looked at the clock, I was stunned that the morning was gone. It had seemed only moments since I'd taken my coffee into my office. Rocky had changed position, trying to keep up with the moving sunny spot.

I printed everything up and got myself together to deliver the proposals. I could have done it online as I had with LaPorte's, but I preferred to deal directly whenever I could. It was good to have a reason to go outside and be in the world. As I approached the papered-over windows of Haley's shop I wondered if she would have some other weird ice cream to taste. But there was no response when I knocked on the door to her place, so I slid the papers under it.

There wasn't even a hint that it had snowed the day before. Chicago was known for weather that changed abruptly. The sun was out and it was warm enough to leave my jacket open, making it a good day for walking, and I looked forward to my trek to 53rd. I passed a row of lilac bushes and looked at the naked brown branches. The softness in the air made me think of spring and how those branches would be covered in green leaves and heavy scented lavender flowers. I could already smell them in my imagination.

There was a bustling feeling to 53rd after the quiet of the side street. Cars clogged the roadway and the sidewalk had a parade of people. When I reached Handelman's shoe store, I glanced through the window before I went in. I had mixed feelings when I saw that Emily and Lewis were behind the counter and all the seats were empty. I would be able to talk to both of them, which was good, but having no customers was bad.

The cow made a shaky trip over the moon with no claps of delight as I walked through the store. The pair looked up with anticipation, but it faded when they saw it was me.

'In no time, this place will be packed with little girls getting party shoes for Easter and sandals for the summer. We just have to get people to understand how special this shop is,' I said in a cheerful voice.

I dropped my messenger bag on one of the chairs and pulled out the proposal. Both Emily and Lewis seemed uncomfortable as they glanced at the paper in my hand. I knew they were getting ready to tell me they couldn't afford my services. I held out the proposal anyway. 'I'm giving you my bare-bones rate because I love this store and I believe in you two. I've made it so you would give me a bonus when the business turns around.'

Lewis took the sheet and read it over. His melancholy expression morphed into a genuine smile. 'This looks good,' he said, looking from the paper to me. 'This seems like something we could manage and the idea of a bonus when things get better seems workable. Our grandparents are still the official owners, so I'll have to pass this along to them, but I'm sure it will be acceptable,' he said.

I had hoped that he would sign it on the spot and give me the deposit check, since I was anxious to get started. It was a habit of mine to view my projects as much more than a job and I was already caught up with the idea of making the shoe store into an iconic destination.

'In the meantime, Emily mentioned that your aunt might be a good resource,' I said.

'Yes, she would. She worked here when she was growing up. Our grandparents believed in making their kids earn their allowance. So she probably has some good anecdotes and photos. I think they hoped she'd join them in the business, but she went to art school and became a jewelry designer. She's local, so I'm sure we can arrange for you to talk to her.'

'Thank you again,' Emily said, taking my hand. 'I just know you're going to be able to help us.'

I was certainly going to give it my best effort.

Since I was in the area, I stopped in at LaPorte's. Neither Rex nor Cocoa were there, but Cocoa had given me a card to show when I came in which explained what I was doing. I started at the top of the menu and chose a green bean salad and a chopped vegetable concoction. I scribbled down notes between bites. *Crisp green beans with hunks of blue cheese and California walnuts in a signature honey-mustard dressing.* I described the other salad as *Bite-size pieces of Persian cucumbers mixed with chopped sugar plum tomatoes flavored with green onions marinated in a homemade garlic dressing.*

I headed home on a high.

I usually only gave a cursory look to the cars parked in front of my building. I didn't currently own one and relied on public transportation and the occasional Uber or Lyft, so parking spaces weren't my concern. I probably wouldn't have noticed the black sedan if it hadn't been parked in front of the 'No Parking' sign. The space was intended to be left empty, but cop cars parked there all the time when they went to the corner coffee shop to eat. I gave the dark car a second look and noticed it had an antenna and a light stuck on the side

– a sure sign it was a cop car. I figured it belonged to a detective who was eating a late lunch. I never thought that it had anything to do with me.

I went up the outside stairs and wiped my feet before I went into the outer vestibule of my building. A man in a dark suit was examining the names on the mailboxes and looked up when I came in. Seeing a formally dressed stranger in the building made me uneasy and I was considering going back outside. He glanced in my direction and picked up on my discomfort.

'Sorry if I scared you, ma'am.' He opened his jacket and pulled out a badge and I noticed he had a gun holstered under his arm. The badge and the gun barely registered. I was too stunned at being called ma'am. It was a first, and I wondered if I had passed some invisible marker and gone from the nice-sounding 'miss' to the frumpy-sounding 'ma'am'. I was only thirty-two and he was clearly much older. 'Detective Jankowski,' he said. He peered closely at me. 'Do you happen to know Veronica Blackstone?'

'It's me. I'm Veronica Blackstone.' My throat had gone instantly dry and I almost choked on my own name. I felt a surge of adrenalin. A detective looking for me couldn't be good. I looked longingly toward the outside and wished I could escape.

'I wonder if I could speak to you,' he said. His words might have made it sound like I had a choice, but his tone made it clear that I didn't.

I asked him what it was about and he wouldn't give a clue. I recognized the lack of expression as what I'd seen on Ben's face. It must be something they taught them in cop school. I certainly didn't want to talk where anybody in the building could pass by and eavesdrop. But I also didn't want to join him on a trip to the police station, so I invited him up to my place.

'No elevator, huh?' he said, following me up the three flights of stairs. There was a tiredness about him that made me think he was already looking forward to retirement, but at the same time he was intent on his job.

'Sorry, it's an old building,' I said as we reached the top-floor landing. I unlocked the door and we went into the small entrance hall. Sunlight was streaming in through the living-room windows, making it seem bright and inviting.

He took a moment to catch his breath after the climb, but nothing showed in his face. It was probably habit now to keep it like a mask with a generic expression. He'd shut the door behind us when we came in but stopped in the entranceway. I wasn't sure what the protocol was, so I simply said, 'Now what?'

He ignored my question and looked around the living room. Was it curiosity or was he trying to gather information on me? His glance moved to the long hall that ended in the dining room. 'Is anyone else home?'

Why was he asking that? 'I live alone,' I stammered. Rocky made an appearance just then and gave me a look as if to remind me I had a cat roommate.

The detective was too busy sizing up my place to notice the feline's arrival. He went from looking around the living room to peering into the open French doors that went into my office and then back to looking down the long hall. 'It's a lot of space for one person.'

'And a cat,' I said, gesturing to Rocky at my feet. The detective gave Rocky a cursory glance and went back looking down the hall and I thought he was counting doors.

I wanted to tell him that only two of them were bedrooms and the other two were a closet and a bathroom, but I said nothing. There was no reason for me to volunteer informa-tion. I thought of a cliché that described how I felt. I let it go since I couldn't think of any better words than that I was on pins and needles waiting to hear why he was there. Obviously it had to do with a crime he was investigating. What could it have to do with me? And how should I answer?

I tried to be calm, reminding myself I wasn't guilty of anything.

He let out a tired sigh. 'Do you mind if I sit down?' Everything was a question with him. Would I speak to him, could he sit down? I thought again that his words gave the illusion that I had a choice, but his tone made it clear I didn't. There was nothing to do but to agree.

'Sure,' I said, gesturing toward the black leather couch. I

sensed that he was glad to sit, even if it put him in less of a power position. I don't know what possessed me to do it, but I offered him a cup of coffee. Or maybe there was method in my . . . I stopped myself right there before I could finish the cliché and changed it to: *I had a good reason behind it.* I remembered something I'd learned when I was writing the first Derek Streeter book. Cops looked to be in charge in a situation like this. But by making it more social there was a tiny shift of power to me.

The offer clearly caught him off guard. It took a moment for it to register and he started to shake his head in refusal, but then I heard another tired sigh. 'Yeah, that would be good,' he said.

I wondered if he'd follow me to the kitchen to make sure I didn't make a hasty exit through the back door. He didn't, and he was looking at his phone when I returned with a couple of mugs of coffee along with cream and sugar. He filled his with so much cream it looked almost beige. Then he dumped in several spoons of sugar. He noticed me watching. 'Afternoon slump,' he said as an explanation.

By now the suspense was killing me – I didn't even bother chiding myself for the cliché under the circumstances.

I had taken the chair adjacent to the couch. He drank half the coffee in one swig and put down the mug before taking out a notebook and pen. I considered commenting that it was my way of taking notes too, but by now I just wanted to find out what he was there about and get it over with.

'How do you know Ted Roberts?' he asked.

'Ted Roberts? The name's not familiar,' I said with a shrug. I felt a gush of relief. Clearly it was a mistake. But something niggled at me. I knew that cops were known not to ask questions they didn't already know the answer to, particularly for a first one. He also didn't get up and start apologizing that he'd made a mistake.

'Are you sure, ma'am?' he asked. I cringed at being called 'ma'am' again. But I also began to understand that it was kind of like the expressionless face. Not using my name was a way to make it seem impersonal. Though I wondered what the cut-off for 'miss' was.

'Yes, I'm sure I don't know him, Detective Jankowski,' I said. 'What makes you think that I do?'

There was the hint of a grimace as he recognized that I'd turned the tables on him. 'Just take a moment to think about it,' he said.

'I can take an hour to think about it. I don't know who Ted Roberts is,' I said, getting annoyed.

'Denying you know him isn't going to cut it,' he said. 'I know that you wrote a mystery and were involved with settling the case of that heiress, and you probably think that makes you believe you're some kind of ace detective. I know how those books go. The cops are always stupid, and an amateur who knits or bakes muffins knows more than the police and solves the crime—'

I couldn't resist interrupting. 'They don't have to knit. It could be crochet.' I flashed my eyes. 'How do you know all that?' I asked.

'It's on your website,' he said in a tired voice. 'Now if you could just tell me about your relationship with Ted Roberts, I can be on my way.' He said it in an offhand manner, as if it was all about this Ted Roberts person and not about me.

'I'd be happy to accommodate,' I said, 'but I don't know him.'

He'd finished his coffee by then and looked at the empty mug. Was he expecting me to offer him a refill? No way. I wanted him to accept what I had said and leave. My mug was sitting untouched. My nerves were on edge and coffee was the last thing I needed.

He looked at me squarely. He pulled out a sheet from an envelope I hadn't noticed before. He pushed it toward me. It was a scan of checks like the bank sent with a monthly statement. One of them was circled in red. 'Maybe this will jog your memory,' he said.

The check was clearly made out to me and the fact that it was part of a scan sent out with a monthly statement meant it had been cashed. I looked at the account name TR Enterprises, trying to make sense of it. Then in a flash I remembered getting the check and from whom. 'You mean Tony Richards,' I said.

'That may be what he told you, but his name is Ted Roberts.' He paused a moment. 'Just a little inside dope. People tend to keep the same initials when they use an alias.'

'I knew that,' I said. I regretted that it came out in a snotty tone.

'Sorry, I was just trying to help with your mystery writing. So, why don't you tell me what it was that he paid you for?'

The detective might have known the answer to the first couple of questions, but I had the feeling he didn't know the answer to this question already. I thought of the Miranda warning, which he hadn't read, but then I remembered some research I'd done. The Miranda warning was only given when you were taken into custody. As long as presumably you could get up and leave, they didn't have to say anything. But they didn't mean what I said couldn't be used against me. I was wary of giving him more information than I had to. He noticed me hesitating and his face softened. 'We're just gathering information about Mr Roberts. If you tell me why Mr Roberts paid you, I'll be on my way.'

Now I remembered something else. Cops could lie and act like your ally to get your guard down. Other than his sharp comment when he'd said he'd ask the questions, he'd been acting more and more friendly, even trying to help me with my writing. I'd watched interrogations where the cops made it sound like all someone had to do was tell them what happened and they'd be free to go. Then once the person talked, the next thing they knew they were in handcuffs.

I'd thought over how to answer, which probably wasn't a good idea. The detective most likely thought I was trying to come up with a story. I was OK with telling him the truth, just thinking about what I should leave out.

'You probably saw on my website that in addition to writing the Derek Streeter mystery, I'm a writer for hire. "Have pen will travel", though now it's more "have keyboard will travel". I wrote some letters for him,' I said finally. I hoped my tone made it seem like that was the whole story, but the detective didn't relax his stare.

'Who were the letters to?' he asked.

'I don't know. I just wrote the body of them and he took care of sending them on.'

'And what kind of letters were they?' he asked.

I squirmed, not wanting to answer the question, but having no way out of it. 'Romantic,' I said finally.

'You wrote love letters for him?' He stifled a smile. 'I didn't know people did that anymore. They were actual letters, not emails or texts?'

'I can't say for certain that they went through the mail since, as I said, he took care of the distribution.' I wasn't saying another word until I knew what the problem was.

'I'm sure I could be of more help if you told me what the problem was with Tony, er, Ted,' I went on.

We locked eyes for a moment, and he moved his head just enough to indicate that he was giving up. 'He's dead. And it seems like foul play.' He was peering at me, no doubt to see my reaction. I felt the blood drain from my face; everything seemed out of focus.

Once the detective had spilled the beans – a cliché but I was panicking so it was OK – he asked me when I'd seen Ted Roberts last.

'Tuesday night,' I said. No delay this time. I was too stunned to stall. The detective nodded and wrote something down.

There was a moment of dead air and then he looked over at me. 'I guess that's it,' he said, flipping his notebook shut. He took his time getting up and gave me a hard stare as he went to the door. 'You're not planning to leave town or anything?' he said. Before I could even give him a 'no', he said, 'I'll be in touch.'

What did that mean? Was I a suspect, or at the very least a person of interest, which was really just another way of saying the same thing?

SEVEN

I was still in shock the next morning. Tony, or Ted, dead? Foul play meant murder, though I suppose the Detective Jankowski would have called it homicide. Whatever you called it, somebody had killed my client and the police were connecting me to him.

The whole name thing was confusing. I'd known him as Tony Richards and the cop was calling him Ted Roberts. I had to assume the police had the correct name, so from that moment going forward I was going to try to refer to him in my thoughts as Ted Roberts, even though I thought Tony suited him better.

I wondered what else the cops knew about him that I didn't. I wanted to kick myself for ever getting involved with him. All that secrecy should have been a red flag, but he'd been so charming, going on about how he'd been so impressed with my website, and there was the fact that he'd offered to pay me more than I asked. At least to start with. Now he'd run up a tab. And when I brought it up, he'd said, 'I'll catch you next time'; I guessed that wasn't going to happen now.

As I was mulling it all over, there was a sharp rap on my door and I heard Sara calling out that it was her. I opened the door and she seemed relieved to see me. 'I texted you, but you didn't answer. I was going to take Mikey out for lunch. I thought maybe you'd like to go.'

I knew the unsaid message. Mikey was a toddler, and it was easier to go out when you had a spare person to corral him and keep him out of trouble while food was ordered or she made a bathroom stop.

Sara was my neighbor and my friend, but I think she was working on another title – sister-in-law. She was the one who had gifted Ben the writing classes, hoping it would give him another outlet other than going out drinking with his cop buddies. And also as a way to put him together with me. She dismissed all the divorce excuses for him staying single. She was convinced she knew better than he did what would make him happy. I think she felt the same way about me.

Her husband was a pharmacist at the local Walgreens and worked all kind of crazy hours since they were open 24/7. Spending all that time with a toddler got to Sara, and I was the one she turned to for girl talk and assistance at times like this. I instantly agreed, glad, frankly, to get out and away from thinking about my dead client.

Sara had the mom look of sneakers, jeans and a black T-shirt. Her brown hair was pulled in a ponytail. She'd told me once that she wore the dark shirts because Mikey invariably left chocolate fingerprints on her shoulder and they didn't show on those shirts.

I grabbed my jacket, beanie, scarf, gloves and purse and followed her downstairs. Quentin was standing by the open door, holding Mikey in his arms. He was the antithesis of Sara. Quiet and thoughtful while she pretty much said what was on her mind without much filtering. Quentin was not a modern dad who dove in and changed diapers and took over when Sara needed a break. He seemed oblivious to the chocolate-milk mustache Mikey had, or the fingerprints the toddler had left on his light blue dress shirt. Sara and I both noticed, but neither said a word. It didn't matter since he'd put on a white pharmacist jacket when he went to work.

Sara took the toddler and in no time had his face wiped off and his jacket on. Quentin leaned over and gave his wife a quick kiss and wished us a good day as we prepared to leave. I grabbed the umbrella stroller and followed Sara down the stairs. The temperature had dropped in a reminder that winter hadn't completely left. The sky was leaden, so there wasn't enough sun to warm things up. It was back to bundle-up time before we went outside. It was getting tiresome to have to zip my jacket, tie my scarf and pull on my gloves. Sara had double duty of doing the same for herself and Mikey. Being a typical toddler, he resisted, and I was getting overheated by the time she got him zipped up.

It was gloomy outside, but at least the wind was quiet. Sometimes I'd walk outside and the wind would literally take away my breath. We got to the corner and I stopped. 'Where to?' I asked.

'I thought we'd go to LaPorte's,' Sara said. 'It's a good place for Mikey.'

'And it happens they're one of my clients,' I said. 'We can have lunch and I can get more background for what I'm going to write.'

Now that we'd agreed on a destination, we started down the street. Mikey waved his arms and called out an excited greeting as we passed a few people walking their dogs. They all had on little sweaters to protect them from the March chill. I saw some crocuses poking out of the dirt along an apartment building. It was a reassuring sign that spring was on its way. Quentin caught up with us. There was something purposeful in his step and he greeted us with a quick wave in greeting as he walked on ahead to the drugstore.

'I guess I should be happy that he likes his work so much, but I wish he looked that excited when he came home.' Her shoulders slumped a little. 'But then I understand. I love Mikey dearly, but it's hard all day, every day, putting someone's needs ahead of your own. I'm at least used to that. It always seems to catch Quentin by surprise. He still doesn't get that Mikey isn't going to stay on the couch and watch basketball with him.'

I nodded in understanding, though I could only imagine what it was like. Sara had left me with Mikey on occasion and, well, I felt a little guilty about it, but I was always relieved when she came home.

A Metra train pulled away from the station on its way downtown. The tracks were on an embankment and I looked up at some passengers walking on the platform to the stairs that led to the street. Sara and I were joined by some other people as we continued along the street that paralleled the tracks.

It was quiet in LaPorte's. It was the calm between their breakfast business and the lunch crowd. We picked a table in the corner where Mikey's misdeeds would be less noticed. It was a relief to unpeel the winter wear and put it all on one of the light wood chairs.

Mikey wanted out of the stroller and I went to grab one of the high chairs. Rex LaPorte was behind the counter and he looked up as I pulled the wooden chair off the stack. 'Did we have a meeting set?' he asked with a concerned look.

'No. I'm just here as a customer,' I said. His face relaxed. 'There's so much going on, I forget about appointments. Just a recommendation, try the beet and spinach salad. It's a new item and my creation.' I thanked him and took the high chair back to our table. LaPorte's was my dream kind of client. I liked the place and it seemed like they would be easy to deal with. I looked forward to tasting the different dishes and writing up descriptions. There was heart in the story how an unemployed teacher created a recipe that ended up being the foundation for a business. And now her children and their children were taking it into something more.

Sara was tussling with Mikey when I returned with the high chair. She was trying to hold him and he wanted to get loose. He took one look at the high chair and started to cry. 'Could you do the ordering. Get me anything and get him the kid's grilled cheese. And coffee, lots of coffee,' she said.

I was glad I'd agreed to come along, imagining what it would have been like if she was there alone. Rex wasn't behind the counter when I returned to place the order, but I did keep his salad in mind. He'd already told the helper that I was working for them and my food should be comped. I took care of Sara and Mikey's. It was the least I could do after all the plates she'd sent up to me, even if they were a ploy for Ben to spend time there.

Mikey was back in the stroller when I returned to the table. 'His choice,' Sara said, rolling her eyes at her son. At the moment he looked like the perfect kid. A warm beam of sunlight highlighted his tousled strawberry-blond hair. The longish locks framed his chubby cheeks and he was looking around the restaurant with a happy smile.

'The food will be here shortly,' I said, setting down two mugs of coffee. She gazed at the mug like it was a magic elixir and was drinking it before I had pulled out my chair.

'I have to do everything on the run. I can't wait until he gets old enough to understand how to stay put while Mommy takes a shower.' She gave Mikey a quick look and he was still content in the stroller and rubbing his eyes. She blew out her breath in relief. 'He's going to sleep,' she whispered. I leaned closer, and sure enough his eyes were on the verge of closing and then did. 'He's out,' she said and her whole body relaxed.

The food arrived and we put it in the middle to share. Sara changed when she was away from Mikey or, like this, when he was asleep. She went back to being herself. We divvied up the food. In addition to the veggie wrap sandwich, and the spinach and beet salad we'd ordered, Rex had added a curry vegetable salad for me to taste. They'd included a list of the ingredients. Mikey's food got pushed to the side.

'I heard you in the hall yesterday with a man,' she said, as she stabbed a hunk of beet and tidbit of blue cheese. 'Anybody I know?'

'Oh,' I said. I thought I'd been stealthy enough to get upstairs unnoticed. There was no reason not to tell her the truth. 'It was a cop, a detective, who was asking about a client of mine.'

'Really,' she said, leaning a little closer. 'Which one?'

I hesitated. I was still trying to deal with the fact that Ted was dead. I had to keep reminding myself his real name wasn't Tony. The whole thing creeped me out and I wanted to push it from my mind, but at the same time I needed to talk about it.

'I never told you about this one. I knew him as Tony, but it turns out his real name is Ted,' I said. I told her how he'd been coming to my place. Then she asked what he looked like.

'I think I know who you mean. Real good looking in a black wool overcoat. I've seen him in the hall a few times. He always paused and smiled at me.' She stopped and appeared embarrassed. 'I hate to sound so needy, but the way he looked at me made me forget I had orange juice on my shirt, and for a moment I felt like Cinderella.'

'I understand. I fell for the smile too, even though he was a little too perfect for me. I'm more into the flawed type.'

'Then Ben's just right for you,' she said quickly. 'He can't seem to get past his divorce and he has a hard time showing emotion.'

I let out a sigh, thinking how glad I was that she didn't know my arrangement with her brother. 'I suppose those would count as flaws, but since we're just friends, it's not an issue.'

'Friends?' she said, rolling her eyes. 'When are the two of you going to wake up and see you belong together?' When I didn't answer, she gave up and went back to asking about my client.

'I get it. I'm wasting my breath. So, what did the detective want?'

Mikey was sound asleep in the stroller, making it easy to talk. I was feeling a little light-headed as I thought back to the cop's visit, and the background of the restaurant kind of blurred out.

'He's dead,' I said, and Sara gasped.

'Was it a heart attack or something like that?' she asked.

I shook my head and swallowed hard. 'The detective didn't give any details, but mentioned foul play, which is a toned-down way to say murder.'

Sara gasped again. 'It's just so shocking.' My neighbor seemed to be trying to process the situation. 'The detective was just looking for background information, right?' she said.

'I don't know,' I said, thinking back to his comment about not leaving town.

'He can't think you had anything to do with it.' Sara seemed indignant. 'What sort of work did you do for Ted?' she asked.

'He hired me to write some love letters.'

'That guy needed someone to write love letters for him?' She seemed incredulous. 'He was charm personified.' She appeared uncomfortable. 'It never occurred to me that he was on his way to your place. I just assumed he was going to the new people who bought the place across the hall from you. I'm embarrassed to admit it, but getting a smile from him kind of made my day.' She looked down at herself. 'For a moment I felt like a person, instead of just Mikey's mom.'

'He said he traveled a lot and he wanted to make sure his girlfriend knew he was thinking of her.'

She checked on Mikey and saw that he was still asleep and took a sip of her coffee. 'I wonder what happened.' She turned to me. 'What about the person the letters were for?'

I shook my head and shrugged. 'I don't know anything about her. Not even her name. He always had me use something like "dearest" or "my angel". He picked up the letters and handled the delivery, so I have no idea where she lived or for that matter where he lived. The client is always right, so I went along with all of it. I had a cell-phone number for him and that's all. He was vague about where he lived and said he was staying somewhere temporarily while his condo was being remodeled. He never explained why he traveled a lot. He told me to write the kind of letter I would like to receive. Lately, he'd still wanted some letters, but also a lot of short notes she could get daily while he was gone. I think they'd made a commitment or were going to.' I shrugged again, inwardly berating myself for how little I knew.

'Wow. His poor lady friend.' Sara stopped and her eyes widened. 'Unless she's the one who did it.'

'I'd say she was the most likely suspect, but since I know so little about his life, there's no way to tell if that's true. I don't know if the detective believed me when I said I had no information about him.' As I said it to Sara I realized that he probably didn't.

Sara's face softened and she reached across the table and gave my arm a reassuring pat. 'There's no way you could have known what was going to happen to him,' she said.

'That's true, but now I'm regretting that I was operating in the dark.'

'You should talk to Ben. You don't want the cops pinning a murder on you. He knows how cops operate. He's supposed to come over tonight. I'll send him up.'

I chuckled in amazement. She never missed an opportunity to throw us together. I was doubly glad she didn't know that Ben and I were practicing to be each other's plus one. Even though I longed to tell her about what a hero he'd been at the fondue restaurant.

It was useless to argue with her, so I simply agreed.

EIGHT

I sat staring at my computer screen, trying to imagine what my fictional detective Derek Streeter would do if I gave him the case. Sara and I had stayed at LaPorte's until Mikey woke up. It was such a treat for her to have time to drink coffee, eat and talk uninterrupted, that I gladly sat there even though I was anxious to get home. Mikey made up for the peaceful time by being cranky on the whole walk home. I felt bad for Sara when they went into her place, and guiltily grateful that I could escape to the quiet of my apartment. Rocky appeared as soon as I came in. He always seemed so happy to see me and I realized how empty my place had been before he'd moved in. He was truly a companion and followed me into my office, jumping on the burgundy chair as I went to my desk.

The cursor was blinking, making me nervous as I continued to look at the screen hoping an answer would appear. Suddenly it was like Derek was talking to me, telling me that I knew more than I thought. Great, my imaginary detective had thrown me a puzzle. Since he was me, I took it as my unconscious tossing me the clue.

I kept getting a mental image of my smartphone and finally went to get it to see if actually looking at it would trigger something. I glanced over the screen at all the apps and then the clue popped out at me. I'd done a mobile deposit with the check that Ted had given me which meant I still had it. The bank had said to keep it for five days, but I'd never disposed of it. I thumbed through the side drawer until I found it. The detective had just waved the copy of it in front of my face and I hadn't had a chance to study it. Now I went over it carefully. It said TR Enterprises, the address was a post-office box and the phone number was the cell number he'd given me. I looked at his handwriting and it was eerily precise. My eye went back to the post-office box number and noted that the zip code was one of the two in Hyde Park. The particular zip code had a limited commercial area on 55th and 53rd. I was sure the post-office box was in one of those places that did shipping and had office services. Finally the computer came in handy, and I typed in what I wanted and waited to see what would come up. There was a MailBox Biz Center on 53rd that I'd never noticed before. I decided my best shot to get information was if I went in person, so I threw on my jacket and went out.

On the way there, I practiced what I would say. I already knew that they would have required a physical address to rent him the post-office box. I just had to get them to give it to me.

By the time I got to the place, I was ready with my story. It was a small storefront with the post-office boxes and a display of shipping supplies in the front and everything else behind a counter. A youngish man was in the back with an older man who I assumed was the owner. I watched them for a few minutes while examining the shipping supplies. It quickly became clear the younger man was new and having some trouble taking in all the instructions he was getting from the owner. I didn't need Derek to tell me who I had the best shot with. I was considering how I would manage to get the younger man to wait on me when luck struck and the older man left to get some lunch.

As soon as the door shut behind him, I moved to the counter and put on my best smile. 'I wonder if you could help me,' I said. 'My aunt has a post-office box here. She's having her appendix out even as we speak. I came in from out of town to take care of her dog Trixie while she's laid up, but I realized when I got here that the only address I had was her post-office box. So could you give me her address?' I took some breaths, hoping it made me seem worried and concerned. The kid looked at me and seemed uncertain.

'Mr Orwell didn't cover that,' he said. 'Maybe you should wait until he comes back.'

'I suppose I could wait, but poor Trixie hasn't had her meds. My aunt said that the poor dog has seizures if she doesn't get them on time.' I threw my best pleading look at the kid and he shrugged.

'There's nothing to say that we have to keep addresses secret,' he said. 'I wouldn't want Trixie to miss her meds.' I gave him the post-office box number. A few moments later, I walked out of the place with my first clue in hand.

The red-brick high-rise was a few blocks from my place. But any plans of nosing around were killed when I saw the cop cars parked out front. I'd have to come back another time. Deflated, I turned to go home. 57th Street had a parade of foot traffic between the people employed at the university getting off from work and students ready to do something on a Friday evening.

I'd barely taken off my jacket when there was a rap on my front door.

True to her word, Sara had sent Ben upstairs, and not empty-handed either.

'Pizza?' I said, looking at the plate in his hand.

'Yes, homemade and, take it from me, delicious. She did a whole number on me telling me that you and I could share the pizza while we discussed your situation.'

'Then she told you,' I said with a sigh.

'I told you that guy didn't pass the smell test,' he said, coming inside.

'You did say that, didn't you,' I said, closing the door. 'I hope you're not going to give me a lecture because I already feel bad enough that I got charmed by him and now I'm in the middle of a murder investigation.'

He stood at the entrance to the hall. 'Where should we have the pie? Dining room or living room?'

We usually spent our time in my living room, but I'd always been the only one eating. I pointed back to the dining room. 'I could make a salad to go with it,' I offered.

He chuckled. 'I guess to a vegetarian, no meal is complete without a bunch of veggies.'

He followed me to the back and I turned on the oven to keep the pizza hot while I made my version of the chopped vegetable salad I'd had at LaPorte's.

'I'll set the table,' he said as I came into the kitchen. By now he knew his way around it and found everything on his own.

'Do you want something to drink?' Before I could offer him the cooking wine, he'd pulled a bottle of beer out of his pocket.

'I'm covered. Sparkling water for you?' he asked.

'That's it,' I said. 'The kind of thing we need to do when we operate as each other's plus one.' I looked at the brand of the beer in his hand. 'I'll know you like Coors.'

'Do you have a preference for sparkling water?' he asked.

I shrugged. 'Just as long as it has bubbles. But knowing it's my drink of choice ought to be enough. We'll still have to figure out some gestures. We can do another reconnaissance to see what we notice.'

'Sure,' he said as he carried my drink into the dining room. I brought in the pizza and salad and we sat down.

For a few minutes we just passed food around and began to eat. Sara did make great pizza and Ben admitted my salad made him like vegetables.

'OK,' he began. 'Sara told me a scattershot of what happened. The guy is a victim of a homicide and a detective showed up to talk to you. Why don't you tell me the whole story?' He'd gone into cop mode. I suppose it was natural for him to take on that tone, particularly when he was asking about something connected to a crime. Even so, I mentioned it.

'You can stand down,' I said, trying to get him to soften his demeanor.

'Sorry, force of habit. The job takes over. My wife used to complain that it was like I was in uniform even when I was in my pajamas.'

'You wear pajamas?' I said with a smile. 'I didn't see you as a pajama sort of guy.'

'Pajamas is probably the wrong word. It's more like a T-shirt with some random bottoms.' He shook his head in disbelief at the topic of conversation. 'You were about to tell me what happened.'

I told him about Detective Jankowski's visit. 'Do you think I'm a suspect? He did say that thing about not leaving town.'

'He probably just meant they might want to talk to you again. As for being a suspect, he was probably looking to see how you were connected to the guy. Did he ask you what you did for him?'

I nodded and said I'd told him the truth. Ben raised his eyebrows.

'Probably not something he expected to hear.'

'I couldn't really tell since he didn't show much reaction. He wanted to know who the letters were sent to, but I couldn't help him since Tony, I mean Ted, took care of the delivery and used terms of endearment instead of names.' Ben and I had finished eating by then and I suggested we continue our conversation in the living room over coffee.

I set the tray of coffee things on the low table as he sat on the couch. I took the wing chair.

'How did you end up with that guy as a client?' Ben asked.

It took me a moment to remember it all. 'He said that he'd seen me on the PBS show explaining how I'd helped the couple – whose engagement party we're going to – find their happily ever after. The article led him to my website. He sent me an email, but wanted to meet in person to discuss what he wanted. The problem was that he traveled a lot and his girlfriend felt neglected. He really cared for her and was afraid she was going to break things off. He wanted something that would make her realize how much he was thinking about her even when he was away. It sounded good to me,' I said with a shrug. 'I asked him to tell me about the woman, but it was pretty general. She was wonderful, successful, beautiful, all like that. He didn't offer much about himself.' I thought back to that meeting and realized I'd fallen under his spell. The smile, the looks and the way he touched my arm when we talked. I wasn't about to share that with Ben. It was so not like me, but there was something about Tony that totally sucked me in.

'What was he doing at your place?' Ben asked.

'I offered to send him the letters by email, but he didn't want to do it that way. So we arranged it so that he'd come to my place and print up what I'd created for him.' I shrugged again. 'I'm in a service business, so whatever the client wants.'

'Could I see one of the letters?' Ben asked.

'Why not?' My client had always deleted what I'd written

for him after he'd made any changes and printed them up. But it was my habit to always create a backup copy, so I had copies of everything I'd done for him. We went into my office and I pulled up one of the early letters I'd done. Ben read it over my shoulder.

Dearest One,
You have made me believe in love at first sight. From the moment our eyes met, I sensed something phenomenal had just happened. And now that we've spent more time together there is no doubt in my mind that you are the one. It probably sounds selfish, but it is all about how I feel when I'm with you. It is as if my whole world went from black and white to technicolor. I only hope you feel the same. I look forward to getting to know everything about you. I long to toast the sunset with you and welcome the sunrise with you, too, my dear.
Xoxo

'The rest of the letters were similar, but lately he'd also been having me write short notes that he either left around for her or mailed. He said they were to remind her of him during his travels. They said things like, *It's hard to get through a Monday without seeing you.* I quoted lines from poems and songs.'

'Is that what women want?' Ben asked.

I shrugged. 'I don't know. Personally, I'm more of an "actions speak louder than words" type.'

He looked at me and smiled. 'Wow, you uttered a cliché.'

I hung my head. 'Here's another one – guilty as charged. The trouble is they just say things in such a quick way. So, there you have the whole story.' I picked up my coffee mug. 'Well, almost.' I told him about how I'd found out Ted's address.

'I hope that doesn't mean that you've decided to play detective again.'

'I suppose I have. I need to make sure that detective doesn't try to pin it on me.'

'I understand, but you might do yourself more harm than good if he thinks you're interfering with his case.'

'Spoken like a brother cop,' I said.

'I'm just trying to help. By the way, do you think that engagement party is going to include dancing? I have the weekend off. Maybe we could do some more research.'

NINE

Saturday morning I was sitting at my computer, starting to work on the assortment of clients. Even though I hadn't gotten a response from Haley about my proposal, I felt confident that she was going to go ahead with hiring me. I was already rethinking what she was calling the place. I thought that having 'ice cream' in the name of the shop gave people the expectation of pastel colors and traditional flavors, but the inside had a high-tech look and she seemed bent on having odd flavors. I thought of suggesting either The Frozen Experience or maybe The Taste Experience. As a joke to myself I thought of I Can't Believe It's Ice Cream. I'd keep that one to myself, since Haley didn't seem to have much of a sense of humor about how weird her flavors were. I hoped she'd rethink going ahead on a Caesar salad flavor. Just thinking about it made me gag.

But that wasn't my business, was it? I was just hired to write some copy, not give her advice. It was my tendency to get too involved with my clients. I had to remind myself not to care too much.

I started brainstorming about how to describe the place. How to make it clear that it wasn't an old-time ice-cream parlor, but rather a taste experience. I stopped and thought about how Haley saw herself. She seemed to view herself more as a food scientist than a treat provider. When I'd asked her if she kept a list of the recipes for the different flavors, she called them formulas.

I reached a dead end for now and decided to let it go for the moment and moved on to describing the flavor I'd tried. I came up with the description of *a delightful mélange of your favorite breakfast items. Bite-size pieces of buttermilk pancakes laced with amber maple syrup, wrapped in frozen sweet cream and finished with a sprinkling of crispy bits of maple-wood-smoked bacon.*

I saved the file and closed it, opening up the one I'd set up for LaPorte's menu items. I thought back to the chopped vegetable salad and typed in *a mélange of carrots, peas, corn, beans and more swirled in a creamy dressing with a hint of curry*. I stared at the word mélange and made a mental note not to repeat it too much in other descriptions. I thought of possible substitutes like 'mixture', 'combination', and 'symphony of'.

I sat back in my chair, considering what to do next. I could see the hard copy of the chapters of the second Derek Streeter mystery sitting on the bookshelf. It was easier to ignore a file on my computer, but the actual pile of papers was a persistent reminder. I pulled out the last few pages to see where I'd left Derek. When I saw that I'd stopped in mid-sentence, I remembered I'd read something suggesting it was good to stop in the middle of a scene or sentence because it was easier to pick up when you next went to work on it. That might work if it was a matter of one day to the next of working on the manuscript, but not when it was weeks. Maybe even many weeks. I had to go back a number of pages to figure out what was going on with my detective and his current murder.

I'd made Derek a thoroughly modern private investigator in terms of his attitude, but he still relied on his instincts and observations rather than a bunch of technological tools.

The story had him hired by a man who thought his scientist wife was selling secrets to the enemy. Since who-knew-who'd be an enemy of the US when the book came out, I decided to make up a country. She was working for Urlandia, which was located somewhere near Russia and China. I was going to call it *The Girl with the Valuable Vial*. I realized that I probably should have said woman, but it didn't roll off the tongue the same way *Girl with* . . . whatever I chose to put after it. I was about to attempt to finish the sentence I'd left half done, when my cell phone rang.

I didn't even get out a hello before Ben said, 'Help!' The word *help* was enough to send a surge of adrenalin, but it was somewhat tempered by his tone which didn't sound like it was a true emergency.

'What's wrong?' I asked, sitting straighter.

'My sister left me alone with Mikey. Quentin's father had a heart attack and they rushed off to the hospital. She left a lot of instructions, but Mikey isn't cooperating, even when I used my cop voice. Could you come downstairs?'

I saved my work and went down to the second floor. Ben had the door open. Mikey was holding on to his leg, wearing only a shirt with a teddy bear on it and a diaper that dangled on one side.

'I tried to change his diaper, but he wouldn't cooperate. The best I could do was stick the wet one back on.'

'So, since I'm a woman, I'm supposed to be a diaper-changing expert?'

He nodded with a sheepish expression.

I was hardly an expert, but I'd done my share of babysitting. I peeled Mikey off of his leg and took him into his room. I used my old trick of telling the toddler that I needed his help. I had him in a dry diaper in no time and dressed in pants. Ben gave us a smile and a thumbs up when we emerged a few minutes later.

'I'm supposed to feed him, too,' Ben said, pointing toward the kitchen. I used more stuff from my babysitting days and made peanut butter and jelly pinwheel sandwiches.

'Can I have one?' Ben said, watching as Mikey grabbed one of the circle-shaped slices in each hand.

I made another sandwich and sliced it up. Ben watched as if I was a super magician.

'Sara said something about taking him out for a walk,' Ben said between bites. 'My compliments to the chef.' He held up one of the slices before popping it in his mouth.

'Are you saying you want me to go with you?' I said and he nodded.

'I am embarrassed to admit that I am befuddled by a three-year-old. It would be so much easier if I could give him a beer and a salami sandwich and we could watch basketball together.'

I got my jacket and we gathered up Mikey and his stroller and headed outside.

It was another reminder-that-spring-was-on-its-way day. There was no need to zip my jacket or add a hat and gloves.

Ben had no problem unfolding the umbrella stroller and Mikey climbed into it.

We didn't mention a destination, but I must have still been in Derek Streeter mode because, without any conscious effort, I directed us to the red-brick high-rise that Ted had listed as his address.

There were no cop cars this time. The building was on a corner with two wings and a grassy area with trees in between. I knew the apartment number was 406 and looked up at the fourth floor, wondering which windows had belonged to him.

We were almost past the building when a black Crown Victoria pulled up to the curb and I saw the driver. I nudged Ben. 'That's his car. Detective Jankowski, the one who came to my place.'

We kept walking, but I looked back. The detective got out of the driver's side and a woman got out of the passenger side. She seemed about my age and there was something haphazard about her appearance. Her honey-colored hair was pulled back into a tiny ponytail and it looked like she was wearing sweats under her coat. 'I bet she's connected to Ted,' I said, staring at her. 'The fact that Detective Jankowski brought her here makes me think she lives in the building. Maybe Ted's neighbor.' I realized it sounded kind of random, so I explained that I'd found out Ted's address.

Ben tried to get me to turn away. 'He probably took her in for questioning and is bringing her back. The apartment would have been taped off and she had to stay somewhere else.'

'You got all that from a few glances at her?' I said, impressed.

'I might have cheated a bit. I called in a favor and got some inside information. I'm assuming she's the one who found him. Her name is Rita Sandusky and they were living together.'

I looked at her more intently. 'She must have been the one who got the letters.'

'I don't know about that, but it appears he interrupted a burglary and got stabbed with a knife from the kitchen.'

'How do they know he interrupted a burglary?' I asked.

'If you notice, I said it *appears* he interrupted a burglary.

The place had been tossed.' He looked at me intently. 'That's cop talk for ransacked.'

'I know what the word means,' I said. 'Derek Streeter said it in *The Girl with the Golden Throat.*'

'That's right, you did,' Ben said.

I stopped and looked at him. 'You read *The Girl with the Golden Throat*?'

'Yeah,' he answered with a smile. 'When my sister gave me the series of workshops, I wanted to see what kind of person was leading them. It was good, but speaking as a cop, I hate to see an amateur out-think a professional.' He added a little chuckle to the last comment. 'Ed could learn a lesson or two from you. The way you described Derek's encounters with his client were pretty hot without being obvious.'

I felt kind of weird. It hadn't occurred to me that anyone in the group had read my book, least of all him. I suppose it was fair play since I got to look at their writing and I felt myself blushing, but I didn't let it deter me from taking in what was going on around me.

I took a last look back, inadvertently making eye contact with Detective Jankowski. There was no doubt he recognized me. I started to walk faster. 'The detective made me.' I leaned toward Ben. 'That's detective talk for recognized.'

Ben rolled his eyes just as Mikey decided to jump out of the stroller and took off down the sidewalk.

'Didn't you belt him in?' I said.

'I forgot and please don't tell my sister,' he said as the two of us ran off after the toddler.

My front door didn't do much of blotting out the noise in the hall and I heard Sara's and Quentin's voices when they returned. We'd caught up with Mikey and secured him in the stroller for the ride home. All the activity had left Mikey worn out and, when I'd left to go upstairs, he was asleep on the floor, hugging a stuffed animal.

I'd gone back to my computer as soon as I'd gotten home and been so inspired by our little adventure that I went right back to working on the Derek Streeter book, and was so deep in it that I jumped when I heard someone at my front door.

Ben was standing with his fingers to his lips when I opened it. I motioned for him to come in and closed the door behind him. 'You can speak now,' I said with a smile.

He led me out of the entrance hall into the living room. 'Sara thinks I went home,' he said, finally feeling free to speak. 'We talked about taking another shot at checking out couple's behavior. As long as I'm here and it is Saturday night.'

I saw his point but, before I responded to it, I asked about Quentin's father. It turned out the heart attack had seemed mild and the prognosis for now looked good. 'So, what do you say we get some dinner and check out the other diners?'

'Well, as long as you're here and it is dinner time,' I said, going to get my coat. 'The funny thing is that we probably both instinctively know the moves, and if we were a real couple we'd just do it naturally.'

'But we're not,' he said, 'and I'm not a smooth operator like your dead client.'

We decided to stay local and go to the Mezze down the street. We were sure to encounter a lot of students on dates and our attire was fine. He was dressed for Mikey duty in well-broken-in jeans and a long sleeve teal blue knit shirt. I had on dark wash jeans and a black turtleneck. We both were wearing sneakers. We tiptoed down the stairs, barely holding in chuckles as we passed Sara's door.

As we walked toward the sunset, the Unitarian Church steeple was in silhouette and the carillon from Rockefeller Chapel was chiming. We had to wait for a table at the Mezze. I used the time to examine the body language of the people waiting with us.

I nudged Ben and pointed with my shoulder to the couple in front of us. He had his arm hanging over her shoulder. 'I like that. It somehow says they're close and comfortable with each other,' I said.

'Like this?' Ben said, putting his arm around my neck so it dangled along my arm. The woman in front of me leaned her head toward the guy and I did the same. 'I think we found something.' And then we both sort of freaked at our closeness and he abruptly retracted his arm as I pulled my head away.

We finally got a table and ordered burgers. His was meat

and mine a plant-based version. Then we started glancing
around at the crowd. I offered to take notes.

'To your right,' he said. I turned and saw a couple sitting
adjacent to each other at the next table. 'Look how close
they're sitting. They are definitely in each other's bubble of
space.'

'Very good,' I said, scribbling it down. When I looked up,
I nudged him. 'That spells true love.' The couple at another
table were sharing a piece of apple pie. She had finished the
portion on her plate and glanced at the hunk still sitting on
his. He glanced up at her and smiled as he transferred the
piece to her plate. 'If you'd had their apple pie you'd understand. It's that delicious,' I said.

I looked toward the front and was surprised to see Tizzy
come in. She glanced around the tables and when she saw me,
her face lit in a smile. Then she saw who I was with and her
eyebrows went up as she came over to the table.

'I'm picking up a pizza. I thought it would be ready,' she
said. 'Love the thick crust, but it takes so long.' She had
stopped next to my seat. 'Mind if I join you while I wait?'

'Of course,' I said as Ben pulled out the chair next to him.
I realized any moment she was going to make a comment
about Ben and me being there together, so I stepped in before
she could and told her about Ted.

'The dreamboat? He's dead?' she said, surprised. 'Did he
live in that high-rise a few blocks over?' I nodded in answer.
'That must have been why there were all the cop cars. What
happened?'

Ben and I exchanged glances and it was clear he wanted
me to answer. I told her what I knew, but she seemed dis-
believing. 'Stabbed with a kitchen knife and his girlfriend is
the one to find him. Sounds pretty convenient for her. What
were you doing for him?'

There was no reason to keep it a secret now, so I told her.
'You think the letters were for his girlfriend?' she asked.

'Maybe, probably.' I felt my shoulders slump. It was a
reminder that I had compromised my way of doing business
with him. 'He barely told me anything about the person the
letters were for. I will never do that again,' I said. 'If someone

wants love letters, I'm going to know who I'm writing them to and what kind of person they are.'

The hostess waved at Tizzy and she got up. 'Pizza's ready. See you Tuesday.' She walked off in a purposeful manner.

'It'll be all over the neighborhood by then,' I said, shaking my head. 'I probably shouldn't have told her about the love letters or the mistake I made.'

Ben smiled. 'There's the Internet and then there's Tizzy.'

After my observation about the apple pie, we shared a piece, though we kept to our own portions. When the check came, he went to take it, but I objected. 'We could split it,' I said.

He shook his head. 'I was brought up to believe the guy pays.'

'But that's if it's a date,' I said.

'But you helped me with Mikey,' he said, still holding on to the check. He finally agreed to let me leave the tip.

We walked back to my building and stopped out front. When I glanced up the street, I saw Ed approaching. No doubt on his way to the market around the corner. I dreaded having another member of the writing workshop see us together. Particularly Ed. He was the most likely to say something embarrassing, but it was too late to duck inside. He stopped next to us, looking us both over with what could be best described as a leer. 'You two together on a Saturday night. What's going on here?' he said, adding an all too obvious wink.

'Nothing,' we said in unison. Ed rolled his eyes and went on to the corner.

TEN

It was my ritual to make myself a nice breakfast along with French press coffee on Sunday mornings. I used the nice china and put the newspaper on the table next to my place. As I brought in my plate of food, I looked at the whole scene with fresh eyes. Single woman with cat who writes love letters for others' lives with just her memories and has habitual pattern for Sunday morning. It was just another reminder of how stuffy I'd become. I was so out of touch that I had to look at others to realize how couples acted. In a desperate act to do something different, I took my plate and sat on the couch in the dining room to eat and read the paper. This is what I've come to: that the wild and crazy thing I did amounted to moving my meal a few feet.

I needed to liven up my life.

Maybe if I played detective. I left the newspaper half read and didn't bother clearing my plate before I went to my computer. I'd been so interested in the post-office box before, I'd ignored the so-called company name. This time I did a search of TR Enterprises. There were actually quite a few, but none of them seemed to be connected to the person I'd known. It shouldn't have been a surprise that his business was bogus, now that I knew he had at least one alias. Was he pulling some kind of scam? Were the letters I'd written involved? I criticized myself all over again for being taken in by his charm. I hadn't really thought about it until now because it had never been an issue, but writing love letters came with a responsibility. I should never have been OK with the glossed-over story he'd given me about the purpose of them.

I tried to put everything about Tony or Ted out of my mind and instead focused on my clients. I would go ahead, even without signed proposals or getting retainer fees. I needed more information about them specifically to write their copy, but in the meantime I could do some research. Not only did I have the Internet, but my place was like a library. There were bookcases in every room but the bathroom. I had books on everything. I had vaguely organized them and found a book with the history of food, one about kitchen science and another that I used a lot that had the origin of common things.

I lost track of time as I searched for information about the history of ice cream. In no time I forgot about the research being for a client and it became for my own curiosity. One thing led to another and before I knew it I was researching ice harvesting, ice houses, and how they kept the ice from melting. Who knew that ice was cut from rivers and lakes in the winter and brought to ice houses where sawdust was used as insulation to keep the ice from melting.

I found out that something resembling ice cream was made in China in 2000 BC. A mixture of a paste made from over-cooked rice, spices and milk was packed in snow to solidify. Needless to say it was only available to the wealthy.

It was a long journey to the ice cream of today which is rated as Americans' favorite dessert. A big change happened when a man in Italy figured out that if you added saltpeter to the ice bath around the ice cream, it froze faster. It had to do with it lowering the freezing point of water, which drew the heat out of the cream mixture. And while I found out that chocolate and vanilla were the preferred flavors, Haley wasn't the first person to come up with unusual flavors. How about in Japan, there was an amusement park that offered raw horse-meat ice cream. Other places had flavors like lobster ice cream and ghost pepper ice cream, which was apparently so hot that a waiver had to be signed before it was served. It wasn't clear how popular any of the weird flavors were, though.

I wrote up a bunch of notes to use in the copy and saved them before sitting back and glancing toward the window. If I craned my neck, I could see past the brick wall of the next building and catch a glimpse of the sky and, if I really pushed it, I got a view of the space between our building and the next and caught sight of the dome of the Museum of Science and Industry. The lights that ringed the dome were on and the sky was darkening. How long had I been working?

I sat back in my chair and stretched out my arms. They felt cramped after the hours at the computer. In the process my hand brushed the mouse and the screen switched to the letter I'd pulled up to show Ben. It stirred up all the thoughts about Ted that I'd tried to push away. The best case was to take his death at face value. That he'd interrupted a burglary and gotten stabbed. It was a random murder. But two things popped into my mind. Ben saying that it *appeared to be a burglary* and Tizzy saying that it seemed convenient that his girlfriend had been the one to find him. I'd had the thought in passing, but hearing someone else say it made more of an imprint. If it was the girlfriend and she was the recipient of my letters, did that mean I was somehow involved?

The random burglary was a possibility. It happened all too often that someone went through an apartment looking for cash or jewelry. Ted could have walked into the place and the burglar panicked, grabbed one of the kitchen knives and they scuffled, or Ted could have tried to use the knife to confront the burglar and they'd scuffled. Either way, it left me and my letters uninvolved with his death.

I went back to wishing that I'd never taken Ted on as a client. I got myself so worked up I had to get away from the computer and go into my living room. Just walking around the room lifted my mood. It was full of color from the artwork on the walls and the patterned rugs on the floor and felt warm and cheerful. I checked the view out the windows. Lights were coming on in the building across the street. Somehow the view made me feel connected to the outside world.

I grabbed the bag with one of my crochet projects from the straw basket at the end of the couch and settled into the wing chair. Crocheting was for me like having a glass of wine was to other people. Just a few minutes of working my hook with some yarn and I began to relax. It was one of the reasons I'd settled into making squares. They were easy to make and the end was in sight as soon as I'd started. Because I varied the stitches, yarns and motifs, it was never boring. And when I sewed them together they became unique blankets. I looked with a bittersweet feeling at my first attempt that hung on the wall behind the black leather couch.

I'd given that one to my father and he'd proudly hung it in his office at the university. It had just been the two of us then, trying to muddle through it after my mother died.

And now he was gone too. I thought back to Detective Jankowski's comment about me living in the condo alone. It was a lot of space for one person. Condo seemed like a too-modern term for such an old building. There were still pipes in the ceiling that had carried gas when it was still used for lighting. Of course, they were sealed off now, but the idea of flickering flames in a fixture hanging from the ceiling seemed incredible in this time of smartphones and international space stations.

My mind tended to wander when I crocheted. I wondered what my parents would think of my profession as a writer for hire. They probably wouldn't approve if they knew it had connected me to a murder. And there I was, back again to thinking that working for Ted had pulled me into trouble. There would be no peace until I knew the truth about what happened.

ELEVEN

M uch as I wanted to stop everything and investigate what happened to Tony, I mean Ted, my life had to go on and I had clients to deal with the next morning. I took my coffee in the living room to have a look at the weather and consider my day. The sky was a gun-metal-gray and gave no hint that the sun was up there above it all. The light coming in the windows was so low I had to turn on a lamp.

I hadn't heard back from Haley or the Handelmans about getting the proposals and the deposit checks. I knew the best way to deal with it was by asking for them in person. It was my least favorite part of the job, but also necessary. And then I thought about Ted again. He'd been quick to give me back the signed proposal and a check for even more than I'd required as a retainer and look how that had turned out.

I was dealing with neighborhood people, but I still needed to look professional, though thankfully that didn't mean dressing up in a suit with a pencil skirt or heels. I had several *work* outfits to choose from and decided on the black turtleneck and gray slacks. The outfit seemed about as gloomy as the day. Thinking about it, all my *work* clothes were on the gloomy side. Professional didn't mean that I had to look like a funeral director. I needed to inject some color in that part of my life too.

I waited until I walked out of the vestibule to zip my jacket and pull on my beanie. It was one of the non-square items I'd crocheted and I loved it, though by now I was already longing for it to be warm enough to go hatless.

Spring couldn't come fast enough for me. Everything looked brown and dead. The blades of grass looked sad and bent. It was hard to believe they would ever be green again. The bushes I passed had a few dried-up leaves still clinging to the branches.

There was a moment of hope as I passed some violets growing in a crack in the sidewalk. It amazed me how the dainty blossoms could manage to bloom in such cold weather. But they were tough little flowers, which might be why they'd been chosen as the state flower of Illinois. Somehow they managed to thrive in such a hostile environment. They were also an urban forager's dream because they could be used in salad or even candied. I wondered if Haley had considered using them in ice cream.

The door was locked at the ice-cream place and I had to knock. Haley seemed surprised when she opened it and saw me.

'I thought I'd stop by and see if you had looked over the proposal.'

'Oh, right.' She seemed a little distracted, but stepped aside to let me in. I could see how she could lose track of everything. With the windows papered over, it was easy to forget that outside even existed. The blue-gray walls seemed even darker with the gloom outside. I got that she was going for a stark look, but it seemed a little depressing.

'As long as you're here, you might as well taste my new creations,' she said. I realized this was going to be more than a quick stop and took off my jacket.

'Can we take care of the proposal first and deposit check?' I said. I was doing my best to sound business-like.

She seemed uncomfortable and I had a dark thought. She might have rethought hiring me since it seemed like she was being forced to do it. I'd gone on good faith before and it had backfired.

There was no point in prolonging this, so I put it out there. 'Let me know if you've changed your mind,' I said.

'I do want your services. It's been pointed out to me that I can be too literal and my website and promotional material need something more poetic.' She stopped and seemed upset. 'I'm the boss, but my investor is the one to sign the proposal and the check. It's no problem since it was their idea. I'm sure they will.' She looked around her and pulled out her purse. 'I can give some cash if it's a problem.' She pulled out a couple of twenties. 'I don't want to wait to get started.' She peered at me from behind the big glasses. There was just the hint of desperation in her eyes.

I would never make it as a tough businessperson. I agreed to start working with her even without the signed proposal. I refused her cash saying it would confuse my bookkeeping. 'But I appreciate your effort.'

'OK, then,' she said. 'What do we do now?'

'I just thought you might want to reconsider what you're going to call the place.' I chose my words carefully. 'You are clearly a frozen treat artist, but calling it the Ice-Cream Experience might make people expect a traditional ice-cream parlor. I thought you might want to call it something else like Just the Experience, or maybe the Iced Experience or the Frozen Experience.' I looked at her for her reaction.

With the large frames of her glasses it was hard to tell, but then I saw some light in her eyes. 'I don't know what to do. I've been in a dither about it. There are rules about what can be called ice cream. It has to be made with dairy products and contain at least ten percent milk fat. But after seeing how you didn't eat bacon, I started thinking about people who are vegan or lactose intolerant and I started working on a mix using coconut and different nut milk. So using "ice cream" in the name of the place is really incorrect. Also, I wouldn't want people to come in expecting pink walls and regular flavors. Maybe I should call it what it is – Frozen Unusual Flavors.' She looked to me for my reaction.

I forced myself not to make a face at the name. 'That says what your shop is, but there's no magic. Maybe we should table the name for a moment and focus on the story of the place.' We talked back and forth. I brought up what she'd said about mixing ice-cream flavors when she was a kid and how she was now a flavor artist with ice cream as her canvas.

'Artist, hmm?' she said. 'I don't know. Artist implies some out-there person who's erratic and undependable. Would people trust that person for a consistent experience? I see myself more as a scientist.'

'You're selling what people think of as a treat and something with fun connected to it,' I said.

'I don't see why it has to be that way,' she said.

I felt myself hitting a wall. I would write what she wanted, but I also wanted to help her succeed. She seemed to want to turn ice cream into a bitter pill. I tried another tactic. 'What is it that you are trying to do with this place?'

She thought a moment. 'Prove that I'm right. That I can make flavors that nobody has ever thought of for ice cream.' I listened to what she said and considered what to tell her.

'I'm assuming you also want this place to be a financial success.'

'Well, yeah,' she said.

'Maybe you also need to consider what your customers might want.' What I was thinking, but didn't say, was there might not be enough people interested in tasting smoked whitefish ice cream to make the place more than a short-term pop-up business.

'I am. I decided to table the Caesar salad flavor,' she said. 'The texture of lettuce doesn't seem to work in ice cream.' She went in the back and returned with a tiny scoop of something with a yellowish color. I was almost afraid to ask her what she'd flavored it with.

She urged me to taste it and I scraped a small bit off with the spoon. Reluctantly, I took a tiny taste.

It was spicy hot and there were raisins and cashews mixed in with the creamy mixture. It left a nice aftertaste. 'It's one of the vegan flavors I came up with,' she said. 'I made it with coconut milk and I thought I'd call it yellow curry.'

'It's definitely a taste experience,' I said.

She seemed relieved by my comment. 'My investor didn't like it.' She sounded deflated. 'They actually said I should have vanilla ice cream. Are you kidding me? What's special about that?'

Reading into everything she'd said, I got a sinking feeling. 'Are you worried about losing your financing?'

She nodded with a groan. 'I thought the money was supposed to be a graduation present and mine to handle, but now it turns out they're trying to use it to impose their will on me. I don't want to be just another ice-cream place.' Her lips twisted into a pout.

'I understand your mission,' I said. I also should have

said that now I understood how shaky her business was, but I felt for her. 'Let me think about it. Maybe I can figure something out.'

'Really?' she said. She pulled out the two twenties again and pushed them on me. 'Please take them. Thank you for believing in my vision.'

The weather wasn't any more cheerful when I got outside. Dreary was probably the best way to describe it. The world around me seemed to be in a dingy monochrome. Maybe it was the way I felt, too. The ice-cream project was melting into nothing. Haley was obstinate. What could I possibly come up with that could please her, her investor and customers? I was a writer not a magician, though I did have a pretty good imagination.

I'd stuffed the two twenties in my pocket, realizing it might well be the only profit I saw from that project. And then there was the ridiculously low offer to do the work for the Handelmans because I liked them. It came back to me how I had let Ted slide. I just didn't have it in me to be a tough businessperson. At least the LaPorte Bakery and Café had given me a signed proposal, paid a deposit and seemed pretty straightforward in what they wanted.

A Metra train was just pulling out of the station on the tracks above me and someone on a bicycle zoomed past me as I turned on to Lake Park. After that I was too deep in thought about my crumbling current situation to notice my surroundings as I continued on my trek, until I turned on to 53rd Street and all the activity of traffic and people cut through my mental ramblings and zapped me back to the present. I passed LaPorte's as a woman came out carrying a sunny-yellow pastry box and I got a whiff of the sweet smell. The kids' shoe store was barely half a block away. I was hoping to catch the sister and brother, or at least one of them, to deal with the contract and deposit. This was definitely not my favorite part of the job, but there was no way out of it.

Both of them were waiting on customers. Lewis looked up and smiled at me, pointing to a seat. He was dealing with a girl and a boy who didn't seem to be able to sit still.

Somehow he'd turned the whole shoe-fitting into a game and the kids got to jiggle while they tried on shoes. The mother was sitting on the edge of her chair with a tense expression as she watched the proceedings. She only relaxed when Lewis had packed up the shoes they were getting and he'd brought out the prize jar.

'Thank you,' she said with a grateful smile. 'They're special needs and this is the first time they haven't thrown tantrums when we went for shoes. You're a miracle worker.'

Lewis turned around the compliment. 'I wish all our customers were as much fun as your two,' he said.

'That's not the usual response I get,' she said, looking at the kids who were practicing jumping up from their chairs. 'We're definitely coming back to this store. I'm going to tell all the people in my mommy group, too.'

I had edged in by now and, after asking Lewis if it was OK, explained to the mother what I was doing for the store. 'Could we include a quote from you?' I asked.

'With pleasure,' she said. I had already noted what she'd said and read it back to her and she nodded an OK.

Lewis asked about taking some photos of the kids reaching in the prize jar. The mother agreed and the kids seemed so used to someone taking a picture of them with a phone, they actually posed.

'Great work asking her for a quote,' Lewis said when they'd gone.

'You did a perfect job of waiting on them.'

'Being a gym teacher helps,' he said.

I'd been thinking of something as I'd watched the kids trying out their shoes by walking around the store. 'I don't know if you want to add anything new to the décor, but have you ever considered a mat with a hopscotch layout on it. The kids could jump around on it to try out their shoes.'

'Wow, that's a great idea,' Lewis said. 'Before anything else . . .' He pulled out a copy of the proposal with a check attached to it and handed it to me. I smiled with relief that I hadn't had to ask for it.

Emily was still with her customer. A little girl was getting a pair of party shoes. Instead of waiting for Emily to check the fit, she jumped up and started dancing around the store. She stopped at the counter next to me and looked up at the wall decoration. The cow was caught in mid-jump on the painted blue background. 'Make it go,' she said, doing a twirl.

'I don't know if the cow is going to jump,' Lewis said. 'She only jumps over the moon when she feels like it.'

'Oh, no,' the little girl lamented.

'Maybe if you ask her very nicely to jump, she'll do it,' Lewis said.

The little girl appeared very serious as she gazed up at the cow. 'Please, oh please lady cow. Jump over the moon.' By now we'd been joined by the mother who had taken out her phone and was recording it all. I don't think the little girl even noticed that Emily had gone in the back. There was the sound of something starting up and the cow swung back and forth as if it was dancing before – with a rather jerking move – it made its way over the moon. Then the dish and the spoon started to run away together. The little girl jumped up and down, clapping with delight.

'I can't tell you how nice it is to deal with a shop like this that isn't part of a big chain. There are so few places like this left,' the mother said. Lewis gave me a nod and I repeated what I'd done with the other customer. The woman was only too glad to be quoted and the little girl was posing before I even brought up the idea of a picture.

The bell over the door jangled as the mother and daughter left, and the three of us congratulated each other. 'You heard her. There are people who want to shop at a place like this. I bet they will come from other neighborhoods. We just need to let people know we are here.'

We talked a bit about what to put on the website and decided that a combination of old and new would be good. 'Aunt Laurel can help with the old stuff,' Emily said, looking at her brother. She turned to me. 'She worked here when she was in high school. Then she moved on and went to art school. She's a jewelry designer.' She shook her head with regret. 'I already told you that, didn't I?'

To cover the awkward moment, I asked if her aunt had made the silver dangle earrings she was wearing. She nodded and smiled. 'I'd be happy to talk to her. Maybe we can set up a time to talk.'

'How about now?' Emily said. 'She's at LaPorte's. They're having a meeting about the neighborhood spring garden fair.'

'Sounds good,' I said, heading to the door.

When I got to LaPorte's, I looked around for a crowd at a table. Before I'd finished surveying the place, I saw a hand waving at me. When I got closer, I recognized Tizzy and smiled to myself. She seemed to be everywhere. She was sitting with three other women. I noticed a nursery catalog on the table. 'Is this the garden fair committee?' I asked.

Tizzy rushed to answer that it was. 'Are you interested in joining?' she added quickly. She'd dressed for the occasion in a flower-print long duster over a pair of jeans that fit like slacks.

She started introducing me around, offering much more than my name. I felt a blush coming as she went on that I was her writing teacher, the author of a wonderful mystery, and that I did all kinds of other writing for people. 'Whatever you need, she can do it for you,' my booster said.

'Actually, that's why I'm here,' I said. My gaze moved to the other three women who were all about the same age. 'I'm looking for Laurel.'

The woman next to Tizzy raised her hand and I did a quick appraisal. She seemed somewhere in her fifties. Her dark hair was threaded with some silver and pulled off her face with a hair tie. There was something artistic about her appearance, which made sense since she was a jewelry designer. Then the writer in me took over and I studied her for a moment, trying to think how I could be specific about her artistic aura. I decided the impression came from the grouping of silver pins shaped like flowers on her charcoal gray sweater, the dangle earrings, silver choker necklace and colorful scarf. It seemed more nonchalant than planned.

'I didn't mean to interrupt,' I said, but the other two women were already pushing back their chairs.

'We were done,' one of them said, and all but Laurel got up.

Tizzy gave me a quick hug. 'I'm off to a Hyde Park Historical Society meeting. You know me, I'm involved with everything in the neighborhood – the garden fair, the used-book sale, and the historical society.' She went on talking about how much she loved delving into the history of the neighborhood, which made sense since she was writing a time-travel novel that took place in Hyde Park. She dropped some facts on me before she left. I was surprised to hear that the shoreline of the lake had only been a block from my place at one time and that the Metra tracks and the whole area on the other side of them, which included Jackson Park and the Museum of Science and Industry, was all landfill. Just before she walked out the door, she called out that she had a lead on another client for me.

I was torn between hearing who the possible client was and talking to Laurel. Finally I decided to deal with what was right in front of me and I told her she could tell me about the client later.

'So you're the one my niece and nephew hired,' Laurel said. Her dark eyes had a lively expression as she seemed to be checking me out. 'I'm glad to see you're a neighborhood person. You understand the feeling of the area,' Laurel said. She looked at the empty chairs. 'We've worked together on the garden fair together for years. There's just something about Hyde Park that's different, special.'

'I grew up here,' I said, 'so I know what you mean.'

Her expression deflated and she let out a sigh. 'But it has its shortcomings.' She glanced at the spots where her committee members had been sitting. 'It's kind of like a small town when it comes to spreading news. I knew that anything I said to them would be all over everywhere in no time.'

'Someone joked that there's the Internet and there's Tizzy,' I said, and she nodded.

'I love her, but I'd never tell her anything that wasn't for public consumption.' Something in Laurel's expression made me think she was referring to something specific that she didn't want spread around the neighborhood. She folded her hands on the table. 'But that's not what you're here to talk about,' she said.

The smell of food had reminded me that I'd skipped breakfast. 'Would you mind if I got some food first?' I asked.

'By all means, go ahead.'

It was actually a two-fer. I was hungry and it was a chance for me to taste some more of their offerings for my description writing.

I had a list of their menu items in my bag and took it out. I marked off the things that I'd already tasted. I skipped right to the sandwiches and chose what was listed as Swiss cheese on a croissant. As a side I picked the potato salad.

'That looks good,' Laurel said when I set the food down on the table.

'Would you believe it's work?' I said with a smile, and explained what I was doing for LaPorte's.

'Another neighborhood business,' she said. 'I used to hang out with Rex and Cocoa when we were teens. We all worked at our family's businesses. We've lost touch though. Now, we just wave when we see each other.' I was listening to her and hadn't touched my food. 'Go on and eat.'

I had my notebook out to jot down any notes along with the ingredient list, and took a bite of the sandwich. I immediately added words to the description. The croissant was now a flaky all-butter croissant, and I added that it was spread with their special mustard mayonnaise. I moved on to the potato salad and was surprised at the taste of curry. I jotted down that it was a cool salad with a twist of curry that gave it a touch of heat. She asked what I'd written and I read it to her.

'That's wonderful. Now, what did you want to talk to me about.'

I started to explain what I'd been hired to do for the children's shoe store and mentioned how the story-branding concept worked. It occurred to me that she might even be interested in it for herself. She wasn't familiar with the term. 'The point is to get the consumer emotionally involved with a business. Wouldn't you rather shop at a small grocery store if you knew how it had come into being and who the people behind it were?'

She considered what I'd said for a moment. 'You're right, you're absolutely right. So then, what you want to know is how the shoe store came to be.' Laurel took another moment to compose her thoughts. 'When my parents started the store, things were a lot different than the kid-centric world out there now. There were department stores downtown that sold kids' shoes and there were some neighborhood places that sold shoes including children's. But my folks decided to open a store just for kids. It probably had to do with me. I had a problem buying shoes.' She seemed a little embarrassed. 'I might have thrown a few tantrums in some stores.' She went on to say that her parents had designed the store with her in mind. 'The first time I saw the cow going over the moon and those footstools that looked like elephants, I never wanted to leave the store.'

I nodded and wrote down some notes. She was giving me just what I needed and I urged her to continue. 'My brother was indifferent to the place, but then he was older and I don't think he cared one way or another about shoes. I helped my parents all the time, and then when I was in high school, I worked as a clerk. We made an event out of it. I was taught to make sure the shoes fit properly and were comfortable. We never rushed customers, but had the kids walk around the store a bit to make sure they were happy with what was on their feet.' Laurel's eyes were dancing as she went on. 'We never got returns. Oh, and you should have seen how the kids' eyes would light up when I brought out the prize jar.' She turned to me. 'You have to get all of that across. I know it all seems old-fashioned, but all the service and attention in this digital world would be appealing.'

'That's what I thought,' I said.

'I haven't really thought about how the store used to be in a long time. There's an old fluoroscope in the back room.' She noticed that the word didn't register with me. 'It would strike horror in parents' hearts now,' she said. 'The child would put their feet in it, and you could look at an X-ray image of their feet in the shoes.' She waited while what she'd said sunk in.

'Really? X-rays of kids' feet,' I said, understanding what she meant about parents being horrified at the radiation.

'I wouldn't mention it if I were you,' she said with a laugh.

'Good idea,' I said. I mentioned the quotes and photos that

I'd just gotten and that it would be nice to balance them with something from the past.

'I have pictures,' she said. 'It's too late to get quotes, but if I think about it, I'm sure I can come up with some anecdotes.' Her face lit up in a smile. 'This stirred up a lot of happy memories, which got my mind off of other, less happy thoughts.'

'I'm sorry. Anything you want to talk about?' I asked. I'd liked her immediately and it seemed like we'd connected.

Her face seemed to dim. 'Not your worry,' she said, getting up to leave. 'Take it from me, you can be older, but not wiser when it comes to men.'

TWELVE

I went right to my computer when I got home. There was already an email from Tizzy about the client she'd recommended me to. She wanted to handle the introduction, so we arranged to meet the next day.

With that settled, I started to transcribe my notes, starting with my description of Haley's latest ice-cream flavor. Between getting the signed proposal, the check, the experiences in the store and meeting Laurel, I felt inspired to work on the copy for the kids' shoe store. I did research on kids' shoes and the fluoroscope that Laurel had mentioned. Once I read about how common they'd been and the radiation they gave off, I understood about Laurel's caution about mentioning it. I thought back on meeting Laurel. I'd liked her immediately and wondered about her man trouble.

I moved on to writing up the descriptions of my lunch at LaPorte's. As I read it over, I had a thought about Haley's dilemma. But since the proposal hadn't been signed and there was no deposit, I was uncertain if I was going to be working for her. I decided to leave it be for now and see how things played out before I passed on my idea.

The afternoon had melted and I hadn't thought about the Ted situation once. I hadn't heard any more from the detective, which seemed like a good sign. Maybe they were sticking with the idea that Ted had interrupted a burglary. I tried to push the whole thing out of my thoughts as I did chores around the house, but it kept popping back up. Somehow I got stuck on the idea of checking out the scene of the crime.

It was still on my mind the next morning. With all the sitting I did, I needed a walk anyway. It was another dull-sky day. Everything seemed gray and to blend together, making it a good time to go prowling around. Prowling sounded a lot more dramatic than what I really planned to do, but it made it feel more exciting. Would a single woman who had a cat and no social life do something as exciting as prowl?

It was a short walk to the red-brick building. The high-rise seemed like an anomaly. It was taller than the other buildings and a much more modern design. More modern was a relative term. My building was over a hundred years old and this one was probably sixty years old. I didn't expect to be able to find out much, but at least wanted to see what name went with apartment 406.

The outer lobby was small with a list of tenants and their apartment numbers on the wall. An intercom was set up next to the bells. Everything else was on the other side of the security door. I looked for 406 and there wasn't a Richards or Roberts – the only name listed was Sandusky. That meant it was her place which implied that he was merely staying there. It hinted that she was paying the rent.

I was thinking it over when I heard some noise from the other side of the security door. The door was solid but there were glass panels on either side. I stepped close to it and peered into the hall on the other side. A tall woman was holding open a door at the back. I could just make out the word 'Lounge' on it. She had a tense expression and was nervously tugging on the red fabric scarf she had hanging loose around her neck. A man exited the lounge and I swallowed my breath as I realized it was Detective Jankowski. He seemed in investigative mode as he walked into the hall, peering around the area. I tried to step back and disappear, but it was too late. He'd already seen me. It was pointless to try to escape since he knew where I lived, and besides, it would make it look like I had something to hide.

He came through the security door and the woman disappeared down a hallway.

'Ms Blackstone,' he said. 'So we meet again.' It seemed like he was making an effort to keep his tone friendly. The heavy door shut behind him as he stopped next to me. 'I was going to grab a coffee at a place I noticed down the street. I owe you a cup. We could talk about things. Maybe I could give you some hints for your mystery writing,' he said.

None of what he said was really a question, or for that

manner an order, but there didn't seem to be a way to refuse. The worst was I knew what he was doing. I'd heard about it at a mystery writers' conference I'd gone to. A former cop was offering some tricks of the trade when it came to inter- rogation. The coffee ploy was a way to make it seem like something off the record. Just a friendly chat where nothing would be used against you, but of course it could be.

He left his car parked out front and we walked down to 55th Street. It had once been all commercial, just like 53rd, but now there were only scattered businesses after almost everything had been torn down during what had been called urban renewal. Some of the space had been given over to bland-looking townhouses, but much of it had been left empty. The street felt sterile compared to the liveliness of 53rd.

HP Brew was a new place in one of the blocks that still had storefronts. Normally, I would have looked forward to trying a new place, but under the circumstances, all I felt was tension. The pungent fragrance of coffee was evident the moment we walked inside. Though the place had only recently opened, it had a lived-in look. I'd read about it in the neighborhood newspaper. The owner had deliberately used repurposed wood tables and secondhand chairs to make it seem like the place had been around for a long time. Most of the tables were taken up by student types who were hovering over some kind of screen.

Heads turned our way as we walked in. It was no surprise. Detective Jankowski stuck out like . . . I stopped myself before I could complete the cliché. There had to be a more original way to say it. The best I could come up with was that he was like a banana in a bowl of oranges. It didn't really capture the thought and I decided sometimes the only thing that worked was the cliché. Detective Jankowski did stick out like a sore thumb. The students were dressed in what I'd call grungy casual, which meant well-worn jeans or sweat pants with something comfortable on top. All of their hair was on the longish side and seemed a little askew.

The detective wore a dark suit with a fit that said it had been bought off the rack with no alterations. I guessed the material was synthetic that fought off stains and refused to wrinkle. His dark hair had a touch of gray and was cut in a no-fuss short style. In other words, he looked like what he was, and I was pretty sure everyone in the place had it figured out.

I could only imagine what they thought I was. I was probably around twenty years younger and, since I hadn't expected to have any professional encounters, was dressed in leggings, a sweatshirt and sneakers with a down jacket on top.

He led the way to a table in a corner with a window that looked out on the street and went to get the drinks. I was left with a few minutes to think about what I was going to say. I was a very bad liar. I could leave something out or put a spin on the truth to make it sound better, but if asked a direct question, I had a hard time doing anything but telling the truth.

He returned with two cups of coffee. 'You drink yours black, right?' he said holding out one of the cups. I nodded and took it from him. He took his back to the counter to doctor it up.

He noticed me looking at the light beige color of his drink as he poured in two packets of sugar. 'Otherwise it has no nutritional value,' he said with a half-smile.

He slid into the seat across from me and didn't say anything more.

It was making me nervous and I knew I should wait for him to say something, but I couldn't help it. 'So how does this go? Are you going to ask me questions?' I said.

'I don't know if they're questions exactly. I was thinking more of like talking over things. You mentioned that you wrote letters for Mr Roberts. I know you said they were of a romantic nature, but I was wondering if you could tell me more about them. To begin with, who were they to?'

He'd already asked me that the first time we met. Was he trying to see if I gave a different answer? I shrugged. 'Like I told you before, I don't know. He never used her name. It was always something like "dearest" or "my angel".'

'He must have told you something about her,' he said.

'No.' I was going to leave it at that, but I couldn't help myself and started explaining that it wasn't the way I usually worked.

'Then why did you agree to it?'

'In my business, the client is the boss. If he was OK with non-specific letters, who was I to object?'

'Did he ask for anything in them?'

'Why all the questions about the letters? I thought they didn't matter. That he interrupted a burglary and was stabbed by the burglar.'

He seemed surprised. 'Where did you hear that?'

I didn't want to tell him about Ben. 'It's just the word on the street,' I said. 'Everybody knows everything that happens in this neighborhood.'

'Well, they shouldn't know that. It wasn't meant to be made public. Anyway, we're not so sure that's what happened. You probably know that most murders happen between people who know each other, seeing that you write mysteries. We're just checking around to find out about people he was involved with,' he said. He was all friendly smiles now, which made me even more sure he was trying to do what that cop at the conference had talked about.

I hated to think that the letters I'd written were involved, but I really had nothing to hide. When I didn't seem to be answering, he rephrased his question. 'Were there any requests in the letters?'

'Indirectly I suppose, he was asking for the woman's love.'

The detective closed his eyes for a moment and was clearly not happy with my answer.

I probably shouldn't have, but I began to volunteer information. I explained that Ted had told me he traveled a lot and he was afraid his lady friend was going to break up with him. The letters were meant to make her feel valued when he wasn't around.

'Where'd he go?' the detective asked and I shrugged.

'He never told me. He just wanted me to come up with lovey-dovey words,' I said. I was itching to ask him about Rita Sandusky now that I knew Ted had been living with her and she was the one who found his body. What had she told him when he questioned her? Did he ask her about the letters? And I wanted to ask him who the woman with the red scarf was. But I knew there was no chance he'd tell me anything.

'Did he owe you money?' the detective said.

'A little bit,' I said. The detective had touched a sore spot, but I wasn't about to admit it and let him think I had an issue with Ted. 'I figured he was going to pay me when we were done with the letters,' I said, keeping my tone light.

'And when was that going to be?'

'We didn't exactly talk about it, but I thought when he'd achieved his goal.'

Detective Jankowski sat forward and had a gleam in his eye, as if he was going in for the kill.

'And that goal was?'

'He talked about her making a commitment. I figured he meant that they'd get married.'

The detective seemed disappointed. 'It would probably help if I could see them. Can I see them?' I got it. He was asking because he couldn't demand them without a search warrant.

I took a moment to answer. I didn't want to be too abrupt, but I didn't want to leave any doubt to my answer either. 'I'd rather not,' I said finally.

His bland expression flashed a moment of annoyance and he took a sip of his coffee to cover it.

'Then I guess we're done . . . for now,' he said. He emphasized the *for now* and it was obvious he was trying to intimidate me, and maybe to imply that I was a person of interest, which was just another way of saying suspect.

All this had taken so long, there was no time to go home and spruce up my look to meet the potential client that Tizzy had talked about. I wasn't surprised that they'd changed their mind about the randomness of Ted's death, but I also wasn't happy about it, since it seemed to have pulled me into it. I began to think about everything I didn't know about Ted. Why did he travel so much? Did he have a profession? What about Rita? It made sense that the letters were meant for her. I was so lost in thought I barely noticed the walk to meet Tizzy.

I entered the campus through the Gothic-style gateway on 57th, which led directly to my favorite spot. Botany Pond was nestled next to an ivy-covered gray stone building. It had recently been refilled after being mostly drained for the winter, and it was coming back to life. A sweet little curved bridge went over a narrow portion of it and seemed like something out of a fairy tale. I'd spent many hours hanging over the side of it, watching goldfish swim by. I loved the fan-shaped leaves of the ginko tree that grew at one end of the small body of water. It was always my first stop whenever there'd been a leaf-collecting project for school. Right now, the lily pads looked a little sad and the bushes around the perimeter were bare, but soon there'd be blossoms, leaves and baby ducks swimming behind their mother.

The campus was a big square divided into small squares called quadrangles. It had been like my backyard growing up. After my mother died, I'd gone to my father's office after school and done my homework while he taught a class or met with students. I'd spent many a happy hour wandering through the quadrangles as a kid.

But oddly enough I hadn't been a student there. It was too familiar, too close to home, so when it came to college, I'd gone downtown to Roosevelt University.

Classes must have been in session because there were only a scattering of students walking toward me as I crossed through the large center area. Squirrels skittered across the ground. A particularly frisky one rushed up to me and got on its hind legs, begging for a treat. I used to always carry some nuts in my pocket for them. All I could do was offer the gray creature an apology and promise of next time.

The door to Tizzy's office was open and she was staring at a computer screen. She looked up as I came in and her face became animated. 'Sit, sit,' she said, pointing to a chair next to her desk. She left whatever she was working on and turned her attention to me. 'No one's here, so we can talk.'

I knew how it went with Tizzy and, before we got enmeshed in conversation, I wanted to ask her about Rita Sandusky.

Tizzy let the name roll around her mind for a moment before she answered. 'No. The name isn't familiar. Who is she?'

I told her what little I knew.

'So she was the dreamboat's girlfriend,' Tizzy said.

'I think so. It appears they were living together.'

'That high-rise building,' she said, shaking her head with

distaste. 'Have you seen how it towers over everything around it?' She did a few minutes on the style and the placement of the building before stopping herself abruptly. 'I do go on,' she said with a laugh. 'I'd much rather know what you wanted to talk to Laurel about?' she asked.

I chuckled to myself. I was seeing firsthand how Tizzy gathered her information.

'I'm doing some work for Handelman's Children's Shoes,' I said. She nodded in understanding before taking off on Emily and Lewis and how they'd been friends with her kids. 'I hope you can help them keep that store going.' She went off on a tangent about how the flavor of the neighborhood came from having small individual businesses compared with the sameness of chain stores. Something popped up on her computer screen and she glanced at it before turning back to me. 'Laurel's had something on her mind lately. I've known her for years. I tried to get her to talk about it, but she just changed the subject. I thought maybe it came up in your conversation with her.'

'Mostly, we just talked about the shoe store,' I said.

'I think it has something to do with a man she was seeing,' Tizzy said. 'She stopped talking about him a while ago. I don't think she has the best sense about men. Her focus was always on her career. You know, she's a very successful jewelry designer,' Tizzy said, looking to me for acknowledgment.

'I knew she was a jewelry designer.'

'She never seemed to have time for a relationship. She even joked that her only social life came from all the neighborhood committees she was on. And then she got involved with this guy. I never met him and, from what I gathered, nobody else around her did either. They were in their own little cocoon. She didn't say much about him, but she had a sort of glow that said more than words could about their relationship. I did see her scribbling drawings of wedding rings. And then a month or so ago, she suddenly seemed different. The glow was gone and her brows seemed glued into a permanent furrow.' Tizzy stopped and I thought she'd reached the end, but her eyes lit up as she did a pivot.

'What's going on with you and Ben? You seem to be spending a lot of time together.'

'It's just a friend thing,' I said, figuring I might as well fill
her in on what was going on. 'He's never talked about his
personal life to the writers' group, but he's messed up from
a divorce and not interested in getting involved with anyone.
You know that his sister lives downstairs and I run into him
a lot when he visits,' I said. 'We realized we could help each
other out by being each other's plus one when we get invited
to events or parties.' I mentioned the engagement party and
how it would look if I came alone.

She nodded with a smile. 'The queen of romance letters
has no romance in her own life. I get it. I'm so grateful for
Theo,' she said, referring to her husband. 'If you need someone
in a pinch, I could lend him out.' Then she laughed at the
idea.

'You were going to give me a lead on a client,' I said, trying
to get the subject off my barren love life.

'Of course, that's what you're here for,' Tizzy said, hitting
the side of her head in a gesture of remembering. 'Her name
is Zooey. She was a student here and now she's running a
coffee stand in the food area off of the Reynolds Club. She
did the business plan as part of her class work and then decided
to make it real. She's a good kid and it's a great concept, but
I think she needs some help bringing in more steady business.'
Tizzy's face brightened. 'I forgot. She lives in that red-brick
high-rise. We were talking about neighborhood architecture
and apartments like yours and she told me how cramped her
studio unit was in comparison.'

I saw that Tizzy was going off on a tangent again and tried
to reel her back into the matter at hand. 'So she knows what
I do and she's interested?' I asked.

'I'm sure she will be as soon as you meet her. Don't worry,
I'll pitch her on your skills. I thought we could go over there
now. We could have coffee and strike up a conversation with
her.' She started to get up, but just then her boss walked in.
He nodded an acknowledgment at me as if he was used to
Tizzy having company, and asked her to come into his office.

Tizzy looked back at me. 'I'm sorry, you'll have to do it
yourself.'

THIRTEEN

The Reynolds Club was the student activity center and was almost back by Botany Pond. The food area she'd talked about was off to the side of the main building, which housed an auditorium and assorted lounges and meeting rooms. It faced a small quadrangle with a fountain in the middle. In the summer there were umbrella tables outside, but now the paved area was bare except for a number of benches.

I hadn't been in the food area lately and was surprised to see it had changed into little boutique stands with some tables and chairs for all of them. There was a vegan burger place, another that featured sub sandwiches, and something called the Pudding Place. There wasn't a sign over the coffee stand, but the fragrance gave it away, along with the espresso machine on the counter. An odd wooden plank hung over an open area of the counter. When I got closer, I saw that it had a series of holes.

'What can I get started for you?' the person behind the counter asked. She had a brick-red scarf tied over her hair, and wore a paisley print jumper with a black turtleneck. I guessed she was in her early twenties. Tizzy had said the idea for the coffee place had been part of a school project. She slid a menu across the counter that amounted to a piece of paper in a plastic sleeve. I glanced over the list of drinks. I expected the usual cappuccinos and lattes, but the list included names like Chocodelite and Lost in the Fog followed by a whole list of different coffees and tea blends.

'You're new. I don't think I've seen you before.' Her smile broadened. 'I like to treat my customers like friends, so I try to get to know them.' She glanced toward the windows. 'Are you visiting the campus?'

I laughed. 'Hardly. I grew up here and my father used to teach English. I live a few blocks away.' I was still holding the menu.

'Tell me what you like and maybe I can assist you in deciding what you want.' She did a little bow. 'Zooey at your service. And you are?' She smiled at my surprise. 'I like to call my customers by name.'

'Veronica,' I said, glancing down at the menu again. I looked over the different coffee offerings. 'You really have all these?' I asked.

'Yes, but I should explain. I make it a cup at a time.' To demonstrate, she put a mug under one of the holes in the hanging wood plank and then dropped a filter holder in the hole. 'I measure the coffee and pour in the hot water and, voilà, you have a cup of French roast or Sumatra or whatever you fancy.'

'What about this Chocodelite?' I asked.

'It's the best. You really have to try it to understand what it is,' she said.

'OK, I'll try that,' I said.

'We have treats, too,' she said pointing to a shelf in a glass case sitting on the counter. Inside there were some cookies and some mugs filled with something. 'The cookies are great, but the mug cakes are exceptional. They're made to order and I have chocolate, vanilla and cinnamon coffee cake.'

'You have really managed to come up with something special,' I said. I instantly liked Zooey and was impressed at how she had created a coffee stand that actually was different.

'That's what I thought,' she said, sounding a little deflated.

I decided to just be straight with her. I told her that Tizzy had sent me. 'She mentioned that you might need some help.' Then I explained what I did.

'Tizzy's the best,' she said. 'She's always trying to help me.' She leaned across the counter. 'She said I need to pull in people from the neighborhood and get some business from people going to the hospital complex.' She pointed vaguely west to the massive group of hospitals connected to the university that were within walking distance.

There were several stools pushed under the counter. I pulled one out and sat down, watching as she went through the motions of making the drink.

I glanced down at the menu again and noticed that she listed the names of the special drinks and the kinds of coffee, but there wasn't any description. 'I was just thinking that it would be great if you had a description for each of your drinks.' I mentioned doing something similar for other food places in the neighborhood.

Her smile faded and she started to look defensive. 'I'm sure you're right. I was in such a rush to open.' She let out a sigh. 'And Tizzy was right for sending you here, but I can't afford anything right now. I get a burst of customers in the morning before their first classes and another bunch of business in the late afternoon when the students and staff need another jolt of caffeine, but I need more of a regular flow. It would be great if people from the neighborhood stopped by, and a game changer if I could get people from the hospital.' She seemed distressed and I felt for her. And wanted to help her if I could.

She finished making the drink and handed me the cup. Chocolate froth was piled above the rim of the mug. I took my first sip and got a wonderful mix of flavors: espresso, intense rich hot chocolate with a touch of cinnamon. 'This is fantastic,' I said, and she started reeling off how she made it with Mexican chocolate she ground up. I looked around at her little area. She really had come up with a great concept, but it needed some tweaking with the descriptions and some publicity to let everyone in the area know she was there. 'We could work out a barter deal. I give you copy and you give me coffee,' I said with a smile.

'Really?' she said perking up. 'That's an interesting proposition. I could certainly do that.'

She looked at the menu with a thoughtful expression. 'I suppose you could write the descriptions from what I tell you, but it would be more authentic if you tasted everything, including the treats.' Her gaze moved up and down the counter nervously, as if she didn't know where to start.

'I could do that. I'm doing it for the other food clients I have. We can start with the Chocodelite and pick up with more tasting the next time. We need to have your story in the publicity copy. I can get that when we meet again.'

'It's a deal,' she said, reaching over the counter and shaking my hand. 'Thank you.'

I walked away feeling jazzed about working with her, totally ignoring it wasn't going to help my bottom line. A description of the chocolate drink was already forming in my mind. It would be interesting doing some research on coffee and coffee stands. And those mug cakes looked delicious. The only problem was, how was I going to keep all the tasting I was doing for my clients from taking up permanent residence on my hips? It was only when I got home that I realized I'd never gotten a chance to ask her if she knew Ms Sandusky. But who knew I was about to get something better?

FOURTEEN

It was late when I finally got home, and it was Tuesday which meant the writing group. I quickly set up a folder for the coffee place, realizing I didn't even know what the name of it was. I typed in the description of the drink I'd had and a rough idea of what I was going to do for her. There was no reason for a proposal since it was going to be a barter arrangement.

The group, as always, had left the pages we'd read out loud for me to look over and comment on. I'd meant to read them over before, but the whole Ted situation had thrown me off. I was going to move to the burgundy-colored wing chair to read, but Rocky was curled up asleep in it.

Instead I moved into the living room. It was easier to read Ed's pages over silently. It wasn't my place to judge what he wanted to write, just help him make it as good as possible. Besides, he'd actually found a place for his work on a website. I had to remind myself that he was writing situations for a fictitious dating show where his hero (who bore a striking resemblance to Ed) got to choose between a plethora of famous women. Most of their time seemed to be spent in the Getting to Know You Suite.

He had put in more conversation, but still most of the time was spent describing body parts and what they were doing. I made a few marks and set it aside.

Tizzy had left the pages we'd read from the time-travel novel she was working on, but also the beginning of a time-travel short story. It took place in the late 1950s Hyde Park. It was fascinating realizing what the neighborhood had been like then. It was before the so-called urban renewal that had meant so many old buildings were torn down. Some of the old buildings had been hotels built for the 1893 World's Fair. The rooms had been grouped together to form apartments. The rent had been cheap and the neighborhood was filled with artists, writers, beatniks, folk singers and improv comedians, along with students from all over the world. She blended the history in with the story by making her time-traveler confused about where she was because the landscape was so different.

Daryl, as always, was too bent on including every step her character took. I drew some lines through a number of passages to eliminate them and wrote a note – *What do you think?* I paused, looking at Ben's pages. He had come a long way from the staccato conversation he'd written at first. Now his cop was showing some emotion, much like Ben was. I made a few grammar changes and wrote on it: *Good work, keep it up.* It was the truth, but I wondered what I would have done if it wasn't. Now that we were friends, would I be able to honestly offer criticism?

When I finally looked up, I was surprised to see it was almost dark. I went around turning on lights and cleared off my dining-room table. I was still in the leggings and sweatshirt and switched out the sweatshirt for a deep purple tunic.

Tizzy was the first arrival, but then she lived in a house just down the street. There was just my building and one more before the block turned into all houses. 'So, what happened? Did you talk to Zooey? Did she hire you?' Tizzy asked as she came in.

'We worked something out,' I said, before leaning out into the hall to see if anyone else was coming before continuing. I didn't want anyone else in the group to hear that I'd looked at some work she hadn't brought to the group. 'I really liked the beginning of your story,' I said. She smiled and got even more animated.

'It was hard to capture everything. Like now, the neighborhood was a real melting pot. I didn't think of it when you were talking before, but I was curious what 53rd was like in those days. Laurel gave me an old photograph of the shoe store and the surrounding places.' She held out her hand. 'I thought you might want to look at it and then you can give it back to her.'

I looked at the black-and-white photo. The family was lined up in the front of the store. Laurel was standing between her parents and her brother. I stared at the picture, putting it together with the woman I'd met. She looked so young in the picture, before life left its stamp on her face.

We were already in the dining room when Ben arrived, which was ironic since he came from his sister's, but I gathered that Mikey put up a fuss about his leaving.

Ed looked down the hall toward the front of the apartment. 'Where's Mr Fancy Dresser?'

I was thinking about how to answer, but Tizzy jumped in. 'He's dead. He lived in that red-brick high-rise. The police think he interrupted a burglary.'

Ed and Daryl both reacted with surprise and Tizzy continued. 'His girlfriend is the one who found him, which I think is suspicious, but Veronica knows more than I do. She was interviewed once by the detective investigating the case.'

'Twice,' I said with a wince.

Ben shot me a troubled look and I glossed over the two meetings with Detective Jankowski. 'He wanted to know about a check Ted had written to me.'

'Ted? I thought his name was Tony,' Ed said.

'Both of them were his names, but it seems that Ted is the real one,' I said.

'If he was killed in a burglary, they can't think you're a suspect,' Daryl said.

'What about the second time you talked to the detective?' Tizzy said.

'It was kind of awkward. I was curious about the name on the apartment and was in the vestibule when the detective came out. He took advantage of our chance meeting and got me to go out for coffee with him.' I watched Ben shaking his head with concern. Obviously, he knew about the 'getting a cup of coffee' ploy. 'He asked me about the letters I wrote for Ted and asked if he could see them.' Ben looked really worried now.

'Of course, I said no,' I said, rolling my eyes. 'You don't write a mystery without learning about cop tricks.' Ben let out his breath and relaxed.

'What do you think happened?' Daryl asked.

'I'm trying to find out,' I said. Ben closed his eyes and shook his head in disapproval.

We finally got to reading and I talked Tizzy into letting the group hear the partial of the story she'd given me. They all liked it, even Ed.

'You gave me an idea of someone my guy could have an encounter with,' he said with a leer. 'Princess Margaret was a babe then.'

They all trooped to the front when we were done. Ben went out last and put the door on the latch.

I was clearing up in the dining room when he came back upstairs from his sister's and let himself in. He was holding up a covered dish. 'It's quiche and salad. Really good, too.' He looked at the table and then toward the kitchen. 'Where do you want it?'

I stopped what I was doing and pointed toward the front. 'I'll grab some drinks.' He popped a bottle of beer out of his pocket.

'I travel prepared,' he said.

I joined him with a glass of sparkling water and cutlery. He was already in his usual spot and had put the food on the coffee table.

The only tasting I'd done that day was the Chocodelite and I was starving. I dug in right away and Ben was right, it was delicious.

'I probably should let you eat first,' he said. 'But what was that you said about finding out what happened to your client? Were you really looking at the names on the bells when you ran into that detective? You know, I told you before that the cops don't appreciate civilians getting involved in their cases. You didn't tell him you were playing detective, did you?' Ben let out his breath and took a slug of his beer.

I put the fork down. 'Wow, that's the most emotional I've ever seen you,' I said. He seemed a little embarrassed and hid it by taking another drink from the bottle. 'To answer everything. Yes, I do want to know what happened to Ted. Yes, I was looking at the bells, but the detective never even asked me about it. No, I didn't tell him I was playing detective. I didn't tell him much of anything.' I let out a groan. 'I didn't find out much either.'

Ben urged me to keep eating, but he seemed troubled, so I

finally put down the fork. 'There's something on your mind. What is it?'

'I don't know if I should tell you now,' he said.

'Now that you've said that, you have to.' I didn't quite put my hand on my hip, but I did cock my head with a touch of attitude.

He took a minute, probably trying to figure out how not to tell me whatever was on his mind, but in the end he relented. 'I asked around and well, they've dropped the random burglary idea. It has to do with how he was stabbed and the fact that usually those random burglar types just want to get out of a place.'

'So tossing the place was a cover-up?' I said.

'Maybe, maybe not. It does seem like someone was looking for something in particular.' Ben put his hand up. 'I'm not saying anymore. You did the right thing not showing Jankowski the letters. He was just seeing what he could get from you.'

'He got nothing,' I said. 'Can't you give me more details about what the cops think happened?'

'You said there might be dancing at the engagement party,' Ben said.

'That's an abrupt change in the conversation,' I said with a surprised smile. 'The answer is yes. What's the problem? You don't know how?'

'Actually, I do,' he said. 'What about you?'

'I did work for a dance gym, remember? It included taking a lot of classes. I'm good on folk dances and I do a mean shuffle ball change. I know my ballet turns,' I said, getting up and doing a twirl across the room. 'See, not even dizzy.'

'But what about your basic slow dance?' he said.

'It's been awhile, but isn't it just holding on to each other and shuffling our feet?'

'Not exactly. Want to give it a shot at practicing?' He'd pulled out his phone, then got up and held out his hand as a slow love song began to play.

'Really? Here? Now? Your sister is going to hear weird footsteps coming from up here.'

'She's putting Mikey to bed and she always falls asleep in

the chair in his room.' He held his hand out again. 'The song's going to be over soon.'

I got up and we assumed the dance position. It felt awkward and strange to be so close to him, but then we fell into the rhythm of the music. As soon as it ended, he backed away so quickly, I almost fell backwards. 'I'm sorry,' he said. 'I really have to go.' He was on his way to the door as he said it.

'What about Sara's plate?' I said. 'It'll just take me a minute to wash it. You always say she wants it back right away.'

'That's just so I'll stay here,' he said. 'You can give it to her tomorrow. She's probably asleep in the chair in Mikey's room anyway. By the time she wakes up, she won't even remember the plate.' He had his hand on the door now and seemed desperate to make a fast exit.

'Was it something I said?'

'No. It's nothing about you. It's all about me.' He went out the door. 'Goodnight,' he said as he closed it behind him.

FIFTEEN

Ben was on my mind when I awoke the next morning. There was what he'd said about the investigation into Ted's death and then there was how he'd acted when he left. Frankly, I was confused. It seemed like we were getting along just fine and since we kept it at being friends there were no demands on him. What could be the problem? The only thing I could figure was that our slow dance made him uncomfortable. I thought about texting him, but what would I say? Oh, well, if I had to go to the engagement party alone it wasn't the end of the world. Or I could take Tizzy up on loaning me Theo, I thought with a chuckle.

As long as I'd made the barter agreement with Zooey, there seemed to be no reason to bother making coffee at home. Besides, hers was far more interesting and better than what I made at home. I'd bring her my description of the Chocodelite, thinking she could start using it.

I knocked on Sara's door on my way out to drop off her plate. She smiled when she saw it was me. 'At last, an adult human to talk to,' she said. Mikey was holding on to her leg, dressed in a diaper and a shirt.

I held out the plate. 'I was just dropping this off.' She appeared disappointed and looked down at Mikey, who had let go of her leg but was now rolling around on the floor.

'Could I persuade you to come in for a few minutes? Just long enough to watch Mikey while I take a shower?' She was wearing sweats and her hair was falling out of whatever she'd used to pull it back. How could I say no?

It was a little strange to walk into her apartment. It was laid out exactly like mine, but at the same time seemed different. The living room was painted lemon yellow and the floor was littered with Mikey's trucks. I followed her down the hall to the dining room, which they had made into a den. There were more toys and a big-screen TV. She took the plate from me and gave me a quizzical look. 'Ben usually brings the plates back,' she said. 'Did something happen?'

I certainly wasn't about to tell her that her brother had freaked out because of a slow dance. 'He just forgot to take it,' I said. 'He said something about you falling asleep in the chair in Mikey's room when you put him to bed. Ben probably didn't want to wake you.'

'He told you about that?' she said, rolling her eyes. 'I put on the lullaby music box for Mikey and it knocks me out every time.' She went on into the kitchen to leave the plate. 'Make yourself at home.' She pointed to the couch in the den as she flipped on the TV to an educational kids' show. She went off for her shower and I let Mikey show me his toys.

'A thousand thank-yous,' she said when she returned. 'I feel like a new person.' She did seem transformed. Her hair was still wet, but pulled into a neat ponytail. She wore jeans and a pale yellow sweatshirt with flowers printed on the front. Mikey rushed over to her and held his arms up for her to pick him up. She did and he immediately put his little hands on her shoulder, leaving some kind of imprints. She looked at them and shook her head with a wry smile. 'It was nice while it lasted.'

She followed me to the front door. 'I know Ben is difficult, but believe me, he's worth the trouble.'

'It's not like that,' I said for the countless time. 'We're just friends.'

She laughed as I went out the door. 'That friend thing never works out.'

I zipped up my jacket just as I was leaving the downstairs vestibule. The cold air was invigorating, but I still was looking forward to Zooey's coffee as I walked down 57th Street. A group of joggers went by as I went into the university's version of a student union. The Gothic design of the gray stone building had a church-like look to me. The food area was off the main hall and had a different feeling in the morning. The coffee place was the only stand open and the smell of the brew permeated the air. A small crowd was clustered around it and they exhibited a vibe of grogginess and impatience while they waited as their individual cups of coffee took their time dripping into the paper cups. I could certainly relate to the grogginess. It made sense since coffee was a drug. I'd done a bunch of research and found out what I knew first-hand – it stimulated alertness and sped up mental performance. It also was addictive to some people, and if they didn't get their morning cup, they got a headache instead. No headache for me, but I certainly longed for that promised alertness and faster mental performance.

I hung back until the group cleared as it got to the time the next session of classes started. She'd just finished handing cups to a few stragglers when she saw me.

'Good, you came. Just let me take care of this.' I saw now that the scarf on her hair and something colorful over a black turtleneck was her look. She started clearing up the mess the rush of customers had caused. 'It doesn't rain, but it pours,' she said, wiping off the counter. 'That's the trouble. They all come at once and then there's just a trickle.'

I hid my reaction to the cliché. She wasn't a student of mine, so there was no reason to bring it up. I had thought over her situation and had come up with what might be the essence of her problem.

'I thought over your situation,' I began. 'I think I know what's at the heart of your problem.' I paused to check her reaction and it was hard to read. 'That is if you want my input.'

'Absolutely,' she said. 'I want to succeed.'

'You get a lot of business in the morning because it's conveni-ent rather than because they specifically want what you offer.'

'I get it. I'm just another coffee place.'

'You need to get the word out about what makes your place special.'

I handed her the description I'd written for her signature drink. She looked it over and nodded. 'That is perfect. I print up the menu sheets at home. Next time I make some, I'll add this and of course anything else you have.' She looked down the counter at the place where she set up the pour-overs. 'I'll brew a couple of mugs for you to taste.' She eyed me. 'Still waking up, huh?'

'Is it that obvious?' I asked.

'When you serve coffee to a lot of people in the morning, you learn to read their faces. It's mostly about the eyes. I can always tell a been-up-all-nighter.' She leaned a little closer and looked over my face. 'I know just what you need. I'll brew you my light morning blends. Just a note you might want to add when you write the descriptions – contrary to what a lot of people think, the light roast offers the biggest hit of caffeine. All those dark roasts with their robust flavors actually lose their wake-up power in the longer roasting.'

'Good to know. And we need to make a point of your expertise at figuring out the right brew for your customer's need,' I said, pulling out my notebooks and taking a stool that was out of the way. I wrote down what she'd said, along with the name of the two blends she was making for me. One was called Brain Starter and the other, Eyes Wide Open. When I looked up from writing I saw that another customer had arrived. My stool was out of her view, so I was free to stare at her. It was obvious she wasn't a student. They dressed for comfort, and she was all about style. I could see the two-piece fitted suit showing through her open black tailored coat. Most of the students wore boots or sneakers. She sported designer heels. Her dark blonde hair appeared recently styled and hung smooth and long. I caught a glimpse of her face. All I could think of was she was absolutely beautiful and there was something familiar about her that I couldn't place.

Zooey regarded her with surprise. 'You look like you're dressed for work.'

The woman let out a tired sigh. 'I am, but I'm having a hard time launching myself off to make my calls. I remembered that special drink you told me about. I thought maybe something like that would help.'

As I listened, I realized who she was. Rita Sandusky. When I'd seen her before she'd been dressed in sweats with no makeup or styled hair on the arm of the police detective. Her expression had been different, too. She'd had a faraway numb sort of look which had altered her features. Now that I knew who she was, I leaned in to be able to eavesdrop better.

'You mean the Chocodelite?' Zooey asked. It was clear that they knew each other, but then they lived in the same building.

'Yes, that sounds like it. I remember you said it had a lot of caffeine and chocolate. I need both of those right now.' She leaned against the counter as if she needed it for support. 'I'd like nothing better than to take some time off, but I can't let my boss know about what happened.' She stopped and looked stricken. 'What happened was horrible, but then to be questioned again.' She shook her head with dismay. 'They asked all kind of crazy stuff and mentioned names I'd never heard of.'

I cringed, wondering if my name was one of the ones they'd mentioned, but neither woman seemed to be paying me any notice as Rita continued, 'They wanted to know if he'd had mail delivered to my address.' She shrugged. 'I never thought about it until they asked me. He probably had his mail sent to the place he was renovating.'

It was hard not to look in her direction as she was talking, but I forced myself to keep looking down at the counter. And she kept on talking while Zooey made her drink. 'The plan was we were going to live there together once it was finished. I never saw the actual unit because he said it was too torn-up.' Her voice began to crack and she dabbed at her eye. 'He said he wanted to do the grand reveal when it was all done and we could move in.' She glanced sideways at Zooey. 'Did you ever see him with somebody else when I was out of town?' she asked.

'No. I never saw him that much.' Zooey seemed to stumble as she said it. I wasn't sure if Rita didn't notice the way Zooey said it or if she simply wanted to believe what she'd said was true because she let it go by. Maybe it was because I wrote a mystery, but I never would have let it slide.

'Sometimes it seemed like we were just ships passing in the night,' Rita said. 'It seemed like one of us was always traveling. He wasn't even supposed to be there that day.' I barely heard past the first sentence. Really? Ships passing in the night. Not only was it an overused phrase, but inaccurate. It was based on a Longfellow poem that described two ships passing in the darkness not likely to encounter each other again. Rita clearly did see Ted more than once. A mental red flag went up in my head. I was a single woman, with a cat, living surrounded by memories, who wasted mental energy fussing about incorrect word usage. It had spinster, dull and no fun written all over it.

'I'll get that drink ready for you,' the barista said, gathering the ingredients. 'Do you need me to take in your mail?' I stopped thinking about myself and went back to listening.

'No, I'm just doing local calls. Thank heavens. About that,' Rita finally looked around and I quickly looked down as if I was reading my notebook. 'I'm not going to leave a key in the umbrella anymore. I'll have to work something else out.'

'Is that how they think the burglar got in?' Zooey asked.

'I suggested it to the detective, and he agreed it seemed likely since the lock wasn't broken. Then he wanted to know who knew about the key and I said I didn't know. Then he told me that leaving a key "hidden" outside the door was the first thing that burglars looked for.' She let out a mirthless laugh. 'And I thought that nobody would look in the spokes of an umbrella.' She looked at Zooey. 'I wonder if this will finally get them to put some cameras in the lobby. I talked to Lois about it a while ago. She said she'd pass it on to the owners. A lot of good that did.'

'Under the circumstance, couldn't you postpone the calls you have scheduled?' Zooey asked as she finished the drink preparation.

'The doctors I'm supposed to meet aren't the problem. I'd have to tell my boss and if he heard anything about an investigation, he'd let me go.' She appeared stricken. 'I can't lose my job.'

I was trying to figure out their relationship. They seemed an unlikely pair to be friends. Rita was probably ten years older and in the vicinity of my age. Her clothes, her job all seemed at the other end of the spectrum from Zooey's funky outfit and struggling business.

'How about some whipped cream,' she said, holding the drink in one hand and a can in the other. 'I don't usually add it, but it seems like that kind of day for you.'

'Go ahead,' Rita said. 'You're right. Who cares about calories?

But you'd better pack it to go. It'll keep me going as I drive.' Zooey poured the mug's contents into a large paper cup and filled the empty space above the hot liquid with mounds of the creamy topping.

Rita took a test taste and closed her eyes as she savored the flavor. 'I think you've discovered the magic elixir.' Zooey tried to give her the drink on the house, but Rita insisted on paying, adding a tip. 'I need you to stay in business,' she said smiling. As she was walking away, the younger woman called out: 'Try to have a good day.'

Rita called back a thanks, but her tone was flat, as if there was no way it was going to happen.

When she was gone, Zooey came down the counter to where I was sitting. 'Sorry for ignoring you.' She looked in the direction that Rita had gone. 'I don't usually like women like her. They seem stuck-up and in love with their own reflection. But not her. She's actually nice. She lives down the hall from me in a much bigger and nicer unit. I have what they call a studio, which means everything is in one room. I'm lucky the bathroom is separate,' she said with a smile. 'She, on the other hand, has a two-bedroom, very nicely furnished. My place is decorated with a bunch of cast-offs from my family.' Zooey seemed a little wistful. 'Maybe someday I'll be able to afford a bigger place, but in the meantime I can't even afford any help. I just shut down for a couple of hours in the afternoon when it's slowest to give me a little time off.' I wanted to hear more about Rita, so I steered the conversation back to her.

'It seems like the Chocodelite saved her day,' I began. 'I like the way she called it a magic elixir. Maybe I should add that to my description.'

'I was glad to do what I could to help her,' Zooey said. 'Something terrible . . .' She stopped herself and glanced around to see who was there. Once she saw it was only us, she came down the bar until she was standing across the counter from me. 'Someone killed her boyfriend. Right there in her apartment.'

I picked up on the word 'her' apartment. 'Then he didn't live there?' I asked.

'It's all about the difference between living there and staying there. She never said too much. We weren't that kind of friends. I heard he was remodeling a condo downtown somewhere and needed a place to stay in the meantime.'

'It must be strange for you. Someone killed in your building. Did you know him?'

'Not exactly.' She suddenly looked uncomfortable. 'I guess I can tell you. It's not like you're involved or anything.' I had to fight to keep from reacting and thought of Ben's neutral expression. If he could manage it when he was reading Ed's descriptions of body parts and whatnot, I could certainly manage it now. 'If you'd met him, you'd understand. He was the kind of guy who could charm the birds out of the trees.'

My cliché warning went off and I could feel my posture change. I took a breath and told myself to let it go. It wasn't as if it was someone in the writers' group or me. She had every right to use as many trite phrases as she wanted. I did ask her to clarify what she meant.

'He wasn't anyone I'd be interested in. Too old and estab-lishment type, but he always added some personal detail about me when he said hello. He'd ask about the coffee place or compliment me on my scarf, and somehow whatever he said seemed to be exactly what I needed to hear. He was gone a lot and I didn't see him that often. He told me he was a pilot for a charter airline. It seemed cool to me that he got to go all over the world and get paid for it.' She let out a tired sigh. 'That's one downside to having your own business. You're kind of tethered to it.' She looked at my notebook. 'You aren't going to put that in, are you? Please don't. I want it to seem like this place is my dream come true and that I love every second that I'm here making a brew.'

'Don't worry, I only put in positive information.' I did what I could to get her back talking about Ted. 'I guess you would know if they hadn't been getting along,' I said.

'They seemed like the perfect couple. You saw her, she's beautiful. And he was – I think the word is "dashing" – sort of like Harrison Ford in his old movies.' There was a definite lull in her business and she came around the counter and sat on the stool next to me.

'I heard her say they traveled a lot. Any idea how they stayed in touch?' I asked, wondering if she'd been the recipient of the letters I created.

Zooey laughed. 'By text, how else?'

'Are you worried, living down the hall from a murder?' I asked.

'The cops told me it seemed as if Ted interrupted a burglar.'

'I guess she must have had fancy jewelry,' I said.

'She's a rep for a drug company. The detective I spoke to said the person might have been looking for drug samples.'

'I'm surprised she'd want to stay there after what happened.'

'She didn't for a couple of nights. First it was a crime scene and she couldn't stay there and then she arranged for a crime cleanup crew to take care of the . . .' she hesitated. 'Blood. They put all the stuff back in the drawer, too. The place looked normal by the time she came back.' Zooey looked down at the counter and fiddled with the napkin dispenser. Something about her body language made it seem like she was holding something back.

'Is there something else?' I asked. She took a couple of deep breaths and finally looked up.

'I haven't told anybody this. Once when Rita was on the road for a couple of days, I saw him on the street with another woman. I thought he was supposed to be out of town too.' Zooey wasn't really looking at me and it seemed as if it was more about getting something off her chest than telling me anything. 'He came to my place afterwards and turned on the charm, asking me not to say anything to her. He said it wasn't what it seemed and there was no reason to upset Rita. He convinced me it would be our little secret, as if we were on a team and Rita was on the opposing side. I wasn't looking to get into the middle of their business anyway, so I agreed.' She seemed relieved when she finished. 'I guess I don't have to tell you not to repeat it.' She shrugged. 'Who would you tell anyway? It's all just a bunch of names to you.' She looked at my empty mugs. 'So, what did you think about the coffee?'

So I had been right when I sensed Zooey stumbled when Rita had asked her about other women when she was out of

town. I kept my triumph to myself and gave her my assessment of the coffee. I suggested focusing on their caffeine
content rather than the flavor and she agreed.

I left there with a lot on my mind from our conversation
and a buzz from the two mugs of highly caffeinated coffee.
The walk to my next appointment helped with both. I'd already
heard that it looked like a burglary, but that it could have been
staged as a cover-up. Nice a person as Zooey said Rita was,
Rita was the most likely suspect. I was sure that Detective
Jankowski thought so too, even without what Zooey had told
me. Most murders were committed by people who knew each
other and spouses or romantic partners were the most likely
of those. I still didn't know if the love letters I'd written had
gone to her – or to someone else? The fact that Detective
Jankowski had asked me about them made me believe Rita
hadn't been the recipient. What about the woman that Zooey
had seen him with? Who was she, and if it was all as innocent
as Ted had tried to make it sound, why had he come on so
strong to Zooey about keeping it under wraps?

SIXTEEN

The walk over to LaPorte's was a good buffer between projects. The buzz from the coffee had subsided a bit and, after I'd gone over everything that Zooey and I had talked about along with the information I'd gotten about Ted, I pushed it out of my mind, ready to deal with my next client. I'd spoken to Rex the day before and we'd set up this time for me to do more tastings. He wanted to speed things up and have me taste a number of the menu items and gather more background information.

The interior of LaPorte's was bright from the blond wood of the table and all the windows. It was the breather between the end of breakfast and the start of lunch. Only a few tables were occupied and there were only a couple of people in line at the counter. The staff was busy making use of the slow time. As I approached the counter, I could see the cooks bustling around the kitchen. A baker came out from the back with a tray of fruit-covered pastries and put it into the refrigerated cases in front just as another baker dumped loaves of freshly baked bread into a basket behind the counter. An interior window looked in on a metal table and one of the bakers was decorating a birthday cake while another was adding decorations to a tray of cookies. The whole place smelled great and, since I hadn't had breakfast, I was really looking forward to the tastings.

I felt uncomfortable about bypassing the line and going right up to the counter, so I stepped to the end of those waiting. When it was my turn, I realized the woman working the counter was Cocoa. She gave me a blank look at first and then remembered who I was and why I was there. 'Maybe if you have a moment, you can tell me what it was like when your mother started baking.'

She seemed exasperated at the suggestions. 'I can't deal with that now.' Rex came out of the back a moment later. He had a tweed sport coat over the white polo shirt and black pants that seemed to be the uniform of the place. He looked at his sister. 'You can't wait on customers when you're like this,' he said. 'It'll be fine, you'll see.' He gave me an apologetic smile before turning back to Cocoa. 'Why don't you take a spa day?'

'Maybe I will,' she said. 'You're right. There's no reason to panic.' She glanced back at me. 'He'll take care of you.' And with that she left.

'Sorry for all that,' Rex said. 'She has a lot going on. We all do with the expansion.' He let out a weary sigh. 'I know why you're here,' he said. 'I was just on my way out, but I'll get someone to bring you a plate of samples.' He turned to the woman who had come from the back to take Cocoa's place. 'Let's do the chicken Waldorf salad, curry chicken salad and German potato salad.'

My heart sank when I heard the list. Even that kind of potato salad had meat in it. Had he forgotten that I was a vegetarian? They all had a lot going on and my non-meat-eating was hardly a priority. There was nothing to do but remind him and face that I might lose the gig. It wasn't a pleasant thought since the job with them was the best one I had going. I'd given the kids' shoe store a real deal, I wasn't sure if Haley would actually ever pay me, and then I'd given Zooey a barter deal. I took a deep breath and reminded him of my eating status.

'You're right. You did tell me that,' he said. 'It's just a minor adjustment.' He told the woman to have them make up vegetarian versions before turning back to me just as a woman came from the back and stopped next to him. 'Irma will take it from here.' He patted her on the shoulder. 'She's been with us for forty years and I'm sure she can give you more background for the part you call *the story of us*.' And then he took off.

She sent me off to a table and came over with a plate of food a few minutes later. 'I'm so glad that Rex hired you. You certainly came highly recommended. Tizzy was in earlier reminding Rex how great you are and how you do all different kinds of writing. It might have worked in the old days to stick with just calling it chicken salad, but now you have to stir their imagination.'

'Then you know Tizzy?' I said.

'Everyone knows Tizzy. It seems like she's on every neighborhood committee and they all meet here,' she said with a laugh. I liked Irma right away. She gave off the vibe of somebody who had been dealing with customers forever and was completely at ease with it. Like Rex and everybody else, she wore a white polo shirt and black pants, but she had a flower pinned to her shirt and glasses hanging around her neck.

She slid into the seat across from me and then noticed I didn't have a drink. She rushed off and returned with two glasses of ice water with lemon wedges stuck to the edge.

'I'm on my feet all the day. It's good to sit for a while,' she said, pulling out the chair. 'You'll have to excuse Rex. Expanding is a big undertaking. His sister is doing a lot, but he sees himself as the big brother who has to take care of things, even though he's actually the younger of the two.'

'I saw her when I came in. She seemed upset about something.'

Irma shook her head. 'She's been in a snit about something all day. There's a lot of stress about the expansion. It's good she finally agreed to the spa day her brother suggested.'

She handed me a sheet of paper with the names and ingredients of what was on the tray in front of me. And I began to taste while she talked.

She began with the story I already knew. Jeanne LaPorte had lost her teaching job and as Irma put it 'turned her spare time into spare change.' She had started with the chocolate mint cake that was really her trademark and then added some other flavors. Eventually, she outgrew her kitchen and moved to a small storefront. She'd barely gotten set up when her husband died. 'You can just imagine how scared she was with two kids and now the storefront. That's where I came in,' Irma said. 'I was her first employee and did a little of everything, but it was Rex who really shone. He was only thirteen but became the man of the family. He made all the deliveries and helped his mother with managing the money. He was the one to suggest they add some of his mother's sandwiches and salads. Cocoa just helped with the baking.' Irma stopped and her expression dipped. 'It's always been hard for Cocoa. She's always been in the shadow of her mother and her brother. Her mother created all the recipes and Rex ran the place with my help.'

Irma went off on a tangent about Cocoa. I listened, but there wasn't much that I could use. It was mostly about how different their lives were. Rex had backup from his family. His son had been working in the place since they were in high school, and his wife filled in whenever it was needed. Cocoa was divorced and her kids had no interest in being part of the place. She oversaw the baking, but there was a little bit of lost soul about her.

The food chased away the last of the jittery feeling I'd gotten from all that coffee on an empty stomach.

I scribbled down some notes about the food. There was no problem writing up the vegetarian versions of the salads because it was the background ingredients I needed to describe. The chicken Waldorf salad had crispy apple pieces, slices of celery, California walnut pieces and a creamy dressing. I would just add that there were generous hunks of white-meat chicken when I wrote up the actual description. I called the other one traditional chicken salad with a twist. White-meat chicken with celery and scallions in a mayonnaise sauce with a sprinkling of dried cranberries and slivered California almonds. The comforting warm potato salad had a dressing with the perfect mix of sweet-sour complemented by the smoky taste of applewood bacon. I had to fudge that one a little since the bacon bits didn't have the taste of real bacon, but like with the ice cream, I remembered the flavor from before I'd become a vegetarian. Irma loved the descriptions.

'Jeanne would definitely approve,' Irma said.

'Then she's still living?' I said.

'They put her out to pasture and set her up at a posh retirement place on Lake Shore Drive. All very nice but not very good, if you know what I mean. She's accustomed to working and being in the middle of things. I talk to her all the time and she'd come back in a second if they'd let her.' She dropped her voice and it seemed like she said, 'If Rex would let her.'

Irma looked down at my empty plate. 'We don't really need a description of this, but you ought to taste it since it's our trademark.' She got up and returned with a slice of the chocolate mint cake. I'd had it numerous times before but I wasn't going to say anything that might convince her I didn't need to taste it.

'That's it, the cake that started it all. I don't even know the recipe. Jeanne wrote it down, but Rex and Cocoa know it by heart anyway, since they both helped her. Cocoa oversees making the dry mix they use to make the cakes.'

The first taste took me back to kids' birthday parties as I savored the dense chocolate flavor with the perfect hint of mint. The white buttercream icing was rich and sweet and lick-your-fork delicious. That description was all for me since Irma was convinced they didn't need it.

After all I'd eaten, I was glad for the walk home. As I neared my building, I scanned the cars for Detective Jankowski's black sedan and, as I went up the outside stairs, I glanced in the vestibule to check if he was hanging around waiting to grab me when I came in. It was negative on both counts. Sara didn't open the door when I went past and I had the feeling Mikey was taking a nap with her sacked out in the chair.

I checked Rocky's food and water as soon as I got into my place, realizing I hadn't checked before I left. My guilt was relieved when I saw that both were close to full. The cat seemed more interested in my company anyway and followed me back to the front. He hung by my chair when I sat at the computer, instead of hopping into the burgundy wing chair.

I was trying to figure out what he wanted when he jumped into my lap and cuddled against me. He started to purr as I stroked his back. Finally, he stretched out in my lap, freeing up my arms so I could type. I transcribed my notes and then leaned back in the chair for a moment.

I considered seeing what Derek Streeter was up to, but before I could open the file, something Zooey had said about Ted popped into my mind. She'd said he'd told her he was a pilot. It certainly would give him a reason to be gone a lot. I started searching around on the computer, seeing if I could get confirmation that it was true. I found out that I'd need his birthday to check if he had a pilot's license. I considered if there was a way I could find it out. I couldn't imagine how I could bring it up in conversation when I saw Zooey again. And that was assuming she even knew. It seemed I'd reached a dead end.

My phone pinged and when I looked at it there was an invite from Tizzy. She had gotten into the habit of having a glass of sherry when she got home from work and invited me to join her. I knew what it was really about. She wanted a download of everything I'd found out.

She lived down the street in what I called a twin house. It probably should be called a conjoined-twin house. The two identical houses shared a common wall between them. I was always fascinated by the different styles of houses in the neighborhood. Hers had two stories and two staircases which was quite common in the local houses. The front staircase was always quite nice and open and the back one narrow, steep and dark. Tizzy greeted me with a hug and took me into what she called the front room, which was accurate – it was in the front part of the house – but to me it was the living room or parlor. A large window looked out on the street and gave her a nice view of what was going on. Her kids were grown and on their own. Theo, the husband she'd offered to lend me, taught English at the downtown university I'd gone to. He was busy working out on his exercise bike in their basement when Tizzy let me in.

Even though I'm sure she knew the answer, she offered me a glass of sherry. It wasn't that I didn't like wine, it was more that it didn't like me. One sip and I felt uncomfortably fuzzy-headed. If I drank a glass, I'd have trouble finding my way home. Instead, she brought me a small pot of Earl Grey tea. I loved the fragrance of the oil of bergamot as it wafted up.

'Isn't this nice,' she said as she sipped her sherry and I my tea. 'I think it's a nice transition to the evening. Then it's dinner and writing time.'

I thought of the story she'd brought in and repeated how much I liked it, which pleased her. We talked about the rest of the group, but she seemed most interested in talking about Ben. I cut it short and told her there was nothing going on. And after his hasty departure, it was absolutely true.

'Have you spent any more time with Laurel?' she asked. I knew exactly why she was asking. It really bugged her not knowing whatever was bothering the jewelry designer and aunt of the pair running the shoe store.

I shook my head and she seemed disappointed. 'But you'll tell me whatever you find out when you do,' she said.

'I'm not so sure her personal life will come up in conversation, since she's supposed to give me information about the early days of selling kids' shoes, but yes, I will report back to you.' To make it up to her, I told her about my second meeting with Zooey. 'She lives down the hall to where the dreamboat lived and unfortunately died.' Tizzy leaned in and wanted all the details. I told her everything I knew.

'So he was a pilot for a charter airline,' Tizzy said. 'He probably flew out of Midway Airport. That's where a lot of charters operate.' She took a sip of her amber wine. 'I know because we flew private once. One of Theo's rich relatives arranged it so we could come to a reunion. It is so nice. You can drive right up to the small terminal and then it's right on the plane with no taking off your shoes and pulling out your computer.' She looked upward, obviously remembering the moment. 'And the plane,' she said. 'It felt like you were strapped to the back of a bird.' Her attention went back to me. 'Sorry, you were talking about a murder and I went off about tiny jets.'

'He claimed to be a pilot, but I'm not so sure. He had several names, after all.' I told her about trying to check if he had a pilot's license, but getting thwarted by not having his birthday.

'What would Derek Streeter do if he was trying to find out if someone like that guy was a pilot?' Tizzy asked.

I thought about it for a moment. 'I guess I'd have him go to the airport and talk to people to see what he could find out. The dreamboat kind of stood out, so someone would probably remember him, even if there was some confusion about his name.'

'Well, there you go,' Tizzy said.

'I should go to the airport and ask around?' She nodded and I reminded her I didn't have a car.

'I could give you a lift and be your sidekick.' Her dark eyes lit up. 'It would be exciting.'

I wasn't sure why I wanted to know if Ted was really a pilot, but I did. Her offer of a ride and coming along pushed it over and I accepted. We agreed to go the next morning.

'How do you manage to get so much time off?' I asked, thinking of her being at LaPorte's and then off to another meeting. And her boss hadn't seemed to object when I was visiting with her in the office.

Her face lit up in a grin. 'It's because I always finish my work, no matter what, and my boss likes to hear all the neighborhood news.'

SEVENTEEN

Night was falling as I walked the half-block or so back to my place. I saw Tizzy's point about how nice it was to have a drink of something at the end of your workday. The only thing for me was that my workday never really ended. The whole conversation with her had inspired me to work on the Derek Streeter manuscript. Why not use what was happening? I dropped my jacket and went right into my office and looked through the last few pages I'd written. It was easy to switch things around a little so that Derek was dealing with someone who had claimed to be a pilot for a charter. Rocky came in and must have sensed that I was deep into what I was doing and didn't jump in my lap as he'd done earlier, but curled up in the burgundy wing chair instead.

I had no sense of time passing and was picturing Derek in his trench coat walking out on the tarmac at the airport. Suddenly there was fog and Derek Streeter looked like Humphrey Bogart and Ingrid Bergman had shown up and I realized I'd put my detective in a scene from *Casablanca*. I was so into it that I literally jumped out of my chair when I heard a knock at the front door.

I pulled myself into focus as I went to answer it, thinking it was Sara looking to borrow something or grab a few minutes of adult talk. My heart did a flip-flop that I attributed to surprise when I saw Ben standing in the doorway.

He peered past me into the dark apartment. 'Were you sleeping?' he asked.

'No, writing,' I said. 'What time is it?'

'Dinner time,' he said, holding up a covered dish. 'Sara sent up some more of the quiche since she said you liked it so much.'

After his abrupt departure the night before, I wasn't sure whether I should just take the plate or invite him in. 'You came for dinner at your sister's again?'

'She called me and said Mikey was asking for me. The kid does like me, but it seemed a little over the top. Still, I'm a pushover when it comes to him.' He paused as if measuring his words. 'We had dinner and the next thing I knew she was pushing this quiche on me, telling me to take it up to you.' He was holding the covered plate up, waiter-style.

I decided it was probably best to just take the plate and let him leave, but when I went to take it from him he pulled his arm back. 'I have specific instructions that I'm supposed to stay while you eat it and then bring her plate back.'

'Oh,' I said, knowing full well what was going on. Despite what I'd said to Sara when I dropped the plate off on my way out, she'd sensed that something had happened between Ben and me. This was her way of trying to fix it. There was no point in fighting it, so I invited him in, though I made him wait while I turned on some lights. There was something different about him. He seemed reserved again and had almost gone back to his neutral cop face. The dancing really must have traumatized him. He'd made it clear that he wasn't ready for a relationship, and the plan to be each other's plus one and then the slow dance must have made him feel he was being pushed into something.

I was absolutely not the needy type, nor the type who saw being rejected as a challenge to try to win the person over. Most of all, I didn't want him to feel uncomfortable around me or feel like he needed to drop out of the writers' group, so I was determined to settle it all right away.

'Let's just forget last night ever happened,' I said. 'It was probably a bad plan for us to be each other's plus one, anyway. We can just go back to the way things were. So we're still friends?' I said, looking him in the eye.

'Yes, friends,' he said, seeming relieved. 'Being each other's escort was pushing it considering how we feel.' I invited him to sit and offered him a glass of my cooking wine. I waited to see if he'd pull a beer out of his pocket, but he didn't, which made me believe he wasn't that comfortable about staying. He accepted the offer of the wine.

I went back into the kitchen to heat up the quiche and get

him the wine. Often, he followed me back, but this time, he stayed in the living room and sat down.

I came back with the warmed-up quiche and drinks for both of us. I noticed that he was sitting forward instead of leaning back on the couch. I thought his body language shouted that – despite what I'd said about erasing everything and going back to the way things were – he was still tense.

'Anything up with the case of the dead Romeo?' he asked.

I was really relieved by the question. I had plenty to tell him and it seemed safe and not personal.

I told him about my new client that Tizzy had found for me. He laughed when he heard our arrangement. 'OK, it's not going to make me rich, but I got a surprise benefit when I went there this morning to taste some of the coffee. I met Rita Sandusky.' I waited a moment for it to sink in.

'The dead Romeo's roommate. What a coincidence,' he said.

'Not exactly. Zooey, the coffee person, lives down the hall from her.' As I began to tell him what I'd found out about Rita through my eavesdropping, it seemed like the spell was broken and he began to relax.

'A drug rep. Hmmm. The burglar could have been looking for drug samples.'

'And if it was a burglar, I found out how they got in.' I explained where the key had been left. He was curious how it had come up in the conversation between Zooey and Rita. I took a moment to remember.

'Rita talked about not leaving the key there anymore, as if Zooey knew about it. They were neighbors after all,' I said.

'Did she know Ted?' he said.

'It seems like she knew Rita better, but told me about an encounter she had with him. He was supposed to be out of town, but she saw him on the street with a woman. He told Zooey it was innocent, but then he also didn't want her to mention it to Rita.' I shrugged. 'I still don't know if Rita got the letters.'

'Love letters seems kind of out of date with everybody texting, sexting and video calling,' Ben said. 'Why would a guy like him want love letters anyway?'

'Yes, but you can't hold any of those in your hand or keep them in a treasure box. That was kind of his point. He said that since nobody wrote letters anymore, they would seem special. He claimed he was old-fashioned and believed in romance. I fell for it completely and I wanted to help him win his girlfriend's heart.'

I put down the fork and put my head in my hands. 'But if the letters weren't for Rita,' I let out a groan, 'it kind of blows the whole scenario. Maybe the letters went to the mystery woman and Rita found out. Like Tizzy said, it seemed suspicious that Rita was the one who found him.'

Ben was really into it now, any signs of his earlier discomfort completely gone. 'It's even better than that,' he began. 'When I got my inside information, I heard that Rita had the building manager with her. It's pretty common that a killer gets someone to go with them when they supposedly discover a body.'

'I heard that too,' I said. 'Rita could have killed him and made it look like the place had been ransacked, then come back later and got the building manager to go up with her.'

'Or,' Ben started, 'the cops could have been right about their first thought that he'd interrupted a burglary. Just that it wasn't random. The coffee girl knew Rita was a drug rep and she knew about the key in the umbrella. You said she's struggling. She could have thought she would find drug samples she could sell.'

'And Ted walked in on it,' I said.

'He could have tried to force himself on Zooey, threatening to call the police if she didn't go along with it. She grabbed a knife in the kitchen and stabbed him as they struggled.'

I hadn't considered the idea she could have been involved. I saw his point, but I didn't agree. Or maybe I didn't want to agree. Something pinged in my thoughts from my conversation with her. She'd mentioned that she took a couple of hours off during the slow time in the middle of the afternoon, which could have been when Ted died. I decided not to bring that up to Ben. He'd gotten the information he'd given me from a source in the police and I was concerned he might feel obligated to give some back as well.

Besides, Detective Jankowski had already talked to her. I wasn't happy with what he was saying, even though I knew it could be true. I liked Zooey, but that didn't really preclude that she could be a burglar and a killer.

'That was fun,' Ben said. 'Maybe fun wasn't the best word. Interesting might be better. I mostly deal with traffic stops and domestic violence and not much investigating.'

It was the most he'd opened up about his job. I really wanted to hear more, but he shook his head and seemed distressed. 'You don't really want to hear about it. It's pretty dark.' He let out a heavy sigh. 'And I guess I don't want to talk about it. Except to other cops. They understand.'

There was a knock at my door and Ben shook his head. 'I think I know who that is. What now?' He got up and went to the door. Sara was holding Mikey. She leaned in and called out a greeting.

'I hope I'm not interrupting anything,' she said, looking around. 'Mikey wanted to say goodnight to Uncle Ben.' Ben glanced back at me and rolled his eyes. He took the little boy out of his sister's arms and walked him to the window. Together they found the moon in the sky and said goodnight to it, along with bidding goodnight to the tree out front, the person in the window in the building across the street who was looking at their computer, and a plane that flew by on the way to Midway Airport. Mikey loved it, and it seemed so did Ben. It was too bad he had such a lock on his emotions when it came to relationships.

Sara made a big deal about leaving. 'Now you can get back to whatever you were doing,' she said. 'Don't you think it's kind of bright in here?' She actually switched off one of the lights before she went to the door.

'That's my sister,' Ben said, shaking his head with amusement. 'Hardly subtle.'

He looked at the plate which was now empty. 'I'd better get going.'

I left him to finish the last of the wine as I went to wash the plate. He was standing when I brought it back. 'So we're good now?' he said. 'Sorry if I let you down about the escort thing.'

'We're good,' I said. 'It was a bad idea.'

We knocked elbows and he went out the door.

When I looked out the front window, another plane flew over on its way to land at Midway. I had deliberately not told Ben about my planned trip to the airport. The cop in him wouldn't approve.

EIGHTEEN

The plan was I would do my coffee tasting at Zooey's coffee stand and then meet Tizzy on the campus.

Tizzy had arranged to leave her office for a few hours on Thursday morning. Her boss must have really liked the stories she brought back because she seemed to be free to decide when she was going to be in the office. It was no problem using the car since Theo took the train downtown.

Zooey had been a little surprised at my attire. I'd gone with what I called my ultra-professional outfit of a pair of black slacks, a black turtleneck sweater and a piece that was either a short coat or a long jacket. It was dark gray and made of boiled wool. It was also the one designer piece I owned and added a touch of class. I'd gotten it on sale, of course. I added a silk scarf for color.

She gave me a cup of Cuban coffee and one from Brazil. They were both strong but smooth. I commented on the lack of bitterness and she smiled. 'It's my secret touch,' she said. She held up a small tin.

'Are you going to tell me?' I asked as I drained the second cup.

Her smile broadened. 'It wouldn't be a secret then, would it?'

'How about calling it Fairy Dust?' I said.

'Good idea,' she said, and took a marker and wrote it on the tin.

I closed my notebook and got a cup of the Cuban coffee to go for Tizzy. As I was waiting outside the business school building, I realized I probably should have talked to Tizzy about clothes and suggested she tone down the colorful kimono jackets she wore all the time. But it turned out to be unnecessary; when she came outside she was wearing a trench coat and a black fedora hat.

She beeped the white Prius parked on the side street and we both got in. With all the one-way streets, she took a circuitous route to get to 57th Street. As we crossed Cottage Grove and passed through Washington Park, Tizzy gave me a tour guide's rundown on the beautiful old park. It had been designed by Olmsted and Vaux with a lagoon and assorted recreational buildings along with all the green areas. The buildings had been designed by Burnham and Root who were renowned architects. Sheep and cows had roamed the open fields, both to keep the grass short with their munching and to give a rural feel to the park.

I didn't think those sheep and cows would have been happy with all the traffic in the present day as we cruised through the park. The streets were convoluted and when we came out of the park, we were on Garfield Boulevard. A center green space separated the two directions of traffic. What had once been a nice neighborhood of apartment buildings and businesses, now looked sad.

'Have you got a plan for what you're going to say?' Tizzy asked. The boulevard continued and we passed into another neighborhood that seemed better kept.

'I thought I'd go with a variation on the truth,' I said.

'I like that,' she said with a laugh. 'You can just say I'm your assistant, though you probably ought to give me an idea what I'm assisting you with.'

I briefly considered asking Tizzy to wait in the car, but since she had generously offered me a lift, she ought to get in on the adventure.

We kept passing through different neighborhoods as I noted planes flying lower and lower. The airport had been the city's main one until O'Hare was built. It had been modernized, but was still kind of like the stepsister of the much bigger O'Hare.

'I'll just follow your lead,' Tizzy said when I'd explained my plan to her. She drove around the perimeter to a driveway that took us to the private terminals. She pulled up next to a small building that looked like a miniature of the main airport. The hangar next to it was open and I saw the nose of a small jet. We walked into the terminal and I noted that it was decorated to be elegant and had a wall of windows that looked out on the tarmac. A fire burned in the fireplace beneath a TV hanging on the wall that was tuned to CNN. A small bar area was set up in the back with a few stools in front of it.

As Tizzy was deciding whether to help herself to the dish of candies on the table next to one of the chairs, a door opened and a tall dark-haired woman came in. She was attractive enough to be a model and made me think of how flight attendants used to look when they were still called stewardesses. She was even wearing a blue pencil skirt and jacket similar to what their uniforms used to look like.

She was all smiles and gracious as she greeted us, but her eyes had a steely look and I knew she was wondering what we were doing there.

I began by introducing myself and explained I was a writer. I offered her a business card as proof. I was afraid that Tizzy was going to chime in that I wrote all different kinds of things including love letters, but Tizzy was subdued as I introduced her as my associate. I thought it sounded better than assistant and it really said nothing. She gave her name as Jewel Stevens.

'I'm working on a mystery. The second book in the series,' I said, hoping that would make me seem legitimate.

'Really?' she said sounding impressed. 'I used to read Nancy Drew books when I was growing up, but now I'm more into romance. What kind of book are you working on?'

'The niche is called traditional. There's not a lot of gore and the reader can follow the clues. My detective is investigating a man who witnesses a crime on a private plane. I wanted to get an idea what a terminal looked like.' I glanced around as if taking it all in. 'I was actually talking to a pilot about what kind of people he flew. I'd really like to get some more information from him, but I lost his card. Maybe you know him. His name is Ted Roberts.' I let it hang in the air, hoping she wouldn't focus too much on what I'd said since I'd left it all pretty vague.

Her long hair brushed her shoulders as she shook her head. 'The name doesn't ring a bell.'

I saw Tizzy's eyes widen at the cliché. Did she really think I was going to say something? Just for a moment I thought back to the list of attributes I'd come up for myself to imply that

I was a stuck-in-her-ways spinster. Certainly attacking a stranger for her word-use fit right in there. I tried to give Tizzy a nod to let her know I wasn't going to react.

I was also remembering that Ted went by several names, maybe even more than I knew. 'He's hard to miss,' I said.

'A real dreamboat,' Tizzy chimed in. 'Kind of a mixture of Brad Pitt and Cary Grant.'

'Very charming and a great dresser,' I added.

Her face lit with recognition. 'I know who you mean. You're right about Brad Pitt. He has the same kind of eyes and that easy smile. I've always known him as T.R. We always joked that he looked like who you'd cast as a pilot in a movie. He really killed it in his uniform.' She glanced around the empty space. 'I haven't seen him lately though.'

'Then he was a pilot for your company?' I said.

'Sort of,' she said. 'He was on our standby list. You know, when someone calls in sick. He might have worked for some of the other charters, too, in the same capacity.'

'Do you know how often he worked?' I asked.

She shrugged. 'Probably a few times a month.' Her brow furrowed as she seemed to be thinking about something. 'I think he used his pilot status to impress his girlfriends. He brought one around once when I was here, and someone else mentioned him coming another time. He acted like he owned the place as he showed them around.'

'Really? I'm just curious as to what his girlfriend looked like. It's for the book,' I added quickly.

Jewel smiled. 'I'd like to help, but honestly I don't remember much about her other than she had dark hair and seemed a little older than him. I can see if we have a phone number for him.'

'Sure,' I said, and went back through the door she'd come in from. Tizzy smiled and gave me a thumbs-up.

'You were great.' She cut herself off abruptly as the woman returned and gave me a piece of paper with a phone number. I thanked her and we left.

'Mission accomplished,' Tizzy said with a giggle as we got into the car.

'Well, sort of. We found out he was really a pilot, but that

he didn't work that much. So where was he during all that
time he told his girlfriend he was off traveling? And I don't
think the woman she mentioned was his girlfriend, unless she
dyed her hair and got older.'

Tizzy dropped me off at my place and went back to work. As
soon as I got upstairs I tried calling the number. I expected
about what I got: a generic message and a full mailbox. After
giving Rocky a few minutes of attention, I sat down at
the computer and stared at the dark screen, thinking over the
morning. Tizzy had asked why I was so interested in finding
out about him. I didn't really have an answer. Detective
Jankowski wasn't hovering over me which made me believe
that he'd given up the idea of me being a person of interest.
It was curiosity and because I wrote the love letters for him,
but maybe it was something else, too. It was inspiring me
to work on the Derek Streeter book.

I might not have gotten all the answers I wanted about
Ted, but I had gotten some information I could use for my
detective. Now that I knew what the terminal looked like, I
rewrote what I'd worked on before and took away the fog
and scene from *Casablanca* I'd imagined and had them
standing outside the very modern hangar. Then I threw the
fog back in for atmosphere.

My stomach rumbled and I remembered all I'd eaten was
a KIND bar to fight off the jitters from all the coffee. I
changed out of my professional outfit to a pair of comfortable jeans and an old soft-from-wear gray sweatshirt. Instead
of eating a proper lunch, I poured out a plate full of popcorn
and doused it with grated cheddar cheese. A short time in
the microwave and it was ready. Instead of sitting at the
dining-room table, I took it in the living room and ate it
standing up while looking out the window at the street below.
I had to fight the feeling of strangeness, but told myself it
was good to do something different. Best of all, it took away
the hunger and was light enough not to make me go into a
food coma.

I was congratulating myself on not being in a rut when my
landline rang. I waited a moment to see if it was a junk call,

but when the mechanical voice said Quentin Wright, I rushed
to answer it.

It was actually Sara, who sounded breathless. 'It's Quentin's
father again,' she said. 'He's back in the hospital. I hate to
ask you like this, but could you take care of Mikey? Ben will
come over when he finishes his shift and take over.'

'Sure, of course,' I said, and told her I'd be downstairs
momentarily. After I hung up, I looked over at Rocky in his
chair. 'Who says I can't be spontaneous?'

Sara gave me a quick hug when I walked in her place and
offered me a lot of thank-yous. She was trying to get ready
and give me instructions at the same time and then she
stopped cold. 'Did something happen between you and
Ben?' she asked.

'Why don't you ask Ben?' I said.

'I tried to, but he answered with a shrug.' She rolled her
eyes.

I hesitated, thinking about answering her in the same way,
but I decided to go with the truth. Maybe if she understood
how he really was, she would finally stop the matchmaking.
I laid out the whole plan of how we'd agreed to be each other's
plus one, but told her that he'd freaked out when we tried
practicing a slow dance. 'He actually ran off,' I said.

'Oh,' she said. 'I didn't realize he was that bad.'

'He's fine if we talk about my client who got murdered.'

Sara suddenly looked uncomfortable. 'I'm really embarrassed to admit this, but we sort of talked a few times.' She
let out a groan. 'It was more like flirting. Don't tell Ben.'

'I won't tell him any more than I'd admit Ted charmed
me,' I said.

She let out a concerned sigh as she came back to the
moment. 'I have to go.' She leaned down to explain to Mikey
that I was staying with him. Mikey seemed unconcerned
as he built a tower with his cardboard blocks. 'I promised to
take him the playground before I knew I'd have to leave. Is
it too much to ask for you to take him there?'

'It's fine. Mikey and I will have a good time. Auntie Veronica
will take you on an adventure,' I said, looking down at the
little boy. She was calling out where the stroller was and what

jacket he should wear as she was pulling on her own. She rushed to the front window and looked out.

'Quentin's here. I don't know about the cell reception at the hospital,' she said before rushing out the door.

I knew enough to check Mikey's diaper and to pack up some snacks before we left. He was a little angel for me, letting me put on his jacket and strap him into the stroller when we got outside. It was a short walk to Bixler Playground. It was fenced in, which meant the kids could run around with no worry they'd go into the street. Mikey just wanted to go on the swings.

He really wanted the big kids' version that was just an open seat, but was talked into the little kid version which reminded me of underwear or maybe what Sumo wrestlers wore. Once I got Mikey seated, he was fine, and I took up a position to push him.

I looked over at the woman and man pushing kids about Mikey's size in the adjacent swings. It was a perfect set-up for them to talk since the girl and boy in the swings seemed content to keep going back and forth. I was curious what their relationship was and tuned in to try to catch what they were talking about. It became clear that they weren't a couple. The man talked about his husband coming home and fussing if dinner wasn't ready and the woman said her husband was about the same. I gathered that they lived in the same building and when I heard the word police, my ears perked up.

'Poor Lois,' the man said. 'She was with his girlfriend Rita when she came home and found him.'

'If that's not bad enough, the cops kept questioning her,' the woman said. I made a point of keeping my gaze straight ahead so they wouldn't think I was listening. 'Do you think Lois had something going with him? His girlfriend was on the road a lot, so he certainly had time.'

'I heard he interrupted a burglary,' the man said. 'But who knows? It could have just been a cover. I'm not sure what's more upsetting – that a burglar was able to get in or that someone killed him and made it look like a burglary. I mean, either way it makes our building not seem very safe.'

'You're right if it was a random burglary, but if he was

murdered it was probably by someone who knew him and you can't expect a security door to protect someone from that. I don't think it was a burglary anyway,' the woman said, seemingly to calm him.

'You know Rita's a drug rep, somebody might have been looking for drugs,' the man still seemed worried.

'Then it would have had to be a desperate teenager. I heard the only samples she had were for an acne cream,' the woman said with a smile.

I was listening so hard that I forgot to push Mikey's swing and it came to a stop which led to a loud protest from him. I gave the swing a quick push and tried to pick up on their conversation, but they'd moved on to some other neighbor who apparently practiced the bongo drums late at night.

Eventually, Mikey wanted out of the swing. After letting him run around the playground for a while, I loaded him back into the stroller. I'd gotten a text from Haley that she had the deposit check for me. When someone had a check, I never wanted to delay picking it up, so I wheeled Mikey down the street.

The windows were still papered over, but I noticed the sign was down with the name of the place. I knocked on the door and she looked surprised when she saw me with the stroller. 'Is he yours?' she said, looking at him, probably to see if he resembled me.

'Nope, just helping out a neighbor,' I said.

'That's very nice of you.' She waved for me to wheel him inside. She kept looking at him and started to play peek-a-boo with him. It was amazing how that never got old, and in no time Mikey was giggling and playing along. 'I bet he would like some ice cream,' she said.

I didn't know quite how to say it, but I was afraid of what Mikey would do with one of the oddball flavors, but she seemed to understand without me saying anything. 'But he probably wouldn't like the chili chocolate that I made up this morning.' She looked at him again. 'I never really thought about kids eating my ice cream.'

It seemed like the perfect time to bring up what I'd thought about when I'd been tasting the salads at LaPorte's.

I knew if I told her what it was, she'd instantly react negatively, feeling like I was telling her what to do. Instead I offered it as a question. 'Have you ever thought about trying to put a twist on traditional flavors instead of trying so hard to be unique?'

I could tell she was listening, but resisting. 'You could have your special flavors as well,' I said.

'So you mean, I could make my own version of vanilla,' she said. I could tell she was already thinking how to do it when I nodded. 'I have some no-flavor ice cream in the back. I was going to mix in some ginger and black pepper, but I could give him some first,' she said.

I agreed and she went into the back. When she returned she had a small cup of the whitish ice cream for him and a scoop of brown ice cream for me. She helped Mikey with his and I prepared myself to taste mine. At first it was just a bitterish dark chocolate, but then the chili hit my tongue. 'Are you looking for an opinion or just a description?' I asked.

'Maybe both,' she said, taking a napkin and wiping Mikey's hand.

'It's interesting, but maybe a little too bitter. The heat of the chili is a surprise,' I said.

'I'll take that into consideration, along with what else you said.' Mikey was finished with his ice cream and she went to get my check.

Mikey seemed to be doing well in the stroller and I decided to walk to the bank and make a deposit there for a change. I realized we'd pass Handelman's on the way. Why not show Mikey the cow jumping over the moon?

NINETEEN

Lewis and Emily looked surprised when I wheeled Mikey into the shop. 'No, he's not mine,' I said and explained about Sara. 'He loves the moon and I thought he'd like to see the cow jump over it.'

'Of course,' Emily said. She looked at his feet in a pair of plastic shoes. 'You ought to tell his mother that we have something much better for his feet.'

I promised I would, before positioning him so he had a good view of the wall piece while Emily went in the back to turn it on. Mikey was entranced.

'I was actually going to call you,' Lewis said coming up to me. 'My aunt said she'd drop off some pictures from the old days.' He looked up as the door to the shop opened and Laurel walked in on a cloud of floral perfume. 'Wow, it's like magic. I say it and it happens.'

I was trying to think of the right words to describe her overall appearance. I'd call it successful-arty. She wore a long loose-fitting burgundy tunic with a black turtleneck underneath. I imagined the silver earrings shaped like long teardrops and silver bracelets were her own designs. Her short hair was somewhere between wavy and curly. I wondered if she was like other people I'd met with curly hair, who always wished it was straight. Her jacket was black wool and she'd pinned an amusing silver cow going over a moon on the outside. I really barely knew her, but I already liked her.

I had to explain to her who Mikey was and she gave me an impromptu hug. 'Aren't you the nice neighbor.'

'Sara keeps me fed, so it's the least I could do,' I said.

'I was going to leave some photographs, but as long as you're here, I can give them to you directly.' She pulled out an envelope and I put it into the bag on the back of the stroller. 'I might as well tell you more about the early days too,' Laurel said. She looked down at Mikey. 'But maybe not. I can't imagine he's going to sit still while I reminisce.'

Mikey kicked his feet a few times and started rubbing his eyes and I saw her point. It was already late afternoon and after our little adventures he was tired. 'He'll probably fall asleep if we walk and talk,' I said.

'That would be fine. I could use the exercise,' she said, patting her soft curves.

As we got ready to leave, Lewis gave his aunt a sympathetic look. 'Everything good?' he asked.

She shook her head trying to dismiss his concern. 'I'm fine,' she said. 'Life goes on. I have my work and you two,' she said, letting her glance take in her niece and nephew. Lewis was hovering and Laurel seemed relieved when a woman came in holding a little girl's hand. The child stumbled a little and looked at the interior with wide eyes. Lewis showed them to seats.

'That's the best,' Laurel said, watching the child. 'When they come in for their first pair of real shoes.' Laurel excused herself and went into the back. She returned holding a pink balloon attached to a weighted ribbon. The little girl's eyes grew even rounder as she reached out for it with a giggle.

'I was going to remind Lewis about the balloon, but it's such fun to do it and watch the look on her face,' Laurel said. 'Now, where were we? We were going to walk and talk.'

I nodded, looking down at Mikey whose eyes were half shut. The way Lewis had asked how she was made me think of what Tizzy had said about Laurel having some sort of issue. Now I was curious too. I wasn't going to pump her, but if she wanted to talk, I certainly wouldn't stop her.

She held the door for me and I wheeled Mikey outside. The air felt soft and the afternoon was fading but there was still time for a walk before it got dark. She suggested we walk to the lakefront.

At first we just walked and it was as if we had to get comfortable with each other. She still seemed tense as we passed through the viaduct that ran under the Metra tracks, so I made small talk, telling her about Mikey and why I was rolling him around in his stroller. His eyes were shut now and he was sound asleep. I tried to transition the conversation to being about her. 'Why don't you tell me a little about yourself? You are one of the owners so you should be included in the "story".'

She seemed hesitant. 'I don't know exactly what you want to know.'

'Don't worry about that. More is always better. I can pick out what I need. How about we start with this? Are you married? Do you have kids?'

She didn't say anything, and when I looked over at her, her eyes looked sad and I realized I must have hit something sensitive and I rushed to apologize. 'I'm sorry, was that a bad question?'

'Probably not for most people, but when you're the spinster aunt, it kind of stings.'

'Believe me, you don't seem like a spinster anything,' I said. 'You're artistic, successful and you seem like fun.' Then I told her the whole thing I was going through, feeling like I'd become a dull, no fun person.

'Listen to us feeling sorry for ourselves,' she said. 'You've got a whole life ahead of you, and I need to let go and move on.'

'Do you want to talk about it?' I said.

'Lewis has made such a big deal out of it and he only knows the barest of details.' She looked over at me. 'You seem like a kindred spirit, so why not.' She stopped talking as we crossed the street and resumed when we got to the other side. 'I know it sounds ridiculous for a woman my age. But I really believed that was it. It was straight out of a rom-com for mature women.' She shook her head with regret. 'Maybe when you hear how it started, you'll understand.' She glanced over at me. 'Have you ever met someone and thought that it was fate, meant to be, and all that other nonsense?'

'Well, actually, no,' I said. 'I had a short bad marriage when I was really young and it made me hesitant to trust my feelings.'

'Now I'm there too,' she said. The street here was lined with apartment buildings with small retail shops on the ground floor.

'So, are you going to tell me how you met?' I said as we passed a small yarn shop.

'It's too embarrassing. I'm supposed to have experience and know better.' It seemed like that was going to be the end of it, but after a moment, she put up her hands. 'It's probably good to talk about it as long as you keep it to yourself.'

I agreed not to tell anyone. And I meant it. I'd make some excuse to Tizzy.

'I could understand it, if I'd met him on a dating site. They are notorious for weirdos and jerks. But we met the natural way. The first time was in an elevator downtown. We both reached for the button at the same time.' She let out a mirthless laugh. 'Sounds like something from a movie, doesn't it? I'd just had a good meeting with a store about showing my line and I was feeling stoked. He commented on me looking happy and we struck up a conversation. It was pouring outside and it turned out we were both heading for the Metra station. I had an umbrella, he didn't, and I offered to share.' She turned to me. 'Can you get more romantic than that?'

'I see what you're saying,' I said.

'We rode the train together to the same stop. By the time we got off the train, the rain had stopped and we started to go our separate ways. He said something about how magical it had all seemed the way we met and our walk in the rain. It seemed like fate that we both had appointments in the same building the next day, and he suggested lunch.

'It seemed like we made this instant connection. Like it was meant to be, so I agreed.' By now she seemed to be lost in her own remembrances with no regard to the listener. Mikey was still asleep as we had reached the underpass that ran under Lake Shore Drive. I asked her if she wanted to turn back, but she shook her head and kept walking. The underpass led to Promontory Point. The manmade peninsula jutted out in Lake Michigan and was rimmed with a seawall made out of rows of stone blocks. At this time of year, the grass was brown and the trees empty, but the views were still spectacular.

I doubted that Laurel was paying much attention to the scenery as she continued on with her tale. The lunch date had been wonderful and they'd agreed to meet again. I gathered that it had combusted into an intense relationship. Her face clouded over. 'I don't know exactly how to explain it, but he seemed to just know what I needed more than I did. I've never had too much luck with relationships, but I thought it had all been leading up to this. Imagine what it's like when you feel like you're going to be the spinster aunt and then you meet someone who turns your world around. It's scary to me now to see how gullible I was. How can I ever trust my judgment again?'

I gathered it was a rhetorical question and only nodded to show I was listening. We were on the path that looped around a grassy area. As we reached the outermost spot on the peninsula, the view was of open water. The mood of the lake seemed calm and reflected the deepening blue of the sky.

'I should have known that when he didn't want to meet any of my friends or family that it was a bad sign. But he said, he didn't want to share me with anyone.' She let out a sad-sounding sigh. 'I was so flattered by his attention, I lost my perspective. Lewis met him once by chance. We'd gone to Gibson's and Lewis was there with his wife and in-laws.' Gibson's was a famous downtown restaurant known for its steaks. 'We stopped by their table for a few minutes and I introduced him.'

She stopped talking suddenly and her brow furrowed. 'What am I doing, telling you all this. I haven't told anybody about this. It's so embarrassing.' The path had begun to curve back and the downtown skyline came into view.

'Sometimes it's easier to talk to a stranger,' I said.

'You know, you're right. No pitying looks from you.'

'You're not the first person to unload something on their mind,' I said. 'I tend to get involved with my clients and I guess I'm a sympathetic listener.'

She nodded but seemed to be done with the story. It was obvious it had turned out badly and I wondered why. It had started out in such a meet-cute way, as they called it in rom-com movies, and she'd made it sound like they really got along. I couldn't let it go without hearing the ending.

'So, what happened?' I said. I was expecting the usual-type twist that he'd cheated on her. I was hardly expecting what she told me. We were back at the underpass and went through, with cars whirling over us as our footsteps made an echoing sound.

'The first time, I didn't think anything of it. He was the kind of guy who always picked up the bill, so when he said he was waiting for a paycheck and he had to make a payment on something, I gave him the money without a second thought. He paid me back right away and I figured that was it. Then he needed some money again, but this time there was a delay in him paying it back. I didn't really think much about it. He'd started talking about us having a life together. He traveled a lot for work, and he said he wanted to give it up and settle down with me. He painted such an appealing picture. All the things we'd do together, places we'd go. It was like a dream come true. What I'd been waiting all my life for. He had a chance to invest in the company he worked for. Then he'd be a boss and stay put. He said he had most of the money in his retirement account and just needed a loan to make up the difference. It was investing in our future. He painted an impressive picture of what it would be like. I could continue on with my jewelry and he'd be there to help with the business end, which is not my favorite part. When I talked to my financial advisor about getting the cash, he asked me about what my plans for it were. He didn't try to talk me out of it or anything, but urged me to wait a little while. It seemed fair enough to me, but when I told my guy about the delay, he got upset and told me I was being manipulated by my financial advisor. He balked and said it felt like I didn't trust him. He urged me to ignore my financial advisor, saying it was my money to do with as I chose. He was very convincing and I was all twisted around. But my philosophy is when in doubt, wait. I told him I couldn't see what difference it would make if I waited a few weeks.' She stopped as she seemed to picture the encounter in her mind.

'He kept going on that I didn't trust him and that he was deeply hurt. When I held my ground, he went ballistic. He said that if I didn't trust him, we had no relationship, and left in a huff. I thought he was just angry and we'd be able to work it out, but that was it.' She dipped her head. 'I can't believe I almost gave him the money. Just like that, he disappeared from my life. No more calls or letters.'

When she said letters, I instinctively stopped walking.

'What kind of letters?' I asked, realizing she'd never mentioned his name.

'He was gone a lot on business, and I'd get these charming notes to let me know he missed me. It was one of the things that cemented the deal with me. The letters were so romantic and not what most people do nowadays. And the things he said. *I saw the moon and I thought of you. I saw the stars and I thought of you. I saw a rose and I thought of you. Everything of beauty reminds me of you and how much I long to take you in my arms.*'

I was mentally mouthing the all too familiar words as she said them. I didn't know what to say.

She seemed relieved to have gotten the story out. 'I'm sure a guy like that will end up getting what he deserves,' she said. 'Lewis knows we're kaput, but no details other than I'd been left. Lewis is so protective of me, I was afraid of what he'd do if he knew what had happened.'

I was too stunned to speak, but I also couldn't let on how I was feeling. I had a bunch of questions I would have liked to have asked. Where did he say he lived? What name did he use, and did she know that he was dead? But the only thing I managed to ask was how long ago the breakup had happened. When she said it had been about a month ago, I realized something even more unsettling. I'd written a love letter for him just a week ago. It meant there had to be someone else.

TWENTY

M ikey didn't stir until we got home and I was glad to have the time to think. I had to wrap my head around not only what Tony or Ted had done, but that he'd used my letters to do it. Did that mean I was an accessory? How could I have known? I really wanted to talk to somebody about it.

The little boy finally awoke when I started pulling the stroller up the stairs to the entrance of our building. Every step meant a bump, so it wasn't surprising. It was easier anyway, since he wanted out so he could go up the stairs himself. I folded the stroller up and followed behind him.

The door to their apartment was open when we reached the second floor and Sara, Quentin and Ben were standing in the entranceway.

After a quick greeting, Mikey ran off to play with his toys.

I gave a report of his long nap in the stroller and his parents thanked me for taking care of him. Quentin's father was back in the hospital but for now all was well.

'Then I guess you don't need me,' Ben said. As Sara was apologizing to him for having him come over, I realized he was the best one to talk with about what I'd just found out.

'As long as you're here,' I said, 'there is something I'd like to discuss with you. It's not personal,' I added quickly. After his reaction the other night, I hoped it would put him at ease. And tamp down any expectations Sara had.

'Actually,' he said, 'I wanted to show you some pages before I brought them to the group.'

'I was just going to order a pizza,' Quentin said. 'How about I order one for you two as well? It's the least I can do after what you both have done for us.'

After agreeing to the offer, Ben and I went up to my place. I hoped that Sara understood that this didn't change what I'd told her earlier. I wasn't trying to lasso her brother, who'd made it abundantly clear he didn't want any entanglements.

Rocky came to the door when we walked in. He really liked Ben and followed him into the living room and jumped on the couch to be next to him. 'He remembers that you were the one looking out for his needs when I first brought him home,' I said.

Ben's face softened as he reached out to stroke the cat's back. 'Just doing my job, buddy,' he said to the cat. Then he looked up at me. 'So how should we do this? Do you want to go first, or should I?' He held out the sheaf of pages.

I could tell he was tense and I knew where he was coming from. Showing your work to someone was always nerve-wracking, even for me now. I always felt a knot in my stomach when I gave a client some copy to look over. When I offered him the first spot, he seemed relieved and I gathered he wanted to get it over with.

'I'm not sure how the group will react to this scene, particularly Ed. He might think I made the cop look soft. I wanted to see what you thought first. Be kind,' he said with a worried smile.

Now I was curious, and I quickly read them over. The scene had his character driving through a rundown area on a cold winter's night. He was looking for someone and I assumed it was a suspect for a robbery or some other crime. When he saw who he had been hunting for, he pulled his cruiser to the curb. I expected the cop to get out with handcuffs jangling and do his usual tough talk, but instead Ben had described him approaching a homeless man. He was described as bone thin with nothing to protect him from the frigid night but a raggedy coat and shoes worn thin. There was some dialogue where the cop tried to get the man to go to a shelter, but the man was clearly mentally ill and too paranoid to take the offer of help. The cop finally gave up, and went back to his cruiser, returning with a coat, a pair of shoes and a bag of food. He helped the man take off his ratty coat and put on the new warmer one. He did the same with the shoes. He unloaded the bag of food and unwrapped a sandwich for him. The man looked up at him and for a moment they connect, not cop and homeless man, but as just two humans out on the street on a cold night. As a last gesture, the cop tucks a twenty into the man's pocket before letting out a heavy sigh and going back to his cruiser.

I was stunned. It was as if everything the group and I had been saying to him had finally gotten through to him. All along his cop character had spoken in short sentences and seemed more robot than person. In these pages, he'd given him dimension – he had given him a heart. Ben had put in descriptions like: *There was a desolate feeling to the dark street in a neglected neighborhood bypassed by everyone who had someplace else to go. Windblown plastic grocery bags hung like sad decorations from the bare branches of a lonely tree. Desperate creatures skittered amongst the abandoned fast-food wrappings and empty bottles that languished in the gutter.* It felt so real and I teared up at the kindness of the cop. It was so different than everything else he'd brought to the group; those pieces had always seemed brittle and cold.

'I don't know what to say.' I looked up from the papers on my lap.

He looked stricken and reached to grab them back. 'I knew it was a mistake. I should have kept on the way I was going.'

I put my hand on his to stop him from taking the papers. 'You misunderstood. I don't know what to say because what you wrote is wonderful. It's full of life, touching. Frankly, your character always seemed like a kind of jerk. This changed everything. Now the reader will know there is something simmering beneath the surface. You put in such great detail. It was absolutely poetic.' I looked at his face. His brow was furrowed and he seemed unglued as he ran hands through his dark hair nervously.

'Poetic, me?' he said with an uneasy laugh. 'The best I've ever done is roses are red, violets are blue.'

'It's a different kind of poetic,' I said. 'I was just wondering – was it based on a real experience?'

He took a couple of heavy breaths. 'It was a buddy,' he began. He stopped and seemed to be having an internal argument. 'I can't believe that I said that. I can't lie – it was me. You don't think it makes me, er, him, seem soft?' he asked.

'No. It makes both of you seem like you have hearts.' He didn't seem to know what to do with what I said and seemed relieved when there was a knock on the door.

'Pizza delivery,' Quentin said when I opened the door. He was so different than his wife. She would have looked inside, trying to figure out what was going on. He just handed over the pizza and a couple of bottles of beer, thanked us again and told us to enjoy.

'You get both the beers,' I said, handing them to him.

'Thanks,' Ben said, uncapping one. 'And about what you said. I know I said to be kind, but really you know you don't have to sugarcoat anything to protect my feelings. If you think it's too mushy, I can change it.'

'I wasn't being kind,' I said. 'I was being honest. It was your best work ever and you should share it with the group.' I put the pizza box on the coffee table. It came with paper plates and utensils.

He still appeared a little overwhelmed with the praise and seemed anxious to get the spotlight off of himself. 'OK, now it's your turn,' he said.

'Why don't you dig in,' I said opening the pizza box.

'No. You tell me whatever you have and then we can both relax and eat. Maybe you'll even have some beer,' he said with a smile.

'Nope, they're all yours,' I said. 'And now for what I wanted to talk to you about.' I told him the whole story. What Laurel had said and how I felt about having written the letters she'd gotten.

'Whew,' he said, blowing out his breath when I was through. 'That guy was a worse slime than I thought. But there's no way you could have known what he was doing with the letters he hired you to write.'

'Do I tell that detective about what Laurel told me? It makes her a suspect, and her nephew. She said he was protective of her. But they're clients of mine. I don't want to stir something up if they're innocent.' I'd gotten up by now and was walking around the room thinking. 'I know you aren't going to approve since you're a cop, but I think the only thing I can do is keep poking around until I find out who killed Ted.' I reminded him that there was another recipient of the letters I'd written after Ted had broken up with Laurel.

Ben thought about it. 'I see your point.' He looked around, as if to see if anyone was listening. 'But don't tell anyone I said that.' He took a slug of the beer. 'But you really should stay out of it. If that detective found out, it might make him take another look at you as a suspect. I told you cops don't like civilians mucking around in their business.'

'He won't find out. Well, until I move in on the guilty party,' I said.

'I can't stop you anyway, can I?' I shook my head as an answer. 'Just remember I'm here if you need me,' he said. 'And now let's eat.'

Friday morning I was at Zooey's coffee stand bright and early. I was after coffee and information. As before, there was a throng of impatient students and faculty hanging by the counter, grabbing a cup of coffee before class. I waited until the place cleared. 'You really ought to give this place a name,' I said. 'Why not call it what it is: A Cup of Joe?'

'What does that mean anyway?' she said.

Thank heavens for smartphones. I typed it in and had an answer the next moment. I told her that the term came from the Secretary of the Navy in 1914 whose nickname was Joe. He banned alcohol on the ships and the strongest drink allowed was a cup of coffee. The sailors started calling it a cup of Joe.

She shook her head, 'I was thinking of something more personal, like calling it Coffee by the Cup by Zooey.' I pointed out the two bys made it awkward and suggested Zooey's Coffee by the Cup. She liked it and wanted to let it germinate in her mind for a few days. 'I have more than coffee drinks,' she said.

She brewed up a cup of her own blend and – probably to prove her point – made me a tea drink called Lost in the Fog. I scribbled down notes as I tasted the drinks. I commented again on how smooth all of her coffees tasted and she smiled. 'That's because I add my secret tweak,' she said. She didn't want to share what it was, so I changed the subject to the death in her building.

'Have the cops figured out who did it?' I asked.

She rocked her head with annoyance and made a face. 'The word is that they can't decide if it was a burglary gone wrong or he was actually targeted. Either way, the manager sent around a note warning the tenants not to let anyone tag along when they went through the security door and no more keys left in flowerpots or umbrellas in front of apartment doors. Lois – she's the onsite manager – will hold spare keys. Of course, there was no word about adding some security cameras.'

Lois must have been the woman I saw Detective Jankowski talking with when I'd gone to see what name was on the apartment number Ted had given when he rented the post-office box. The people at the playground had mentioned the name as well. And what was it they'd said about Rita's samples? As I remembered, I brought it up to Zooey.

'It's true, she does sell acne medicine, but she has other stuff, too,' Zooey said.

A couple of students rushed up asking for whatever was quickest. She filled two cups from an air pot and pushed them across the counter. As I watched her moving around the place, I thought of Ben's assessment that she could have been the burglar. She'd just given away that she knew about Rita's drug samples beyond the acne medicine. But the fact she had drug samples seemed to be common knowledge, judging by the pair I'd heard at the playground. I wondered what Lois had to say about the whole thing. I was definitely going to find a way to talk to her. Just not now.

I left the coffee place and started down 57th Street on my way to LaPorte's. It had already been arranged for me to go there and do more tastings. The sky was a gloomy metal-gray, and with the low light and no shadows it was easy to let everything blend into the background as I walked to LaPorte's. I thought back to the night before. I understood now what Sara kept trying to tell me about Ben. There was a whole lot more than I'd realized under that cop-face surface. She might be right that he was worth the effort to get past it, but he had to want it. And the way Ben had pushed me away after the few minutes of closeness in that stupid slow dance, he was staying locked in the castle with the drawbridge up.

Funny how he'd been fine talking about motives in Ted's death. Crime was comfortable to deal with, but not getting past his divorce. The conclusion we'd come to was that there were a number of possible motives for Ted's death. Different motives pointed to different suspects.

He was living with Rita and it seemed as though she was paying the bills. He wasn't working much, according to the charter company woman, and after what he'd tried to pull with Laurel, it seemed likely he'd hit on Rita for money too. I knew for a fact that he'd had at least one other woman while he was living with Rita. What if she found out?

But if it had been a burglary, was it random or someone who knew what was there? It seemed as if more than Zooey knew about the drug samples. What if it wasn't exactly a burglary? What if someone was looking for something in particular? Like what? I shrugged off the thought as I turned on to 53rd Street and joined the parade of foot traffic.

I checked out a blank wall near the windows as I walked into LaPorte's. I'd had an idea and emailed it to Rex. Why not put a photo mural of pictures from the bakery and café's history along with a blow-up of the family's story? Once the layout was designed, it could be put in the new stores as well. He was all for the idea and wanted me to write a special version for it.

I was glad to see Irma was behind the counter since she knew why I was there. Even so I waited my turn in line.

While I was waiting, Cocoa came from the back carrying a large cake box. I was going to wave a greeting at her, but she seemed distracted and appeared rather grim as she presented the customer with the box. She returned from where she'd come with no notice of anything.

I finally advanced to the counter. Irma's face lit with recognition and she was about to say something, when I saw her look toward the door with amazement. 'Oh, my,' she said, 'Rex isn't going to be happy.'

Curious as to what had gotten that response from her, I

turned and saw a woman coming across the restaurant. She looked vaguely familiar and as soon as Irma spoke her name I understood why.

'Jeanne, what a surprise,' Irma said. I couldn't tell if it was a good surprise or a bad one that Rex's mother, the matriarch of the whole business, had just shown up. I could see the resemblance to both Rex and Cocoa in her features.

She took a long look around the place and took in a deep breath. 'Ah, the sweet baking smell of chocolate mint cake. It brings back memories.' She came behind the counter, and everything in her body language said she felt like she was home.

'No one said you were coming in,' Irma said.

Jeanne laughed. 'That's because they didn't know. If I'd told Rex, he would have tried to talk me out of it. I'm tired of hearing everything secondhand about what's going on. I wanted to see for myself.'

Just then Cocoa came out from the back with another cake box. She had the same glum expression. Before she'd even noticed that her mother was there, Jeanne was on her case.

'Honey, remember what I taught you. Our cakes are connected to happy events and no matter what your day is like, when it comes to dealing with customers, you have to smile.'

Cocoa grunted in protest before seeming to will her face into a cheerful expression. Jeanne patted her daughter's shoulder. 'That's better. You can tell me whatever's bothering you later.' Cocoa moved on to deliver the cake.

Jeanne noticed me standing near the counter. 'I'm so sorry we neglected you,' she said, giving me a warm smile. Irma stopped her and explained what I was doing there.

'It certainly sounds like a good idea, not that anybody told me about it,' Jeanne said, sounding a little irked.

'As long as you're here, it would be great to talk to you. I've heard the story of how you started out, but I'm sure you have extra details,' I said, hoping to smooth things over.

Irma stepped in and suggested I deal with the tasting first and told me that Rex had left instructions for me to be given a platter with the remaining eight salads for me to taste.

'That's ridiculous. It's too many to taste at once. Make it just four,' Jeanne interjected. As an afterthought, she seemed puzzled by the number of salads and asked for a list. Irma handed her a paper menu. As Jeanne read it over, she kept shaking her head and muttering to herself something about not getting an OK from her.

Irma leaned closer and told me to find a table and she'd bring the food. When I looked back, Jeanne was on her way into the kitchen with Irma trying to keep up with her. I found a small table near the door and took out my notebook and pen. I kept looking toward the kitchen expectantly, but time kept passing and there was no Irma. I was debating what to do when she finally came up to the table with a plate of salads and some freshly baked dinner rolls.

'Sorry for the delay.' She seemed frustrated about something and then decided to share the details. 'I had no idea that Jeanne wasn't in on all the additions of foods or the changes around here. She had to taste the salads before she'd let me give them to you. She nixed four of them.' Irma rolled her eyes. 'She's very upset about how Rex has standardized everything. It's not the way she likes to do things. If she says anything to you, please don't use it in what you're writing.'

'Of course not,' I said.

She put the plate on the table along with a piece of paper that had a map of the plate with each salad's name and the ingredients. 'Jeanne's idea.'

I began to taste and write down notes. The coleslaw was creamy with a hint of celery salt. The egg salad had a crunch from slivers of celery and subtle onion taste from scallions blended with mayonnaise and a dab of mustard. I jotted down balsamic vinegar dressing over fresh mozzarella and chunks of tomato in the aptly named tomato and mozzarella salad. The final salad was a puree of carrots and walnuts with honey and ginger. Middle Eastern heritage? Since I hadn't had breakfast, I not only tasted the salads but finished them off, and all the rolls I'd used to clear my palate between salads.

I was finishing up my notes when Jeanne came up to the table with two cups of coffee and a piece of the chocolate mint cake. Her manner made me feel as if we were at her kitchen table.

I thanked her for the cake and coffee, explaining I'd already written up something on the cake.

'Then we'll just get it boxed for you to take home,' she said, taking the seat across from me. When I looked at her and the piece of cake, it seemed like the perfect picture to include. After asking her if it was OK, I grabbed a couple of shots with my phone and showed them to her. I explained the plan of having a photomontage on the wall along with the story of the place.

'That sounds wonderful,' she said. She picked up my phone and examined the picture I'd taken. 'I like your thinking,' she said. 'Casual shots like this are better than something staged. The whole feeling I've wanted for this place is that it was like you stopped at a friend's place.' She started to tell me about the start of the business. It was basically the same story I'd heard about her baking cakes from her kitchen, but she added an element of emotion that I hadn't heard before. Her husband had died shortly after she moved to the storefront and she didn't know if she'd be able to manage. 'But somehow I did,' she said brightly. 'This cake was the start of it all. Other bakeries have tried to make it, but it's never quite the same. They don't know my secret to the taste. That recipe is the key to the castle. It still took a lot of hard work. I was lucky to have Irma and my kids to help out, but the buck always stopped with me.'

I didn't even consider that she'd used a cliché because it seemed to fit what she was trying to say so perfectly. She glanced toward the counter and her face took on a stern look. Rex had just come in and was talking to Irma. As he glanced toward his mother, he didn't look happy. Jeanne reached across the table and put her hand on mine. 'I can't wait to see what you put together.' Then, after saying she'd send somebody over with a container for the cake, she pushed away from the table and marched toward the counter, gesturing that they should go upstairs to the office area.

I decided to give it a couple of minutes to see if someone did show up with a container, and it gave me a chance to look over my notes again and finish the coffee. Since I'd only had one cup at Zooey's, by now I was more than ready for another.

I was reading over my notes when I sensed someone standing next to the table. I absently picked up the plate of cake as if to hand it to them before looking up.

'If you're offering, I'll take it,' Lewis said. I pulled my hand back with a laugh.

'No way am I giving up a piece of this legendary cake,' I said before explaining I was waiting for a container. Something seemed different about him as I looked him over.

He noticed my puzzled expression. 'It's the clothes,' he said, showing off his tracksuit. 'I got a last-minute call this morning to take over for the coach at St Mel's.' He reminded me that he was a substitute gym teacher, which covered acting as a coach, too. 'I just picked up lunch for Emily and me,' he said, holding up the bag.

He started to walk away and then turned back. 'Aunt Laurel seemed to be in a better mood than I've seen her in a while when she came back from your walk. I don't know what you talked about, but if she said anything about that boyfriend of hers, please don't repeat it to anyone.' He checked the area to see if anyone was in earshot. 'She doesn't know it, but the guy's dead. There's nothing to connect him to her and it's better to leave it that way.'

He waited until I agreed and then, before I could ask him anything like how he knew Ted was dead, he was on his way out the door.

No one brought the container for the cake and eventually I got one myself. It had been quite a morning.

TWENTY-ONE

I spent the walk home thinking about meeting Jeanne LaPorte and how she had offered a different feeling about the place. She was the heart of the endeavor and looked at it as being an extension of their home. Rex was all about business.

I'd heard enough from Jeanne and Irma to read between the lines that Jeanne wasn't happy about being sidelined. Rex had presented himself as being in total charge of the business. Irma, too, had made it sound like he did a lot when his father died, but Jeanne still saw herself as the boss. I could only imagine the battle going on between them after I'd left. Personally, I was relieved that Jeanne seemed happy with what I'd been hired for. The work for LaPorte's was the biggest job I had and I would have hated to lose it.

I was already reframing how I was going to handle the background story. I just needed an opening line. Somehow, when I had that, the rest of it seemed to fall into place.

I had the same issue with the backstory for Handelman's Children's Shoes. I regretted that I hadn't managed to get some more about the beginnings of the place from Laurel, but she'd gotten sidetracked with telling me about Ted. Of course, I hadn't realized that was who she was talking about until she'd got to the end and mentioned the letters. I'd paid attention when she was telling how they met and such, but not the way I would have if I'd known who she was talking about. I tried to remember what she'd said, but mostly I was left with sort of an overview. It appeared he'd wooed her to get his hands on her money. She seemed hurt, and also angry at herself for falling for him. Maybe she'd realized she should have been wary since he was younger than she was. What she'd said about Lewis stuck in my mind. He was protective of her and he'd met Ted. For a moment my mind wandered away from thoughts about what had happened to Ted to the concept of having family who were protective of you.

It was something I knew nothing about. I was an only child with parents who'd been only children themselves, which meant no aunts, uncles or cousins. With my parents gone I was really alone in the world. So, now I was a single woman with a cat, living alone with her memories, slightly stuck in her ways, not much fun, who had no one watching her back.

Rocky came to the door when I got home. He seemed to pick up on my mood and stuck with me as I went into my office. When I sat down at the computer, he jumped in my lap and went into full cuddle mode, leaning against my shoulder and hugging me with his paws.

'Thanks, I needed that,' I said to the cat. 'And in case you're wondering, I'm absolutely watching your back.' As I said it, I ran my hand along his back and he began to purr so loudly he seemed to rumble.

I pulled out my notebook, intending to transcribe everything into its right file. I opened the LaPorte's file first, intending to put in the descriptions of the latest things I'd tasted while it was fresh in my mind. Somehow I thought I'd taken more extensive notes, but really they read more like a list of ingredients with a few buzzwords thrown in. I put my hands on the keys prepared to type, but I hit a snag. It should have been quick and easy, the point was to make word sketches of the taste of each menu item, but I found myself agonizing over every word. I called it word constipation and I needed something to free up the flow. A walk often worked, but I'd been out enough. I considered other options. If I hadn't had so little tolerance to alcohol that a mere sip gave me an uncomfortable buzz, I would have considered taking a hit of the cooking wine. It seemed like a writerly thing to do, but would have hindered me more than helped. I thought about crocheting. Wasn't that kind of like taking a walk with my fingers? It was certainly rhythmic and meditative. I had a number of squares I was working on, but I couldn't really let my mind go. I had to be sure not to lose or gain a stitch at the end of the row and pay attention to the pattern of stitches. All that really mattered now was that my hook kept moving to release my block. I found some leftover yarn and grabbed the first hook I saw. I made a long chain as a foundation and then turned back on it doing single crochet stitches. Since it wasn't a particular project, I didn't have to measure the length or worry about gaining or losing stitches. As my hook moved, my shoulders relaxed and my mind cleared, and after a few minutes I felt the words ready to move out.

I looked down at the snake of stitches which, even with such little regard, had turned out quite nicely. Amazed that I hadn't thought of this before, I stashed the whole thing in a dark corner of my desk.

I smiled to myself as the first salad became *sweet spheres of fresh mozzarella coupled with bite-size hunks of vine-ripened tomatoes flavored with a splash of balsamic vinegar-based dressing.*

Even though the chocolate mint cake was their signature item, it had only been described as chocolate mint cake with white buttercream icing. I flipped open the container with the slice that Jeanne had given me and broke off a piece that had both cake and frosting. As soon as I tasted it, I was reminded of birthday parties, pink dresses and happy times in my life. Just as Jeanne had said, their cakes were connected to happy moments. Wasn't all that really part of the taste? And so I wrote: *the legendary cake that started it all. With a perfect undertone of mint, the dense chocolate cake is complemented by the buttery white frosting evoking memories of birthday parties and smiles.*

I went back to thinking about the wall montage and looked at the photos I'd taken, hoping they'd inspire me to come up with the opening line.

When I finally took a break, I texted Sara to ask how Quentin's father was and to offer my services if needed. I'd barely hit send when there was a knock at the door. I opened it and Sara was standing in the doorway dressed in her mom wear of leggings and a big T-shirt with a blob of something orange on it. 'I hope you're not disappointed that it isn't Ben,' she said.

I shook my head as an answer and invited her in. Was I disappointed that it wasn't Ben? I had gotten used to talking over the whole Ted thing with him, so maybe I was. Not that I would ever let on to Sara.

I started to offer her some of my cooking wine, but all I had to say was *would you like* . . . and she was nodding yes.

'Quentin just got home,' she began. 'All that's going on with his father made him want to get closer to Mikey. I couldn't agree more, particularly if it gives me a few minutes off. He and his sister spent the day at the hospital and I got to stay home with Mikey.' She let out a tired sigh and held up the shirt showing off the orange blob. 'Thought it would be fun to finger-paint. Mikey was more into throwing the paint.' I asked her about Quentin's father and she said they were still evaluating whether to do surgery. 'I'm sorry for the guy, even though he doesn't like me.' She made a face. 'He thought Quentin should have married Suzy Blake whose father owns a car dealership.' She settled on the couch just where Ben always sat while I went to get the wine. I mentioned that it seemed like the family seating arrangement when I handed her the glass of wine and she laughed. 'Yeah, it's in our genes that we like sitting in the center of the couch.' She took a healthy drag of the wine. I'd gone fancy and added a slice of lemon to my sparkling water.

She wanted to talk about anything but kids and I told her about Zooey and my trip to LaPorte's. She was very interested in hearing about Jeanne's visit to the place. 'It's got to be hard having all those family members working together.'

'Sometimes it works,' I said, thinking of the Handelmans. They seemed to get along and look out for each other. I described their situation to Sara, though I didn't repeat anything Laurel had said as she had requested. 'I'm fascinated by the whole family dynamic. It seems pretty nice, but then I probably have a romanticized view of it since I'm looking from the outside.' I adjusted my glass. 'You and Ben seem to look out for each other. How many times has he come over this week?'

'Yes, my brother always comes through when I need anything. It helps that he loves Mikey.' She put her wine glass down and faced me. 'I'm sorry for trying to push you together with him. Until you told me how he acted the other night, I had no idea he was that messed up from the divorce. I just want him to be happy. I appreciate that you didn't take it personally and push him out of the writing group and such. And for the record, you might be right about the friend thing working this time.' She took another sip. 'I'm not sure if it helps, but I look at you as family. I guess that's why I kept hoping there'd be something more than friends with Ben.'

I got up and gave her a hug. 'The best family are the people you pick to be part of it.'

'Good one,' Sara said. 'Now that we've gotten past the mushy stuff, is there anything new about that too-charming client of yours who got killed?'

'If you mean, have I figured out who killed him – no. But I did find out more about him and how somebody could have gotten in,' I said.

She shuddered when I told her about the key left in the umbrella spokes and then shrugged. 'I guess it's pretty common to leave a spare key hidden somewhere.'

'I'd thought of leaving one in the boots I leave in the hall,' I said. 'But since you have one to my place, I didn't.'

'Good,' she said. 'I'm taking my spare key from under the mat and giving it to you.' Her cell pinged and we looked at each other knowingly. Quentin had run out of patience.

The interruption turned out to be a blessing because when I went back to the computer, I had the first line I was looking for. *It all started with a birthday cake . . .*

I was off and running after that and lost track of time. I'd missed the sunset, dinner time and even the late news. I made myself a bowl of soup and a grilled cheese sandwich and called it dinner just before I went to bed.

Zooey kept the coffee place open on Saturdays, but just for the morning. There were a few classes and she wanted to have a consistent presence even if it was barely worth her while. What she really needed was to grab some of the neighborhood people I passed who used the campus as a spot for their exercise walks. I was going to be sorry when this assignment was over. It got me out of the house early and her coffee was much better than mine.

There were just three people clustered around the stand

when I came in. She acknowledged me with a wave and I grabbed one of the stools at the far end of the counter.

'Hey there,' she said, joining me when she was done with her customers. I handed the descriptions of the two drinks from the day before. Writing about the coffee blends was pretty redundant. I did make a point to mention how smooth her brews were and that they all contained Zooey's Fairy Dust, which is what I'd named her secret ingredient. The Lost in the Fog tea drink was another matter. The flavors were more obvious and I described them as a symphony of English breakfast tea, frothed milk with a hint of sweetness.

She read them over and nodded with approval. 'These are great.' She set them aside. 'Let's see what we have for you today.' She looked over the list of coffees. 'There's just one medium roast left and a few dark roasts,' she said. She set the mugs up and the filters. I used the opportunity to get some more information for her story. I took a few notes as she told me about working for a couple of coffee places while she was an undergrad. When I had the two mugs of coffee for the day's tasting, she sat down with her own mug of brew.

'Anything new with the investigation of that guy in your building?' I asked, trying to sound casual.

'I think the cops have been around some more.' She let out an annoyed sigh. 'The manager of the building has gone nuts. Every day she's sending out another notice. Today's was that anyone having someone stay at their place for more than a week has to check with her. I heard she's in trouble with the building's owners. I heard it all from Rita.' She took a moment to explain who Rita was in case I didn't remember her from a few days ago. I tried to look as if I really needed my memory refreshed. 'What makes it even worse is that the cops keep talking to Lois because she was with Rita when they found Ted.' She looked toward the door as a couple came in. 'I thought when that guy died it would be the end of the problem, but even dead he's causing trouble.' She got up and went around the counter as the couple approached and I went back to my tasting while thinking about what she'd said.

I had forgotten that Lois was with Rita when Ted's body was discovered. I thought about trying to get more information from Zooey, but why not get it directly? Why not talk to Lois? I finished the first mug and noted that it had a mellow nutty flavor meant to be sipped and savored. All I needed was a few sips of the French roast to write that it had a smooth smoky flavor. I was probably overusing smooth and I was using it to say not bitter, but the fact was that none of the coffees I'd tasted had any harshness to the taste. Whatever she put in the Fairy Dust, it seemed to work.

I had finished the second mug and was getting up to leave when she finished with the couple. They'd both ordered Chocodelites.

Zooey reminded me she was closed on Sunday. 'We can finish up the coffees on Monday,' she said, picking up my mug and putting it in her table-top dishwasher.

I was pretty buzzed from the coffee and as I walked out on to the street a plan was forming that would get me access to Lois. Since Zooey was likely to be around on Sunday and might blow my cover, I wanted to do it now.

I created my backstory as I walked to the red-brick building. I was so deep in thought, I didn't remember walking there. I had no memory of crossing any streets and I hoped in my trance state that I'd looked for traffic.

I put on a purposeful air and walked into the lobby and checked for the doorbell marked office. There was no instant buzz to the security door unlocking it, but a voice crackled through the intercom offering assistance, which was a nice way of asking what I wanted. Without missing a beat, I launched into my story. I had a friend who was interested in moving into the neighborhood and I was checking apartments for him.

Lois came to the security door and looked me over through the windows on the side of it. I smiled at the tall woman with a boyish figure. I must have met her approval because she opened the door and invited me in.

She introduced herself as we walked back to her office, which was a small room across from the building lounge. I gave her my name and said I lived in the area, as I glanced around the interior trying to get a sense of who she was to help me make conversation. Most of her desk was taken up with a computer. The only picture on her desk was of her with a long-haired Siamese cat. A bunch of pens were stuck in a mug shaped like a cat.

She offered me a chair adjacent to her desk. 'What size place was your friend interested in?' she asked, sitting down in front of the computer. The 'friend' was Ben. It was easier to make up answers when I had a real person in mind. I hoped that Ben wouldn't mind that I was using him as the model for my 'friend'.

I had no idea what his real living arrangements were, but I imagined that he'd probably be fine with a one bedroom on a lower floor. The cop in him would want to be able to make an easy exit in an emergency. As soon as I gave her his supposed requirements, she started typing in on the computer. She also started asking questions.

'Who exactly would be living there?' she asked in a pointed voice. I already had an idea why she was asking, based on what Zooey had said about the note being sent around.

'Just him,' I said.

'Then you won't be staying with him?' she asked, turning to look at me directly.

'You mean like overnight?' I asked.

'Overnight is not a problem. I meant like moving in with him.'

I pretended to be embarrassed by her question. 'I think your question is a little intrusive. I don't know where this relationship is going, but he should be able to have who he pleases in his own place.' I waited a beat before continuing. 'I heard there was an incident in this building. Is that why you're asking all these questions?'

At that her business-like demeanor began to melt and she leaned back in her chair. 'If you think that means your friend is going to get a break in the rent, forget it.'

She seemed overwrought and I genuinely felt bad for her. I glanced at the cat picture again. 'What's your cat's name?' I asked.

Changing the subject to something personal worked and her face lit up. I'd used this technique in the first Derek Streeter book and I was glad to see it worked in real life.

'His name is Harry,' she said. She reached in her desk and brought out more pictures of him. I commented on his beauty, which was true. The cream-colored cat had big blue eyes and darker markings on his head and ears. I brought up Rocky. As soon as she recognized me as a cat person, she became friendlier. And when I told her how I'd come to adopt Rocky, she warmed even more and shared that Harry was a rescue, too. Now that we had the bond of giving homes to rescues, she relaxed completely.

'I'm sorry for grilling you about your friend,' she began. 'It's just that everyone living in one of our units has to be on the lease and fill out background information.'

'And that's because of what happened?' I asked innocently.

'Yes and no,' she said. 'It's always been the policy, but I sort of lapsed it with him.' She rocked her head with remorse. 'You would have to have met him to understand. He'd been living here for months, but somehow he kept convincing me it was only going to be for a few weeks longer. He had another place that was being remodeled and each time I brought it up, he said there'd been a glitch.' She rocked her head again. 'I tried to get him to give me an absolute date when he'd be leaving, but he got me so twisted around, I kept letting it slide.'

I gave her an understanding look that was legitimate, too. I'd fallen for his delays in paying me and had done everything his way. It shocked me to realize that I'd let him use my office.

'I think it's called gaslighting,' she said. 'You know, when someone gets you to believe something that you know isn't so.' She put her hands over her face for a moment. 'And it was all a lie. It turned out he had different names and there was no condo being remodeled.'

She sat upright suddenly. 'What am I doing? This is so unprofessional,' she said. 'Please forget everything I just said. Going forward I'm going to be on top of things. So, if you intend to stay at your friend's place, you'll need to be on the lease.'

I realized I'd gotten all the information I was going to get from her and she had also given me an out to leave. I simply told her I didn't feel comfortable bringing it up with my friend. 'I'm afraid it would scare him off if I made it sound like I was moving in,' I said.

'Oh,' she said, looking troubled, as she probably thought she'd lost out on a possible tenant. I was already standing and thanked her for her time. I looked back at her desk and was going to comment on her cat when I saw a sheet of paper. I couldn't make out all the words, but enough to know that it was one of the 'notes' that Ted'd had me compose.

Lois was the other woman getting the letters?

I blinked at the sunlight when I came outside, my mind still reeling. I was off in my thoughts again and was startled when I heard someone call my name. As I brought my focus to the present, Detective Jankowski was standing by his black sedan.

'Just guessing, but were you doing your own investigating?' he said. Without waiting for me to answer, he continued. 'You can put it to rest. We've settled the case in a manner of speaking. Once Ms Sandusky was honest and admitted that she kept samples of cough syrup with codeine, it was what we thought at first. The victim, Mr Roberts, interrupted someone attempting to steal the drug samples. There was a scuffle over a knife and Mr Roberts was stabbed.'

'Then you've arrested a suspect?' I said.

'We're working on it,' he said. 'My point is that your letters had nothing to do with it. So you can stand down.'

I was dumbstruck. It all felt very anticlimactic. 'I don't know what to say.'

'How about "goodbye and I'll stay out of your business"?' he offered.

I didn't move for a moment and he waved for me to go. My head was spinning as I walked the couple of blocks home. My thoughts were disjointed as I went up the outside stairs and through the vestibule. It was a burglary after all. Just not random. My thoughts flitted to meeting the detective. Not good that he'd figured out what I was doing. Derek Streeter would not be proud.

I went up the stairs and when I got to my landing had my key pulled out. As I looked to my door I saw a package on the mat. It was about the size of a shoe box and wrapped in brown paper. My address was written on top, but there was no return address and no postage. It made me feel uneasy. The mail carrier, FedEx, Amazon and UPS always left packages outside the glass security door. It was a general rule that when any of the residents found a package out there, they brought it inside the locked door and left it near the foot of the staircase. The only thing that made sense was that this package had been personally delivered. I shook it and nothing rattled, but it felt like something was in there.

But how had the package ended up in front of my door? I went down to Sara's and knocked on the door, thinking she might know. I'd barely moved my hand away and the door opened. Sara and Quentin were standing in the entrance hall. They both looked drained and were just taking off their coats.

'We just got home from the hospital,' Sara said, handing her coat to Quentin. He nodded a greeting and then left to put their outer wraps away.

Suddenly the box I was holding didn't seem that important and I asked about Quentin's father. Sara let out a weary sigh. 'They did emergency surgery. He is doing OK for now, but the next twenty-four hours are the most critical.'

Mikey came running down the hall from the back with Ben following behind. The toddler's diaper was open on one side and appeared ready to fall off. 'He ran off as soon as he heard you,' Ben said to his sister. He turned to me and smiled, looking at the package in my arms. 'You came bearing gifts?'

I quickly explained finding the box in front of my door. 'I wondered if you knew how it got there.'

Sara shook her head as she made a grab for Mikey. 'Maybe Ben can help you,' she said, hoisting her son on her hip and going down the hall.

Ben glanced after them. 'How about we take this up to your place?'

TWENTY-TWO

'**W**hy don't you start from the beginning?' Ben said when we got upstairs. He went into the living room and took his usual seat on the couch. I sat in the wing chair and put the box on the coffee table. He looked it over as I explained finding it in front of my door.

'No return address, or postage,' Ben said.

'Right, it had to have been delivered.'

'And you're afraid to open it.'

'Yes,' I said feeling embarrassed that I was such a wimp.

He held the box up to his ear. 'I don't hear anything ticking.' He smiled to show he meant it as a joke, though I doubted anybody used wind-up clocks with bombs anymore. 'I'll take care of it.' He pulled out a pocket knife and cut through the brown paper, revealing a lidded rectangular box with all the labels removed. We both looked at the lid as he prepared to lift it off. 'Too bad we don't have a drum roll,' he said. I knew he was keeping it light because I was so tense.

'Just open it,' I said, finally. Then before he could act, I flipped the lid off. We both looked inside at a layer of white tissue paper. I'd gotten up my courage by now and pulled off the top layer of paper only to find more tissue paper. And then more and more until the bottom of the box was visible. 'Nothing?' I said, incredulous. We went back through all the tissue paper, checking to see if something was wrapped in it, but there wasn't.

'Why would somebody send me an empty box?' I said shaking my head. '*Who* would send me an empty box?'

Ben was already on his feet. 'I'll check with the neighbors,' he said, heading out the door. Thanks to all the time he spent at his sister's, he was familiar with everybody in the building. He was only gone for a few minutes.

'The Brewsters on the first floor said someone rang their bell and said they had a delivery and they buzzed the person in. The sound quality on the intercom isn't that good so they couldn't tell if it was a man or woman.'

'I guess that's a dead end,' I said, staring at the box. 'I don't mean to keep you. You probably have to be somewhere.'

He sat back on the couch. 'I've been at my sister's since this morning, and because they might have to go to the hospital during the night, I'm staying over.' He glanced around the peaceful living room. The buildings across the street blocked the late afternoon sun and the room was in a soft twilight. 'I'm glad for the break.'

We sat in silence for a few moments, staring at the empty box.

'It's probably somebody's idea of a prank. The best thing to do is to forget,' he said.

'Is that your personal or professional opinion?'

He hesitated. 'I was trying to make you feel better. It's kind of weird, but if somebody was trying to give you a message or a warning, they probably would have put something in there.'

'Like a dead something,' I said.

'Right. What kind of message is there in a box full of tissue paper?'

We decided to let it go, which seemed like the only alternative anyway. Ben suggested we change the subject. 'My day was filled with kids' TV shows, trying to feed Mikey a peanut butter sandwich, trying to get peanut butter off the curtains, and picking up toys. I don't know how my sister does it.' He looked over at me. 'What about your day?'

In all the fuss about the box, I'd forgotten about the earlier part of my day. 'Just a regular Saturday,' I began. 'Let's see, I tasted some coffee, found out who Ted's other woman was and I had a run-in with Detective Jankowski.' I thought for a moment. 'Maybe run-in is the wrong word choice, more like a dismissal.'

'Your day beats mine, how about some details?' By now the living room was in deep shadows and I couldn't even make out Ben's expression. I got up and started turning on lights as I described talking to Lois. 'I'm afraid I used you,' I said, and told him about the apartment ruse.

'That's what friends are for,' he said with a smile. His smile faded when I got to the part where Lois was talking about Ted and then I told him about the note on her desk.

'Wow,' he said. 'That guy keeps seeming sleazier and sleazier.'

'Yeah,' I said. 'It seems like he used the notes to make it appear he was interested in her and so she wouldn't insist his name was on the lease,' I said. 'He'd have to fill out a whole form with background information.'

'He probably didn't know which name he should use,' Ben said, trying to make a joke.

'She seemed pretty upset with him. I guess he kept saying he was only staying a short time and then he'd get her confused about how long he'd been there and when he was leaving. She claimed he was gaslighting her.'

'She was with Rita when she found Ted, wasn't she?' Ben said. 'Maybe she already knew he was dead.'

'Hold that thought,' I said. 'When I came out of the building, Detective Jankowski had just got there. He figured I was there nosing around. He told me basically to butt out and that I wasn't a person of interest anymore. He didn't even care about the love letters. They found out that Rita kept samples of cough syrup with codeine and figured that's what the burglar was after.'

'It figures the building manager would be one of his ladies. She was convenient and he wanted something from her.' Ben moved on to what the detective had said about the motive for the crime. 'I guess I could see that. Someone stealing drugs could have fought him instead of just running off.' He looked at me. 'Is it case closed for you now that you don't have to worry about being a suspect or having the letters you wrote pulled into it?'

'I really haven't had time to think about it. Finding the box in front of my door took the spotlight away from it.' I let out a breath and looked at the box again. 'I guess I will let it go. Unless something happens that makes it so obvious that the detective is wrong.'

His phone pinged and he glanced at it and winced. 'Sara said dinner's ready and you're invited to join in.' He let out his breath. 'I love Mikey and I'm sure whatever my sister put together is delicious, but I'd settle for just good if it came with some peace. I noticed there's a new barbecue place down the street. Want to try it?'

I hadn't even thought about food until he mentioned it and something different sounded appealing. After making sure they had vegetarian options, I agreed. Sara took the news we weren't coming well. I think she was probably relieved not to have company after the day she'd had.

It wasn't a date or anything, but it was still a nice change to be going out on a Saturday night. The food place was crowded with couples and it would have been a good place to pick up on romantic gestures for me and Ben. Even though I didn't need them to use for the engagement party, the writer in me made note of them anyway. A couple were leaning toward each other across a small table as though they didn't want to miss one breath of the other. Another couple were squeezed into one side of the booths, sharing a plate of food.

Ben ate ribs and I had side dishes. We shared a peach cobbler, assuring each other it had less to do with being a romantic gesture than neither of us had room for a whole one.

When we got back to the building and started up the stairs, Ben looked at his sister's door. He didn't say anything, but I had the feeling he wasn't ready to head back in there. 'You can come upstairs if you like. We could watch a movie or something.'

'That would be great,' he said. He made sure to text Sara and let her know he was upstairs in case they got an emergency call. He looked at my DVD collection and laughed. 'You sure like romantic comedies.' We finally watched *Sleepless in Seattle*, though I'm sure he would have preferred something with car chases.

'Well, I'd better go,' he said when the credits came up on the movie. 'They set up an air bed in Mikey's playroom.' He didn't sound very enthused and I had an idea.

'You could stay up here,' I said. 'There's plenty of room.' I walked him back to the spare bedroom to show him. 'The bed's all made up and everything. You can shut the door and have your own private space. You won't even know that I'm just down the hall.' We both started to walk through the door at the same time and brushed against each other. It was like the slow dance all over again and I backed away quickly. But apparently not fast enough.

'It won't work. I'm going downstairs,' he said, rushing up the hall to the front door. He'd let himself out before I had a chance to follow.

Rocky came out of the office and joined me. 'It was just an innocent offer. He sure took it wrong.'

Sunday morning, I went to set up my breakfast and the Sunday paper as I always did, but this time when I thought about sitting down with my food and French press coffee, I realized how much nicer it would be to have someone on the other side of the table asking for the sports section.

I cancelled my breakfast plans and thought about the crew downstairs. Sara was always making food for me. This time I would make something for them. I whipped up a couple of Dutch babies and – as soon as they came out of the oven – took them downstairs.

Sara was still in her sleepwear and looked at the giant baked pancakes hungrily. 'Thank you,' she said. 'Too bad Ben's not here. As soon as we got the call that Quentin's father was stable, he took off. He wouldn't even let me give him a piece of toast.' She shook her head. 'It was like he was afraid of something.'

Or afraid of someone – like maybe me.

I'd just walked in the door when the text came from Ben. All it said was *Sorry. Hope we can still be friends.* I typed back *Sure.* I was thinking of adding a heart emoji, but I was afraid it might freak him out, so I put in a happy face emoji and hit send. He sent back a thumbs-up. I must remember to maintain my distance from him.

With that I put all thoughts about Ben and the night before to the back of my mind, along with the strange empty box that was still sitting on the coffee table, and went into my office. I spent the rest of the day working. I polished what I'd already written for my clients and wrote new copy.

I had fun writing about Zooey, explaining that she'd used

her interest in coffee drinks as a basis for a business plan for her college class and then used the business plan to make it become real. Under interesting facts, I had a heading that asked if blonds were more fun and then wrote about light roasts, which were also called blonds, offering more buzz for the buck.

I described Haley as being an alchemist when it came to ice cream and mentioned how she looked at it as a medium to mix things in and come up with something new. I took a chance that she would accept my suggestion and made a point to say she created her own renditions of traditional flavors along with her own unique creations. Her mission was to offer a taste experience. I hadn't heard back from her on what she thought of my suggestion for the name of the place.

For Handelman's I wrote about old things becoming new again. I explained the idea for the design of the shoe store had come from the Handelmans' experience with their own kids. At that time the only option they'd had was shopping at a traditional store that served all ages. Shopping for shoes was a traumatic experience and they'd wondered if there was a way to change it. What if they made it fun? I had pictures of the elephant stools and the moving cow going over the moon when they were new. One photo had a crowd of kids staring up at the cow climbing in the sky. I'd added one of the pictures I'd taken that had a similar feel from the current day.

I spent a lot of time talking about how important it was to have a fitologist for children's shoes. I admit to making up the word and I'd be sure to get an OK from Emily and Lewis.

LaPorte's was the biggest job. I had several versions of their story, starting with Jeanne baking in her kitchen, and I'd written the bare bones of bios. I typed up all the menu descriptions and made sure I didn't use mélange too many times. I tweaked the description of the chocolate mint cake and would have to see if they wanted me to describe any more pastries.

It was long past dark when I finally stopped working. I went through the apartment turning on lights and trying to focus on the here and now. I'd taken the French press pot with me to the office, but the newspaper and place setting were still on the dining-room table. My stomach growled, reminding me that I hadn't eaten all day.

I stopped before I walked into the kitchen. I wasn't up for scrounging around for something to make for dinner. And after all the sitting, I was up for a walk anyway. The easiest take-out was a pan pizza from the Mezze and a salad. I ordered it and got ready to pick it up.

The cold air felt refreshing as I walked outside. Everything seemed very quiet. There were few people on the sidewalk and little traffic. The Mezze was getting ready to close and they were wiping down the tables and sweeping the floor when I went in to pick up my food. I was surprised to see Tizzy and Theo on their way out. They waited until I got my food and the three of us walked back together. When we got in front of my building, Tizzy asked if I wanted some company. She wanted to show me something she'd written that she conveniently had on her phone. In addition to being quiet, Sunday nights always felt a little lonely to me, so I was glad to have the company. She sent Theo on home and we went up to my place.

Tizzy took the spot on the couch where Ben usually sat. She noticed the box on the table and asked about it. I explained its strange arrival and shrugged when it came to where it came from and why. 'It's a mystery to me,' I said.

'Do you think it's connected to the death of the dream-boat?' she asked. After she said it, she paused with a smile. 'That sounds like a good title for a mystery. Maybe you could use it for the third Derek Streeter book.'

I let out a mirthless laugh. 'I'll have to finish the second one before I worry about a third.' I set my food on the coffee table as she urged me to eat. 'Speaking of the dreamboat, it seems as if the cops have settled on that he interrupted a burglary. The woman he lived with had drug samples they think the burglar was after. So, whatever he was doing with those letters I wrote doesn't matter. We didn't really have to go to the airport,' I said with a shrug. I suggested she read her work out loud while I ate.

Her piece turned out to be a poem about the changing moods of Lake Michigan. It was quite good and I made a couple of suggestions. She noted them and then got down to why she was really there. Had I found out what was bothering Laurel Handelman? I didn't know what to say, so I did a pivot.

'I was just working on one of the pieces for the shoe store. Let me show it to you. Maybe you have something to add.'

'I'd love to,' she said, getting up and following me into my office. I turned on the wall sconces in addition to the desk lamp to better illuminate the room. She looked around. 'I've always wondered what it was like in here,' she said. 'It's like the inner sanctum.'

Her description seemed a little dramatic, particularly at the moment. 'Sorry for the mess,' I said, seeing the French press coffee pot and cup were still there. I left to take them to the back and when I returned, she was holding the yarn and crochet chain I'd stuck in the corner. Ever curious Tizzy wanted to know what it was about.

I had never discussed that I had moments of getting stuck with the writers' group and they all had the illusion that I merely had to sit in front of the computer screen and the words flowed. I decided to share the truth with Tizzy and at the same time show off my solution.

'I had no idea it happened to you.' She looked at me with surprise. 'It happens to me all the time,' she said. 'If crocheting helps, please show me how to do it.' I didn't want to take a chance that she would remember that I hadn't answered about Laurel and agreed.

'Let me grab some supplies,' I said. I'd been thinking it was a waste to use scrap yarn and make a pointless length of chain stitches and had a new idea. I came back with two skeins of yarn and two hooks.

'When I did that I was just crocheting with no project in mind,' I said. 'But going forward, I think the best thing to do is use the stitches for something. It's kind of a win-win. You get past the block and you have something to show for your time.'

'That sounds great,' Tizzy said with her usual enthusiasm. I handed her the hook and a skein of beige worsted yarn. She was a quick learner and picked up on how to make the slip knot and chain stitches right away. She had no trouble with single crochet stitches either. When she seemed comfortable with the process, I had her undo all the stitches.

'Now we can start the project together,' I said. Rather than explain the plan, it seemed best to have her understand it by doing. We both made a very long chain of stitches and then turned and went back over them with a single crochet in each chain. I held mine up. 'You've already begun a scarf,' I said. 'You just keep turning and doing a row of single crochets. We're working the long way and, after about four or five rows, all you'll need is to add some fringe.'

Tizzy's eyes froze in panic before I assured her I'd be available to help with the fringe. 'Then I can take this with me?' she asked, holding on to the yarn and hook.

'It's yours to keep.' I had stuck my hook in the skein of yarn and had begun winding the long piece of work around the wad of yarn. I started to put it in the corner of the desk, but it took up much more space than the scrap yarn.

'Why don't you put it in that bottom drawer?' Tizzy said.

I nodded with appreciation. 'I usually have just the desk lamp on and the drawers are all in shadow. I forget they're even here.'

'Is that the one you gave to the dreamboat to use?' she asked.

It took a moment to register. 'I can't believe that you remembered and I forgot.' I looked at the file drawer with new interest as I thought back to that first meeting with Ted. He was Tony then and showered me with compliments on the samples of my work he'd seen on my website. I wasn't usually impressed by extremely handsome men, but there was something else about him. I suppose you'd call it charisma. He'd said he was more or less living out of a suitcase and needed some space to keep a few things. Thinking back, it seemed like he told me rather than asked. That kind of thing usually offended me, but somehow not with him. I just kept saying yes to everything. Yes, I didn't have to meet or even know anything about whoever was getting the letters. At the time, I thought he might be gay and the reason for his secrecy was that he didn't want me to know I would be composing letters to a man. And there were all those compliments he gave me and his insistence on giving me a larger retainer than I'd asked for. I chided myself again for letting his charm cloud my good sense, but that was before I knew he had several identities, was wooing women while living with his girlfriend. And then there was the money he'd asked Laurel for. I glanced at Tizzy and thought how she would never hear about that from me.

'And you were never curious about what he had in there?' Tizzy asked, breaking into my reverie. 'I know I would have looked.'

I stared at the wooden drawer with sudden trepidation while Tizzy went on. 'It's not big enough for a dead body.' I'm sure she meant it as a joke, but it fell flat.

My heart had started to thud in anticipation. 'I always gave him a few minutes alone in my office. I assumed he looked over the batch of letters and notes I'd done for him. Maybe made some changes and then printed them up. They were always deleted when I went to my computer later.' We were both staring at the drawer.

'If you're not going to open it, I will,' she said. I would have gladly let her open it, but I had an image to keep up and gave the drawer a pull but it didn't move. It was an old wood desk and the drawers had gotten warped over time. It took some tugs and shifting before I got it open.

After all the trepidation, it was almost a disappointment. There wasn't a gun or a stash of cash. Just a dark green metal box. I pulled it out by the handle on top and tried to open it. No surprise, it didn't budge, and I noticed it had a four-number combination lock on the front.

Maybe it had the gun or stash of cash in it. I picked it up and shook it. I felt something shifting around inside, but no thud that a gun would have made. Would a stash of cash make a sound? Maybe a flutter of bills.

'Maybe he used one of the obvious number sequences,' I said. Tizzy watched as I tried putting 1234 into the lock. Nothing happened. It was the same with four zeros.

'Maybe you can break the lock,' Tizzy offered, and I gave her a look.

I looked around at the box. 'Maybe if I had tools,' I said. Then I had an idea. 'Sometimes there's a code that comes with it on the bottom. Ted could have used that.'

'This is so exciting,' Tizzy said. 'I feel like I'm on a case with Derek Streeter.'

'Don't get too excited,' I warned as I flipped the box. I saw nothing on the bottom but a sticker that said Made in China. Something jumped out at me as I stared at the sticker and I grabbed a paper and pencil. A few moments later, I showed Tizzy the paper with 4145 written on it. 'Let's see if this works.'

I rolled the lock tumblers with the four numbers and paused for a moment, almost afraid to see if it opened. If it didn't work, I was out of ideas. I almost wished I had a drum roll as I tried to lift the lid.

'It opened,' I said. 'I can't believe it actually worked.' When I looked inside there seemed to be just papers. I pulled them out and started to flip through them, glancing at what they were. There was a receipt for the post-office box, several confirmations for hotel reservations, something with a hand-written list and copies of all the things I'd written for him. At the bottom there were some blank envelopes and stamps along with a pen. Tizzy was watching over my arm.

I noticed some scribbling in the corner of the letter that Laurel had recited to me and recognized her initials. As I looked through the letters, they all had initials on them. Some had two sets.

I was thinking what a skunk he was, sending the same letter to two women, but I kept mum on it. It was crazy to think that Tizzy would figure out what the LH stood for, but I wasn't taking any chances.

'Are those the actual letters you wrote for him?' she asked, trying to read them.

Since I was worried about her recognizing the initials, I handed her a couple of the short notes that had a Ch and an L, which I guessed was for Lois.

I'm sending this note since I can't be there in person to wish you a happy day. Just thinking about you brightens mine.

You made my life go from black and white to Technicolor.

Just knowing you're underneath the same sky makes me joyful.

You are like sunshine shining through the clouds.

I'm counting the seconds until I see you again.
I can't live without your love.

Tizzy looked at me after reading the last one. 'OK, I started getting a little melodramatic,' I said. I gathered up the papers and put them all back in the box.

'What are you going to do with it?' she asked.

'That's a good question,' I said. 'I guess my options are ask the detective I talked to if he wants it, but then he'd probably ask a bunch of questions about why I had it. And he did tell me that they'd settled on the scenario that Ted had interrupted someone stealing drug samples, so it's hardly pertinent.' I looked at the box in the drawer. 'I could take it someplace and ditch it.' I had an image of Tizzy and me taking it over to the campus and leaving it sitting on the bridge by Botany Pond. But then someone would probably freak out and call the cops. I pictured a bunch of cops in protective gear that made them look like space people getting out of an armored truck to examine it. Or they'd send a bomb-squad robot to blow it up. It might take out the whole bridge.

'What are you thinking about?' Tizzy said. 'You have a weird expression.' I didn't feel like sharing the bomb squad at Botany Pond. You never knew with Tizzy. She might get the story mixed up and tell someone who just heard 'bomb at Botany Pond' and I'd end up with the FBI knocking at my door.

'I think I'll just keep it here for now,' I said.

'That's probably a good plan,' Tizzy said. 'This has been so exciting, I forgot all about the time. Theo just texted me wondering where I was. He's waiting downstairs to walk me home. He's such a sweetheart. It's only a half a block, but he doesn't want me out alone so late.' She started toward the frosted French doors that led to the entrance hall. 'What a weekend you've had. A mystery box and then the metal one.' She stopped and turned back. 'You didn't tell me how you figured out the combination.'

I was actually quite proud of myself, even though looking back it seemed obvious. 'The combination was four numbers. There was only one word on the sticker that had four letters: *made*. I changed the letters into numbers by their place in the alphabet. M was the thirteenth number but I needed a single digit, so I added the 1 and the 3 to get 4. The A was 1, the D was 4 and the E was 5.'

'Wow,' Tizzy said. 'I never would have thought of that.' She had gotten her coat and was putting it on. 'I know what you said the police think about what happened to the dreamboat, but what do you think?'

I let out my breath as I considered her question. 'I want what they said to be right, but I don't think it is.' I walked the short distance to the front door with her. She thanked me for the help with her poem. She was about to go out the door. She glanced back into the living room where the mystery box was still sitting on the table. 'You know, that looks a lot like a shoe box.'

TWENTY-THREE

I t was late Sunday night now and it felt as if the world was taking a pause before the week began again. Everything seemed peaceful and quiet. Except me. Thinking about the mystery box, Ted's box, Tizzy's visit and the episode with Ben over the last two days had left me feeling wired.

Tizzy's comment about the mystery box was right, it had the dimensions of a shoe box, a small shoe box – like one from Handelman's. But why would someone from the shoe store send me an empty box. Was it supposed to be some kind of warning? How scary was a bunch of tissue paper? But getting an empty package was unsettling, so maybe that's what they intended. Lewis had asked me to keep what Laurel had said to myself. If the package was supposed to get that message across, it should have been a lot clearer.

Thinking about the metal box in the desk made me upset with myself. I was as bad as Lois, letting him convince me to go against the way I worked. Letting him use my office. I never let anyone in there. Tizzy had called it the inner sanctum. But I'd let Ted in like it was nothing and allowed him to be alone in there on top of it.

Tizzy's question stuck in my mind. Did I really think that Ted had been killed by somebody trying to get their hands on some cough syrup with codeine? It was certainly convenient, since it took any heat off of me and lessened the chance of the love letters being made public. But with all I'd found out about Ted it made me wonder. The detective had taken the focus off the victim and put it on the circumstance of his murder. I wondered how much Detective Jankowski even knew about Ted, other than he was a pilot and was living with Rita. I doubted that Lois had told him about getting the affectionate notes from Ted or that she'd let him slip out of having his name on the lease. Would Zooey have told the cop she'd seen him with another woman or that he'd tried to get her to keep it quiet?

I had a different image of Ted. He was clearly juggling women. I had figured out that he was able to go from one to the other by claiming he was off flying a charter jet somewhere. His income from being a pilot seemed sketchy since he was only a standby pilot and didn't appear to work that often. He'd put pressure on Laurel for money, and Rita was paying the bills along with who knew what else. He'd gotten Lois in trouble with her bosses after playing mind games with her. His condo story was merely an excuse as to why he always went to their place or, for that matter, my place. And that was probably only the tip of the iceberg. I didn't bother chiding myself for the clichéd thought. Nothing else said it quite the same.

And then there was Ben. If I was honest, I had started to think of him as more than a friend – maybe it was going toward the level of everything his sister had hoped for. I'd seen past the shell he put up and liked what I saw. He must have sensed it and gotten scared off. I would simply take a few steps back and return to seeing him as a member of the writers' group and the bearer of food from his sister. I wondered if I should send him a text saying as much, but I worried that it would somehow make it worse and decided it was one of those times when saying nothing was the best answer.

Tomorrow was the big reveal. I'd show everything I had so far to my clients. All the pieces were still works in progress and I expected them to want tweaks and some changes, but they needed to be OK with the basic concepts.

I had developed thick skin over the years. It was a necessity for writers. You had to be able to take criticism without falling apart. But there was always that hope that they would love what I'd done and say it was all perfect.

None of the above thoughts were conducive to sleep. Knowing myself by now, I took some action and made myself a cup of chamomile tea. When I brought it into the living room, I realized having the mystery box on the coffee table wasn't helping me to relax. I stowed it in the corner of my office.

After settling on the couch and taking a few sips of flowery herbal tea, I pulled out one of the squares I was working on. It was a basic granny square and the stitch pattern was second nature to me now, which made it good for times like this. I began to work on the square and let my mind go.

It was always the same. As my mind eased, the living room became like a canvas for my memories of events that had taken place in that space over my life.

The first view was always of my mother in her element. She loved to entertain and I saw her mixing with her friends at our annual Christmas Eve party. The scene felt bright and happy.

An image of me practicing the pirouettes that I'd just learned at ballet class showed up in my mind's eye. It was already just my father and me then, and the room seemed less bright and a lot less happy. The scene flipped to my eleventh birthday. I was sitting in the chair by the window crying. I was wearing a burgundy velvet dress and my hair was a mess. My father had done his best to fix it, but he was an English professor not a hair stylist. I needed my mother for that and a whole lot more. Passed on to a better place, people said. I didn't agree.

It became like a movie montage as the seasons changed. The tree out front would have a sprinkling of snow on its brown bare branches. Sparrows with their winter weight of feathers would cling to the branches as they rocked in the cold wind. Then the tree appeared back to life, covered in bright green leaves with a red cardinal landing on a branch. The door to the balcony would be open to let in some air or closed tight with rain beating against the glass as the images moved on.

I saw my father coming home on a winter's evening. His coat smelled of the cold and the radiator hissed as the heat came on. Then one of my last memories of him, sitting in his favorite chair reading the Sunday paper. I looked around the living room with all the artwork and doodads that we'd all accumulated over the years and wondered if there were somehow bits of something left behind from all the moments that had happened in that room. I felt emotional, but no longer tense. I was already half in a dream.

Rocky followed me to my bedroom and took up his position above my head and we both fell into a deep sleep.

TWENTY-FOUR

I knew it was Monday morning before I even opened my eyes. The peace of Sunday night was over and a garbage truck was picking up a load. It rumbled and then whined as the container was raised and its load dropped in with the sound of glass hitting glass.

The truck was just driving away when I looked out the living-room window to check the weather. It was hardly promising. The sky was a yellowish leaden color, and the street was glistened with rain. People either had umbrellas or ran with their hoods pulled up.

I had to take the weather into consideration when I was figuring out what to wear. Instead of going in order of location, I'd had to arrange times when they'd be free to go over things with me. It meant doing a lot of extra walking around the neighborhood. At the same time, since I was presenting my work, I felt the need to dress a little more formally. I went with black slacks because it wouldn't show if they got wet. I picked a white shirt with a black pullover sweater to go with them. The collar and tails were all that would show of the shirt. Sneakers would have been easier for all the walking, but they were the wrong look. I pulled on a pair of ankle boots instead. I topped it with a colorful silk scarf and my trench coat. I had everything packed in my peacock blue messenger bag, confident the leather would keep everything dry. Rocky followed me to the door and seemed sad to be left behind.

Sara and Mikey were coming up the stairs as I went down. She gave me a quick report that Quentin's father was doing well and no emergency babysitter would be needed.

It wasn't as cold outside as I'd expected, but the air felt close from all the moisture. The rain was light at the moment, but I opened my umbrella anyway and went toward the campus and my first stop.

I was hoping for a cup of Zooey's coffee before we talked.

The walk there had helped to get my mind alert, but it didn't compare with a couple of mugs of her fresh brew, particularly the blond roasts, but my plans changed when I walked into the food area. The weather had turned everyone into coffee freaks and the stand was surrounded by a crowd. She viewed them with a look of panic as she rushed to set up mugs of coffee to drip. I heard impatient rumbling coming from the line waiting for their caffeine fix.

I couldn't help myself. I acted without thought and made my way behind the counter. 'Could you use some help?' I asked. She looked at me as if I'd descended from heaven.

'Do you know how to make the drinks?'

I nodded. I'd only become a writer for hire in my twenties. Before that I'd had an array of jobs, including working at one of the neighborhood restaurants. I'd been hired as a server, but often had helped making the espresso drinks. I'd watched Zooey set up the mugs of coffee enough times to know how to do it. She showed me a cheat sheet that had the recipes for the fancy drinks and the canisters with coffees for the individual brews and the tin marked Fairy Dust. I stowed my coat and messenger bag and took the order of the next person in line.

We worked it out that I'd deal with the coffee by the mug while she made the espresso drinks. With the two of us working, we got the line under control and eventually the crowd thinned out.

In the process of measuring all the coffee for the mugs, I saw a lot of the Fairy Dust and by the end had figured out what it was. I wouldn't make it public, but I was going to try adding it to my at-home brew. It was simply unsweetened cocoa with some salt added. The mixture might have been original, but adding salt to coffee grounds had been around for a long time. When I'd been doing research on coffee, I read that cowboys added salt to their coffee.

'That's it,' she said as the last person in line took their paper cup and walked out into the quadrangle. 'Thank you. It was great to have backup. We work well together,' she said with a relieved smile. It was true we had managed to move around each other with ease while we took orders and set up drinks.

'Yup,' I said, looking at the canisters with the names of the different blends on them. 'Time for us. Can I make you a cup?' I asked.

'Absolutely not. You've done enough. How can I ever thank you? I wish I had some Jamaican Blue Mountain or pure Kona,' she said. I knew all about the two coffees from all the research I'd done. Jamaican Blue Mountain was the rarer of the two. Something about being grown at high altitude in Jamaica gave the coffee a unique and tasty flavor. Pure Kona was grown on the big island of Hawaii. The volcanic soil and weather gave the beans a distinctive taste and color. Both had high price tags.

In the end she made us each a cup of the Eyes Wide Open blend. I figured I would go over what I'd brought while we had the coffee. I pulled out a copy of the story about her and the list of coffees I'd tasted. She started to look at it but a customer walked in. 'I'm sorry. I don't know why I told you to come in the morning since it's the time when I get most of my business. I guess it was just habit.' She put down the paper and went to the counter. As she was handing the man a paper cup of coffee, the door to outside opened again and Rita walked in.

She was dressed for work in a suit and heels. She folded up her umbrella and approached the counter. My eyes were locked on her, though she paid no notice of me. She and Zooey exchanged a friendly greeting and Zooey asked for her order.

She seemed in a lighter mood than when I'd seen her there before. 'I'll have a latte with one percent milk. That chocolate thing you made for me last time was delicious and I certainly needed something extra that day. But what's that saying? "A second on the lips, forever on your hips." I've got a ton of clients to see today.'

While she waited for her drink she kept on talking, still paying no notice to me. 'It's such a relief to have that detective off my back. He kept showing up with just one more question.'

'What happened? Why'd he stop coming around?' Zooey asked as she handed her neighbor the drink.

'I figured if they were sure it was all about Ted walking in on someone robbing the place, they'd back off. So I told him that I'd had some samples of cough syrup with codeine.' She leaned close to the counter and dropped her voice. 'I haven't had any samples of that for months, but the detective bought it. He gave me a hard time for not telling him at the beginning. And then Lois came down on me for keeping dangerous drugs that tempted robbers. She wanted me to sign something that said I wouldn't keep any addictive drug samples in the place going forward. I refused and she threatened to break my lease, which is fine with me. I can't wait to move out of that building.'

Rita had it all wrong when she said someone was robbing the place or that the drugs tempted robbers. She really meant burglars. A burglar went into a place without permission with the intent to commit a crime, whereas robbers dealt direct with taking something from a person. Not that I was going to say anything. I was far too interested in what she was saying.

'I want to put everything with that sleaze behind me. The detective asked me if he'd sent me any love letters.' She sounded incredulous. 'Turns out he was sending love letters to someone that wasn't me. He didn't even write them himself but got them from somewhere. It makes me mad all over again,' she said.

I couldn't believe what I was hearing and I had no idea what to do with it. I'm sure Detective Jankowski would be very interested in knowing that she had lied about the cough syrup drug samples. And now with all the anger she was spewing about Ted, I wondered if she was about to admit that she'd been the one to stab him. My smart watch vibrated with a reminder of my next appointment. It was at LaPorte's and they were my biggest clients and I couldn't afford to be late since Rex had chosen the time.

Much as I hated to leave, I had no choice. I had been looking forward to going over what I'd written about her. I thought she would appreciate that I'd mentioned her ability to size up customers and figure the right drink for them. But all I could do was leave the papers for Zooey to look over. I quietly slipped out while Rita continued to rant. Could it be that the obvious was right all along?

There was no time to think about it now. I had to walk to 53rd in the rain. The ankle boots had turned out to not be good rainwear and I had to watch that my feet didn't slip while I was mentally preparing to meet with Rex.

I zigzagged through side streets and cut through the shopping center, only skidding a few times. The rain was letting up as I turned on to 53rd. I checked my watch and was relieved that I'd made it just on time.

I folded my umbrella as I walked into LaPorte's and wiped my feet on the mat, hoping not to go skating across the floor. The light wood tables made the interior seem bright after the gloom outside. I took a deep breath and walked to the counter. I could see why Rex had been so specific about the time. It was the slow time just before the lunch rush. Only one table was occupied and Irma was dealing with a lone customer at the counter. I waited off to the side while she finished.

'I'm supposed to see Rex,' I said when the man moved away.

She seemed to know all about it and told me to pick a table and he'd join me shortly. I couldn't seem to help myself from feeling nervous. It didn't matter that I'd met with Rex numerous times and he was friendly, when it came to showing my work it was different.

I chose a table by the window, and as soon as I was settled in took out the different versions of the backstory, the descriptions of the menu items, and an idea for the layout of the wall piece. I was just finishing when Rex walked up to the table. He was carrying a plate and had a friendly smile.

'I understand you missed these the other day,' he said, putting the plate down. There were dabs of four salads. He pulled out the chair across from me and sat down.

'So you got your mother's approval?' I said, recognizing them as the ones she'd made a point that she hadn't okayed.

He seemed puzzled until I explained what Jeanne had said. 'She likes to be updated on what we're doing. I forgot to mention the new salads.'

'Then they have her stamp of approval?' I asked, pointing at the sheet with the backstory. 'I wrote that she oversaw the menu.'

'You can leave it, but I make all the decisions now.' He picked up the papers and started to read through them. 'You might as well sample them and take your notes, while I do this.'

I had a hard time concentrating on the flavors of the salads, but managed to get the basics and scribbled some notes. He put the stack of pages down and looked at me.

'I marked a few places where it needs to be changed, but most of it's great. The picture of my mother with the piece of cake works for the wall montage. It gives the illusion she's still part of the business.' He leaned back in the chair. 'You seem to have captured an overview of our business, but there are so many stories. Of course, there's no room to include them.' He glanced around the restaurant. 'My wife is always saying I should write them down and make a book out of them.' He shrugged with a hopeless expression. 'But I wouldn't even know how to start.'

'I could probably help you with that,' I said. 'I know you're busy, but I have a writers' workshop. It's a friendly atmosphere and mostly neighborhood people.'

He nodded with interest. 'And they meet at your place?'

I gave him the basic details of the location, day and time. 'You could try it once and see if you think it's something for you. The first one is complimentary. Just let me know when you want to come.'

Irma came up to the table and told him something and he started to move away.

'I don't believe in putting things off. How about I come tomorrow?'

I agreed, and he got up and followed Irma to the back.

I sat back in the chair with a great sense of relief and took a minute to collect myself. Not only was he OK with my work, but I might have gotten another member in the writers' group.

The rain had started up again as I retraced my steps and went up to 57th. I used the walk to unwind from the meeting with Rex, wondering what I'd been so worried about. The time for my meeting with Haley was less exact, so I took my time and managed to make it there without skidding on the wet sidewalk.

The windows were still papered over at the ice-cream place. The 'Coming Soon' sign was still down and I hadn't yet heard what she thought of the name I'd suggested for the place. I knocked on the glass of the locked door.

Haley looked worried when she opened the door. The white apron she wore had smudges of something, meaning she was probably concocting some new flavor. I had allowed plenty of time to go over things with her, however I still had to go back to 53rd to meet with the Handelmans and I intended to get right down to business. But I couldn't help myself and asked her what was wrong.

'I probably shouldn't tell you this, but my investor is being difficult. Something happened and they're taking it out on me.' She slumped on one of the stools.

I set down the messenger bag and pulled out the file with everything I'd written up for her. 'Maybe when they see all this, they'll see everything in a new light.' I held on to the folder for a moment, deciding I wanted to tell Haley about what I'd written before she read it. I'd described her as an alchemist. Technically that was someone who turned lead into gold, but the concept was someone taking something worth less and turning it into something worth more. I thought it worked for her. She did take ingredients and turned them into a frozen delight. But she seemed like a literal sort of person and I thought it might come as a shock unless I explained first.

I eased into it by saying that I'd started the piece with the history of ice cream which was factual. 'When I came to writing about you, I wanted to make you seem as special as you are, so I described you in a unique way.' As I finished, I handed her the pages. It was always nerve-wracking watching someone read what I'd written. I kept tabs on her expression for a hint of her reaction. Between the big glasses that dominated her face and her natural reserve, there wasn't a clue. Finally, she put the pages down and looked up. 'Alchemist, that's different. I like it. And maybe when my investor sees it, they'll finally understand what I'm trying to do.'

'As I was working on it, I realized I didn't have much personal information to include. I could put in something about your family, whether you live in the neighborhood or if you're a dog or cat person. Maybe you like to test out flavors on your boyfriend, partner or husband,' I said with a shrug.

'None of that matters,' she said in a sharp tone. 'It's all about the ice cream.'

It didn't seem like a good time to ask her about my proposed name for the place, so I asked her if she'd come up with any new flavors she wanted me to try.

She seemed to brighten up at the mention of her creations. 'I do. I'm going to call it spiced tea or chai tea. I created my own spice mix of cardamom, cinnamon, ginger and cloves. In your description you might want to mention that the spices have health benefits. Cardamom can be a mood elevator as well as benefit your heart and lungs. And cinnamon has all kinds of health benefits like lowering blood sugar and blood pressure. Maybe I should call it healthy tea ice cream.' She brought me a scoop.

'This one is a keeper,' I said savoring the spicy flavor. 'I don't know about calling it healthy tea ice cream. It sounds like medicine. How about calling it frozen chai tea instead?'

'I think you're right,' she said.

I was back outside a few minutes later, going back to 53rd. But it was three down and one to go. So far all had gone well, though it was hard to count Zooey because I didn't know her take on what I'd written yet. My thoughts went to Rita and I wished I could have stayed and heard more, though I wasn't sure what I could do with the information.

By now the rain had become more a drizzly mist and the umbrella wasn't needed. The light was the same as it had been in the morning and the only way to tell it was afternoon was looking at my watch.

I was ahead of schedule when I got to 53rd and took a detour back to LaPorte's. When I'd been going through the messenger bag for Haley's file, I'd realized I didn't have one of the sheets from the LaPorte papers. It was important because it had Rex's notes on it.

The atmosphere was totally different when I went into the

restaurant now. A lot of the tables were full and there was a
line of people buying pastries. I checked the table where we'd
been sitting, but it was clear, as was the floor below it.

I was giving it another look when I heard someone call
out 'Veronica.' Irma was behind the counter waving, holding
a sheet of paper.

I went to retrieve it, asking who'd found it.

'The busboy gave it to me,' she said. 'Rex was already
gone.'

'Thank you,' I said, sounding relieved. 'I'm afraid it makes
me look like a scatterbrain.'

'No worries,' she said. I slid the paper in the proper file
just as Cocoa came out with a cake box for a customer. She
delivered the cake and came over to where I was standing.

'Rex didn't tell me you were coming. I should have a say
in it. I'd like to look over what you've done.'

I didn't want to get involved with their family dynamic and
pulled out the whole file, handing it to her. She read it over
quickly and spent the longest time on the layout for the
montage. 'There should be a picture of my mother,' she said.

I explained the one I'd taken with the piece of cake and
showed it to her on my phone. 'What about one with a whole
cake and her standing behind it, holding the original recipe?'
she said. I sensed that it was more about her being part of the
decision than the importance of the photo.

'Sure,' I said. 'I'll leave it up to you to arrange it,' I said,
thinking it was better to let her talk it over with Rex.

It was still a little before the appointed time, but I went to
Handelman's down the street.

The messenger bag smacked against my side as I went
into the shoe store. All the seats along the wall were empty
and the cow seemed to have stopped midway over the
moon and appeared to be taking a nap. I stood by the door
for a moment, waiting for someone to appear. When no one
showed I stepped into the middle of the shop and heard voices
coming from the back.

As I neared the counter the voices became clearer and I
stopped to listen, waiting for a break to announce I was there.

I could hear Emily clearly and my ears perked up when I

heard her mention her aunt. 'Don't tell Aunt Laurel. It will only make it worse,' Emily said.

'Don't worry, I won't,' Lewis said. 'Who knows what she'll do with the information. I was only looking out for her best interests. I did what I had to take care of that guy. It's over now anyway.'

I was stunned by what I'd just heard. But I also didn't want Lewis to know that I'd heard it. Being as stealthy as possible, I retraced my steps until I was back at the entrance. I opened the door being as noisy as possible and called out hello as I let it shut.

Lewis and Emily came from the back and were all smiles as they greeted me. I was trying to focus on what I'd brought with me, but I was still shaken by what I'd heard.

The outer door opened and Laurel came in. 'I thought my aunt should be here to look everything over with you,' Lewis said. 'She might have something to add.'

The jewelry designer came up to me and gave me a warm hug. 'Thanks for listening to me the other day,' she whispered in my ear as she slipped a package in my hand. 'It's a pair of earrings I think will suit you.' She released me and turned to her niece and nephew. 'I'm happy to do anything I can do to help these two. We're family and we look out for each other.' I looked at Lewis for his reaction. He nodded with a serious expression.

Lewis suggested we sit in the chairs along the wall and let Laurel read over what I had first, and then pass the sheets on to Emily and she'd pass them on to him.

It was taking all my resolve to keep myself together and I was glad to have been given simple directions to follow. I found their file and handed it to Laurel. I had included some photographs with captions that I'd taken with my phone and some that Laurel had sent.

They looked everything over and did leave a few notes, but in general it was what they'd all hoped for.

I packed everything up and we set up another time to meet. As I left I noticed a shoe box sitting on one of the chairs. It made me think of the one at my place.

TWENTY-FIVE

I was on autopilot on the walk home. Between thinking over what my clients had said and what I'd heard Rita say and then Lewis, my mind was spinning.

It was late afternoon by the time I got home. I dropped the messenger bag and flopped on the couch. Now that the worry over what kind of reaction I was going to get to my work was over, I felt drained and exhausted. I didn't know what to do with what Rita and Lewis had said. Rocky jumped next to me on the black leather couch. It made me think of Ben and how the cat liked to sit next to him. It also made me think of how I really wanted to run everything past him, and in person. But after the way he'd run off when I'd offered him the room and gone home without even a goodbye the next day, and even with the text about still being friends, I was concerned he would think I'd created a reason to see him.

The only thing to do was leave it for tomorrow after the group and hope that he stayed.

I discovered that I was famished. I went into the kitchen and made myself a pot of spaghetti and a green salad. The unread Sunday paper was still sitting next to my unused place setting on the dining-room table from the day before. They both came in handy now. I used the fork on my food and the newspaper was my company.

I decided to take the night off from doing any work.

My plan had been to keep the scarf crochet project for relief when I was stuck writing, but since it was *my* plan, I could change it. Instead of idly watching some romantic fluff, I could work on the scarf while I watched. It hadn't worked with the squares because they required too much attention, but the scarf was simple and repetitious. It was worth a try, anyway. I cued up the movie and went into my office for the yarn and hook. Once I retrieved them, I was about to close the drawer until my gaze hit the green metal box. I pulled it out and set it on my desk. I'd been distracted when Tizzy was there and had gone through everything rather quickly. Why not have another look? Opening it was easy now that I knew the combination. I took my time going through the contents now that I had no one reading over my shoulder. Most of it seemed the same, but then I found something that surprised and confused me. It was one more thing I wanted to run by Ben.

I skipped going to Zooey's coffee stand the next morning. I wanted to get started on the changes for my assorted clients and I had the group's pages from the previous week to go over. I spent some time doing the usual sprucing up I did in anticipation of having company. The final step was to clear off the dining-room table and bring in another chair for Rex.

The doorbell rang right around seven and, when I opened the door, Tizzy and Rex were coming up the stairs together.

'I know you're going to like the group,' she said to him as they came inside. He stopped in the entrance hall and started to walk toward the French doors to my office.

'That's Veronica's office,' Tizzy said. 'We meet in the back.' She waved to him to follow her. I stayed in the front to buzz Ed and Daryl in and they arrived a few minutes later. Ben was late and I had a sinking feeling he wasn't going to come, but I heard the knock at the door just as the others were settling around the table.

I went to let him in and saw that he had on his cop demeanor. His mouth was set in non-expression and even his dark eyes seemed flat. He stopped me as I shut the door. 'I didn't bring the pages we went over,' he said in a low voice. 'Things got kind of out of hand and I'm trying to pull back.'

'Whatever works for you,' I said, disappointed that he seemed to have gone back in his shell. 'We have a new member,' I said as we walked to the back.

Tizzy was explaining to Rex how the workshop went as Ben and I came into the dining room. Rex had already introduced himself and seemed comfortable, but then with all his experience at LaPorte's he was used to dealing with new people. Ben was the only one not familiar with the bakery and restaurant and I handled their introduction.

'OK, we all know each other,' Ed said. 'Let's get going.'

I offered to let Rex go first and tell everybody about what he wanted to write.

'How about I just watch this time,' he said. They all nodded with understanding and Ed handed his pages to Ben. I kept an eye on Rex as the reading continued. I couldn't tell how he felt about the group by his facial expression. The only thing I noticed was that he kept looking at his watch.

Tizzy had brought her poem and Ben's pages were filled with back-to-terse dialogue and no emotion. Daryl was more tense than usual at having to deal with a new critic.

When the last piece was read and we'd finished making comments on it, conversation broke out as the group began to de-stress. They always needed a few minutes before they got ready to leave. Rex stood up, pointing at his watch face. 'I have to go.' He thanked everyone and looked at me. 'I'll be in touch.' He saw that I was getting up to see him out and said he could manage on his own.

They all handed me their pages as they got ready to leave and I followed them up the hall. Ben walked out with them without a look back and closed the door behind him. I hadn't had a chance to say anything to him. I stood looking at the closed door for a moment, thinking it was even worse with him than I'd thought. With a sigh, I went into my office to put their pages on my desk.

Something seemed off and it took a moment to register that all the drawers on my desk were pulled out. I sucked in my breath when I realized I wasn't alone.

'I thought you left,' I said as Rex came out of the shadow. And then I saw that he was holding something against his body – the green metal box.

'Open it,' he commanded. 'It has to be in there.' He was holding up his free hand and the desk lamp reflected off the knife he held in a threatening manner.

'How did you know about the box?' I said, trying to keep calm. Then I knew. 'It was Tizzy, wasn't it?'

'She came in yesterday and I overheard her telling whatever

committee she was meeting with about this box. She had already been most generous with information about you when she recommended I hire you to write the copy for us. I knew about all the different writing you did, the group Tizzy was in, and how you had cared so much about one of your clients that you'd let him use one of the drawers in your desk.'

I stared at the box he was holding by the handle now. I knew exactly what he was after. I'd found it during my second go round with the contents. But I had no idea how Ted had ended up with it.

'What was Ted Roberts, or maybe you knew him as Tony Richards, doing with the recipe for your chocolate mint cake?'

The good nature had gone out of his face. 'I'm just trying to get back what's mine. That bastard stole it and was using it for blackmail.' Rex glared at me. 'Those letters you wrote for him.' He shook his head. 'Do you have any idea what a mess they made?'

'They were for you?' I said.

'No,' he said sounding annoyed. 'They were to my sister. He'd convinced her that he wanted her all to himself when she'd wanted to introduce him to everybody. I only met him by chance when I came back to the restaurant one night after closing. She was baking while he watched.' Rex stopped to take a breath. 'I have to say he was good and I was taken in at first. He had a way of connecting with people so you felt comfortable with him right away. He knew about the expansion and laid it on pretty thick about what a brave move it was and how we'd built the place up from scratch. I was happy for her. Cocoa's husband walked out on her after a couple of years and since then she's had a few failed relationships. Once I'd met him, she felt free to go on and on about how wonderful he was. He was a pilot who flew all over the world and sent her romantic notes when he was off on his travels. She confided in me that she thought he was the one.

'Then she let it slip that she'd given him some money and she started telling me about ideas he had for our business. She thought they were gold and, when I didn't agree, she brought up that she should have equal say in what went on.' He let out an exasperated sigh. 'My mother and sister have dealt with the baking and recipes, but I'm the one who makes the business decisions. The only one.' He looked at me with hard eyes. 'I didn't trust him. He'd started coming by the restaurant during the day, surprising her after he'd returned from a flight, and I followed him after one of his visits – at least to the entrance of the high-rise. I knew the building manager thanks to the deliveries I still make. She gave me an earful about him. The biggest piece of news was that he was living with his girlfriend, who incidentally was footing the bills.

'I confronted him and tried to get him to disappear from Cocoa's life. When he blew me off, I said I was going to tell Cocoa how everything he'd told her was a lie.' Rex stopped and let out a disgruntled sound. 'That's when he told me he had the original recipe of my mother's famous cake. He must have convinced my sister to show it to him and pinched it when she wasn't looking. Stupid us kept it in a safe at the restaurant. If I said anything to Cocoa, he was going to post a scan of it on the Internet. Then every bakery in the world could replicate it. They would know how we got that perfect mint flavor that no one has ever been able to match. That recipe is our fortune. It's like the spice list for Colonel Sanders' chicken or the formula for Coca-Cola.' He peered at me to see if I understood how important the recipe was. I decided the best thing to do was go along with him. I hoped he would plead his case and then leave with the recipe.

'The next thing I knew she was telling me they were getting married and how it would make him part of the business. She wouldn't hear of any sort of prenuptial agreement. He wanted to elope right away, but she'd convinced him to wait a few days so she could put together a family gathering, not telling them that it was actually a wedding party.'

As he said that, I remembered that I'd heard them arguing about a wedding cake when I'd come in to LaPorte's to talk to Rex. I'd assumed it was about the order of a wedding cake, not realizing it was for her. All his talking was making me uneasy. I had no idea how serious he was about the knife in his hand and I didn't want to find out the hard way.

'As long as he had that recipe, my hands were tied. I had

to get it back. I figured it was in the place he was staying. It was easy for me to get into the building. All I had to do was show up with a yellow box and I knew someone would let me in the security door thinking I was making a delivery. I took a chance that his girlfriend had a key hidden somewhere in front of the place and found it in the spokes of an umbrella stuck in a stand outside the door. I rummaged through the place, looking for the recipe, but came up empty. I was actually going to leave, but then he showed up. He'd already grabbed a knife from the kitchen and came after me. We scuffled and I got the knife. There was no way we were both going to walk out of there.'

I understood it was about more than the recipe. Ted viewed Rex as an obstacle to his plan to become a partner in the business. And Rex had been the alpha male since his father had died and he wasn't going to give that up.

'I knew his girlfriend was a drug rep and figured the cops would think he interrupted someone after drugs, which is exactly what I heard they settled on. But I still didn't have the recipe back. I couldn't leave it out there. I couldn't let my mother know that it was lost. I've been running things, but my mother is the sole owner. She'd cut off my power.' The devastation that would do showed in his face.

'If it hadn't been for Tizzy and her nonstop chatter, I never would have gotten a lead on where that bastard had stashed it.'

'The mystery box was from you?' I said, pointing to it in the corner. He looked around at my office. He nodded.

'It was just a prop to get someone to let me in the locked door. I was betting that you left a key hidden someplace. Too bad you didn't and we could have avoided all this. Now how do I open the box?'

I gave him the combination and he had it open with ease. He fumbled through the papers until he came to the hand-written sheet I'd barely noticed the first time and only recognized when I'd gone through everything that second time. My hopes that he'd take it and leave were dashed when he glared at me, waving the knife.

'You're going to have to come with me,' he said. He had

stuffed the recipe in his pocket and with his free hand
grabbed my shirt and pulled me close to him. He poked the
knife toward me and I could feel the sharpness press against
my chest.

'Dinner's here,' Ben said as my front door opened. 'Where
should I put it?' he called out, seeing that I was in my office.
He stepped through the open French doors and saw Rex and
the knife and sized up the situation.

'I don't know what's going on, but I'm sure we can work
things out,' Ben said in a calm voice, instantly going into his
cop mode.

'No, we can't,' Rex said. 'She's coming with me.' To impress
his point, he poked the knife in harder and I cried out. 'Now
turn around and walk,' he commanded me.

We went out the front door and began down the steps with
Ben hovering behind us. There was nothing he could do but
follow us down the stairs. Rex had retracted the knife enough
so it didn't hurt, but the threat was still there. My heart was
thudding and I was trying to keep my anxiety at bay so I could
think straight. If we left the building there was no telling
what Rex would do. I went through the list of attributes I'd
given myself. I was a single woman with a cat, living with
her memories, stuck in her habits. I was sure there was more,
but I couldn't remember. I wanted to be around to add to
and change those attributes. I wanted to make new memories,
change the single thing, loosen up and be more fun. I was not
going to let Rex keep that from happening.

We'd almost reached the second floor and I knew the only
one who could do anything was me. I tried to keep calm by
taking deep breaths, while I frantically searched my mental
arsenal. And then I had an idea. I wasn't sure it would work,
but it was my only hope. I wished there was a way to signal
Ben. I had to hope that he would understand and react fast
enough. I took another deep breath and stepped on to the
second-floor landing. I grabbed at my throat while opening
my mouth and made a loud gagging sound.

Ben's reaction was instantaneous. 'She's choking,' he yelled.
And it seemed like time stood still.

Just like the man with the choking woman at the fondue

restaurant had, Rex froze for a split second, but long enough for Ben to knock the knife away and kick Rex's foot from under him. I was flung against the banister as Rex fell down the stairs, hitting his head on the newel post and knocking himself out.

And just like that it was over. Ben called it in. Rex was just coming to as a flood of uniforms poured into the vestibule.

'Still no elevator, huh,' Detective Jankowski said in a tired voice, before we climbed the stairs to my apartment. His wrinkle-proof suit still looked crisp, but his eyes looked worn out. We had already gone over the basics in the downstairs lobby. He had taken the recipe out of Rex's pocket before the paramedics had taken him to the hospital to be checked out. Rex's next stop was being booked and then jail. The flurry of uniformed officers that had shown up had taken care of gathering the knife for evidence. They'd also dealt with all the neighbors who'd opened their doors at all the racket. Basically, in their usual brusque manner, the officers had told them the show was over and there was nothing more to see. I was going to have to give them a better explanation than that, particularly to Sara who looked aghast as I passed by her place on the way back upstairs. I assumed she saw her brother accompanied by a detective as well.

Detective Jankowski already knew that his cop instinct about the circumstances around Ted's death had been wrong and that I, the amateur sleuth, had gotten to the truth. I hadn't said anything about it and neither had he.

He took a heavy breath as we walked into my place. The detective with Ben came in just behind us and we all stood in the entrance hall for a moment. Knowing police procedure would require that the cops speak to us separately, Ben suggested he and his escort go into the dining room.

'We could start there,' I said to my detective, pointing into my office. The metal box was open on my desk and all the drawers were still pulled out.

'Ms Blackstone, you should have given me this a long time ago,' he said poking through the box with a pencil so as not to disturb it as evidence.

'I didn't know about it until a day ago,' I said. He cocked an eyebrow and then let it relax. He'd probably realized it was best to let it go, for fear I might bring up his mistake thinking Ted had been killed in a drug burglary. I wasn't even going to mention what I knew about the non-existent cough syrup with codeine since it didn't matter anymore. I was truly glad not to have to mention what I'd heard Lewis say since I had clearly misinterpreted it. I felt better about accepting the earrings Laurel had given me. I loved the tiny blue disk with a crescent moon and a rhinestone star. I would have felt too uncomfortable wearing them if it had turned out her brother killed Ted.

Eventually the detective and I sat down in my office. I let him have the burgundy wing chair and I sat at my desk. More than once he looked around as if hoping a cup of his overly sweetened, milk-laden coffee would appear.

The adrenalin rush had mostly disappeared as a sense of relief set in. I was alive and had time to change the list of attributes. I could make more memories, loosen up and have some fun. There were a lot of questions and it seemed to go on forever. The detective wasn't happy when I started discussing whether Rex had really been looking out for his sister when he followed Ted, or was it worry about losing his control of the business. 'How about you stick to the facts,' he said, stifling a yawn.

The detective wanted to know my relationship to Ben and how he had walked in on Rex holding the knife on me. It was pretty straightforward. I told him that Ben was in my writing group. His sister lived downstairs and sent up some of their leftovers after the group. Ben left the door on the latch while he went to get the food.

'Then he's not your boyfriend?' the detective asked. When I said no, the detective looked a little judgy, like maybe he was seeing me as a single woman with a cat, etc., who got mixed up in trouble because she was love-starved. I let it go. When I asked him what would happen to Rex, he gave me a tired look and said it was for a judge to decide.

The night sky had grown pale by the time I walked the detective to the door. Ben and his detective came from the back at the same time. The two men walked out together and Ben and I went into my living room and flopped on the couch side by side.

'That was something,' I said.

'Are you all right? No nicks from the blade that need first aid?'

'I'm all good,' I said, leaning back in the couch.

'Good move to do the fake choking,' he said.

'Good move to figure out what I was doing,' I said. 'Thank you. You pretty much saved my life.'

'But only because you set it up,' he said.

I looked over at him. 'You look pretty chipper considering being up all night.'

'It's cop training,' he said. 'I should probably go home.' He stretched and seemed about to get up.

'Before you go, I need to say something,' I began. He sat back on the couch and turned toward me. I reminded him of what he'd said when he'd arrived at the writing group. 'You said things had gotten out of hand last week.' I took a breath and continued. 'I just want to tell you that I'm sorry. The slow dance, the offer of the room.' I stopped, trying to think of how to continue. 'I know you said you were still getting over your divorce and you didn't want any kind of romantic entanglements. I know the dance and the room offer made you feel uncomfortable and maybe that I was pushing you across a line or something. Anyway, I'm sorry.'

He just stared at me for a moment and then his lips curved into a smile. 'That's what you thought?' He shook his head with disbelief. 'I wasn't uncomfortable at all. If anything I was way too comfortable in the half a slow dance we did. You said you were gun shy after your divorce and you didn't want to get involved in anything. I was afraid that if I had you in my arms any longer, I was going to cross the line from friendship into something more. I like you and I was honoring what you said. And staying overnight?' His eyes went skyward. 'I didn't want to take a chance of losing what we have.'

'Then you didn't run out the door because you were freaked out at being so close to me.'

'Nope, not freaked out in the least.' He put his arm around

my shoulder. 'See. I'm not running to the door.' He looked over at me, seeming to be evaluating something. 'And you don't seem to be pulling away either.'

'So where does that leave us?' I said.

'I think we'll have to figure it out. But for now, how about we grab some breakfast at the place on the corner. They should be just opening. Then I have to go to work.'

As we passed Sara's door, he leaned in and whispered with a chuckle, 'Sara finally got her wish. We spent the night together.'

TWENTY-SIX

figured if Ben could go to work and be a cop all day after the night we'd both had, I could function, too. There were texts and phone calls galore as the story hit the news. Sara sent a text with a big question mark. I couldn't possibly explain it all typing with one finger and promised to give her the whole story in person . . . well, almost the whole story. I was going to leave her thinking my relationship to Ben hadn't changed.

But in the meantime I still had work to do. Tired as I was, I sat down at the computer feeling inspired by all I'd been through to work on the Derek Streeter manuscript. I didn't need to look at the hard copy to know where I was. I was carrying the story in my mind now. All I had to do was open the Derek Streeter Bk 2 file and start to type. I'd left him in a locked room with no way out and suddenly the answer came to me as I remembered something I'd read about a man who built armoires that opened on to secret rooms. I changed it a little bit and when Derek found the false back of the armoire and slid it away, he found a secret passage that led outside. I laughed out loud as I pictured Derek tipping his hat and thanking me for finding him an out before he jumped into an Uber and took off for the private terminal at the airport where he met a tall woman named Jewel. I sat back in my chair and smiled. I knew now that I could finish the manuscript. And maybe, like Tizzy said, there would be a book number three.

Ben called me during his meal break. We talked for a little while, still confused about exactly where we were. The only thing for sure was that being each other's plus one was back on, starting with the engagement party. 'You can tell Theo to stand down,' Ben joked.

The rest of the day was a blur and I fell asleep in my clothes.

* * *

I was back ready for action on Thursday. I took all the notes
from my clients and worked on their pieces. Six hours went
by and it felt like five minutes. Rocky came and went and
came back in the room and seemed surprised that I was still
there. I finally got a chance to fill Sara in on what had happened,
though by then she'd heard the story from Ben. Without me
saying anything to him, he'd left out our change of status, too.

On Friday, I was ready to go back to my clients and show
them the changes I'd made and talk about what had happened.
My first stop was Handelman's. When I saw Lewis, I wanted
to hug him and congratulate him for being innocent, but then
he didn't know that I'd thought he was guilty.

Laurel was there with her niece and nephew and snagged
me the first chance she could and suggested that Lewis
and Emily look over the stock in the back room for a few
minutes. By now the whole story with Rex and Ted/Tony
and my part in it was all over the neighborhood. Here it comes,
I thought as we stood in front of the counter.

'So you wrote those letters,' she said, looking at me. The
only thing I could do was what I'd been doing a lot of –
apologizing. I explained that I'd fallen for his charm and
agreed to work in a different way than I usually did. 'But
will never do again,' I said.

She had gone to the police with her story, but had insisted
on keeping her identity a secret. 'I'm just so embarrassed
about it,' she said.

'You shouldn't be,' I said. 'You got free of him before he
did any real damage. You didn't give him the lump sum
he wanted.'

'It was pure luck and Lewis,' she said. 'He just told me
what he did. When I first asked my financial advisor to get
the money for Todd, as I knew him, he mentioned it to Lewis.
My nephew felt uneasy about it, but he didn't want to say
anything to me. He asked my advisor to stall releasing the
money. It led to Todd going from Dr Jekyll into Mr Hyde.
Lewis did me a big favor even though I was heartbroken at
the time. I feel terrible for Cocoa. Maybe when some time
has passed, I'll let her know he duped me, too. She has to
deal with the whole thing with Rex as well. It seems a pretty

extreme length to go for a recipe, but then I don't know what I'd do if someone ripped off one of my designs.' I thanked Laurel for the earrings and showed I was wearing them. 'And now let me get to why you are here.' She called Lewis and Emily out to join us.

I showed them the new version I'd created. I had the story how the store had started and placed it in a time where service was what all stores offered. I had put in some photos Laurel had sent from the early days of happy kids getting their shoes fitted, reaching in the prize jar and watching the cow going over the moon. Then I'd added a heading that said *times change, but little feet don't*. There was no other store like it in the city. The next section spoke of the present and included the photos I'd taken and the quotes from the moms. There was a quote from Lewis on how they gladly took returns, but there were very few because they made sure the shoes fit before the kids left the store. A section was devoted to how much time they took with every child, letting them walk around the store. I'd included the hopscotch mat I'd suggested so the kids could try out the shoes in action. I'd already researched it and told them where they could get one.

Lewis was going to start uploading it to their website as soon as I sent everything to him electronically. On its own, the cow started her trip over the moon and we all laughed.

I went to see Haley next. I stopped in front of the place and looked up at the banner across the front. Though she'd never told me, she was using my suggestion for the name of the place. I felt a little thrill as I read *Coming Soon: Fro-Zen*. The door was unlocked this time. When I walked in I did a double take. Cocoa LaPorte sat on one of the stools. Haley looked up with a tense expression. 'Meet my investor and my mother,' she said. I must have looked puzzled. 'Hess is my father's last name. She's always gone by LaPorte.'

Cocoa gave me a wan smile. 'I'm sorry for everything. I can't imagine what my brother was thinking. Well, he wasn't thinking. He was trying to be the big brother even though I'm the older of us.' I let her go on, even though I didn't have the same take on why Rex had done what he did. 'I'm hoping that the court will be lenient with Rex.' She hung her head sadly. 'If there's any upside, my daughter and I have made peace. She's willing to listen to my advice and I'm OK with the final decision being hers.'

Haley nodded. 'It's kind of like what you said,' she said, looking at me. 'I'm going to stop trying to reinvent ice cream. I'm going to go for special instead of weird. So no whitefish-flavor ice cream. I'm going to keep most of the flavors I had you try, but I'm also going to have flavors like a dense chocolate ice cream with pieces of my grandmother's famous cake embedded in it.'

'That sounds like a winner,' I said. 'I suppose I'll have to rewrite this now,' I said, looking at the pages in my hand.

'Not completely. Please leave in the part about me being an alchemist,' she said. 'And I have a new flavor for you to taste.' The scoop had vanilla ice cream swirled with ribbons of golden honey and studded with California almond. It was both delicious and different.

Before I left I asked Cocoa how what had happened would affect the plans for LaPorte's expansion.

'We're going ahead with it. Rex's sons will handle the new places and my daughters will help me. My mother is already back working. She didn't like being pushed out by Rex.' I asked her if she still wanted my services.

'You mean because you wrote the letters?' she said and I nodded.

'It's not your fault. Your intent was to bring happiness to a couple. We were all victims of him.' She had a sad smile and I gave her a hug.

Zooey's was my last stop this time. We had communicated by email and she'd left comments on what I'd written which I'd now incorporated. We still had drinks she needed descriptions for, but the end was in sight. She was dressed in a colorful caftan and had a scarf over her hair. Her eyes widened when she saw me. 'I'm glad you're OK.' She reached out and grabbed my arm and held it as her words started to tumble out. 'I had no idea that Uncle Rex would do anything like that. But my mother should have known better. I thought she was seeing someone, but I had no idea that it was Ted or that she was going to marry him. It's doubly creepy now how he came on to me.' She stopped and noted the stunned look on my face. 'You didn't know Cocoa is my mother?'

'You never mentioned your family and you said you just wanted to go by Zooey.'

'Guilty,' she said. 'I was trying to make my own way. I didn't want everybody connecting me with LaPorte's.'

'So, then Haley is your sister?' I said, still processing what she'd said.

'My twin to be exact, though it's fraternal twin. We both wanted to do our own thing. Now we're all going to help each other and my mother. Next time you come in, I'll have the family chocolate mint cake, but with a twist. I convinced my mother to make it in squares.'

Just then Rita came in dressed in a suit and heels. She started to give Zooey her order as she caught sight of me. She looked at me as if she thought she knew me, but didn't know from where. Zooey filled her in on who I was. Then Zooey told Rita her mother was Cocoa LaPorte.

Rita put her head in her hands while she waited for her coffee to brew. 'If he wasn't already dead, I think I'd kill him,' she said.

When the writers' group met the next time, before we got down to business we talked about Rex and Ted. Ed wanted to hear how Ben had saved the day. Ben gave me most of the credit for my plan. He was still keeping his cop persona around them, but every now and then, when he looked my way, his eyes lit up. Daryl was overwhelmed with the whole story and just listened. Tizzy's brows were locked in a furrow. 'It's all my fault. I should never have told Rex about the love letters and you letting that guy keep stuff in your desk.'

I accepted her apology just as the others had accepted mine. Tony or Ted had conned us all in one way or another. I thought back over my reaction to him. The writer in me wanted to find the right words to describe the effect he had on people. The best I could come up with was that he made you feel special, valued, and as though whatever you were saying was the most interesting thing in the world. His looks were charismatic. Just looking at the way his eyes danced made you want to smile and keep gazing at them. I was still upset with myself for having been taken in by him. Obviously, it hadn't been to the degree of Laurel, Cocoa, Lois or Rita, but enough so I'd done things I felt uncomfortable about doing and almost gotten killed for it. I hoped I'd learned something so it wouldn't happen again.

While Ted's death had just been a small story in the newspaper that didn't make it to the TV news, the whole episode with Rex made it all over the media. Rex was charged with attempted kidnapping of me while they figured out the charges in Ted's death. Rex's attorney was already claiming it was self-defense. But there was the issue that it was in the midst of a burglary. The crazy part was that the story really became about Ted and his assorted aliases. How he charmed his way into the lives of women and then hit on them for money. The point was that they were smart, successful women who no one would expect to fall for a con.

Once the story was out, more women came forward, along with more aliases that he had used. It turned out that in his earlier relationships, he had managed to work them without love letters.

But then he'd upped his game, trying to work more than one woman at a time, using the letters to keep whoever he wasn't actually with, interested. The ironic part was that Rita, who claimed to be his real girlfriend, had never gotten a letter or even a love note. It was anyone's guess if he really would have married Cocoa. She thought he would have, though reluctantly admitted that he'd asked her for a large amount of money in advance of their wedding with the same story he'd given Laurel.

The love letters I wrote became part of the story and I thought it would ruin my business. But there's that saying about no such thing as bad publicity. The letters captured people's imaginations and suddenly the idea of a real piece of paper with caring thoughts became a thing. I had a flurry of business as letters from me had a certain cachet. People didn't even want to pretend they wrote them.

*   *   *

Sara knew about the engagement party on Saturday night. She even gave her approval to my attire. I'd splurged on a ballet-length black dress that was cut on the bias. But she had no idea that I even had an escort, let alone who it was.

She opened her door as I went down the stairs and smiled as I opened my coat to reveal the dress. I'd left my hair loose and gone full makeup. She gave me a nod of approval. 'Wow, even mascara. You look great. All you need is someone to appreciate it,' she said. I offered her a Mona Lisa smile in return.

Ben had parked the Wrangler and was leaning against the passenger door when I came outside. He straightened as I came down the stairs and I got a full view of his appearance. He looked perfect in herringbone sport jacket, blue dress shirt and gray slacks and I did my impression of a wolf whistle.

'You clean up well,' I said, walking to the car.

'I could say the same.' He stepped away and opened the car door, offering his arm to help me to manage the high step to get in.

The party was at the fancy downtown hotel where both of the couple worked. It was elegant and I was given a special toast as the fairy godmother who'd brought them together. It was a nice reminder of how my love-letter writing could turn out for the good.

I was glad that Ben and I had worked things out so he could be my plus one. We ate, danced and socialized. I got a number of leads for different writing projects and the evening seemed like it had been a success until I remembered our original plan. 'We forgot,' I said in a panic to Ben.

'Forgot what?'

'The body language. So we'd seem like a real couple and not just friends.'

He laughed and pulled a photo out of his pocket. 'When you were in the ladies' room, the photographer dropped off the picture he took of our table.' He held it out to show me. Ben and I were sitting with our shoulders touching and our heads angled toward each other in the perfect couples' pose. 'Personally, I think we nailed it,' he said.

'You're right.' I looked at the picture and smiled. 'Do you think it means something?'

He leaned toward me, recreating the pose. 'Maybe that it's real.'